A Price for Genius

A PRICE FOR GENIUS

Lin Wilder

A Price For Genius

Lin Wilder

ISBN: 978-1-942545-68-2
Library of Congress Control Number: 2016916371

View from Mt. Pilatus, Lake Luzern, Switzerland
©Throughthelens2014 | Dreamstime.com

Deadly Danger
©Anest | Dreamstime.com

Wilder Books
An Imprint of Wyatt-MacKenzie

"Modern medicine is a negation of health. It isn't organized
to serve human health, but only itself, as an institution.
It makes more people sick than it heals."
Ivan Illich, *Medical Nemesis*

"The more time, toil, and sacrifice spent by a population
in producing medicine as a commodity, the larger will be the
by-product, namely, the fallacy that society has a supply of
health locked away which can be mined and marketed."
Ivan Illich, *Limits to Medicine*

Suddenly regaining consciousness, Rich Jansen attempted to stand, then instantly regretted the abrupt movement. The pain began at the base of his head and exploded in successive and increasingly intense waves of agony, forcing him to close his eyes, hang his head and wait motionless. Remaining on his hands and knees for a minute, then two; waiting for the pain to subside, for the nausea to fade. Jansen finally risked opening his eyes. Squinting at the bright light, he very slowly and carefully moved his head from right to left.

So far so good. Linoleum floor, shiny black and white. That noise… what is that sound? Aw no, don't tell me, please God…

The memories flooded back as Rich raised himself up to a crouch, knowing better than to immediately stand up. Gingerly reaching behind his head with his right hand, he winced when his fingers probed a large wet and tender swelling at the back of his head. Slowly he stood, swaying a bit while the vast room spun about him.

Whatever they hit me with had carried one hell of a wallop.

The phone call from Reardon had happened last night? Or wait, was it yesterday? The minute he hung up the phone, Rich had called the airport to secure a seat on the next flight to Zurich. Sixteen hours later, he was in Lausanne, Switzerland, and had arrived at the animal research labs in the corporate offices of Andrews, Sacks, and Levine, one of the largest pharmaceutical companies in the world.

The elfin-like Ariana had been showing him where the test mice were kept when everything went black. Quickly looking around for her, Jansen saw only a few spots of blood and some scuff marks. And, ugh… hundreds of mice, scrabbling all over the lab; for whatever reason, whoever broke in decided to free the mice. Ariana was nowhere to be seen.

The letter…where is the letter?

Jansen reached into the pocket of his sports jacket, the one he'd had on since leaving San Luis Obispo, and breathed a sigh of relief when his right hand found the single page. A page now smeared with blood from his head wound.

Hello Mr. Reardon,
By the time you get this letter, it will be too late. We'll
already have her.
*Here are the steps you must **NOT** take:*
> *Do not call the cops.*
> *Do not contact Interpol.*
Tell no one. We'll know if you contact the police or Interpol.
We'll know and we'll kill her instantly. But we are civilized
businesspeople; this is all about business after all. Do
nothing at all until you hear from us. And you will hear
from us, Mr. Reardon. You must know Sir, there is a price
for genius. We trust you will pay it if you want to see your
daughter alive.

In the other pocket of his jacket, Jansen found his cell. He hit her number. *Please pick up, please pick up.*

Heart hammering as he counted the rings, Jansen's knees

nearly buckled with relief when his wife answered her phone. "Lindsey, where are you?"

"At the track—I was just starting a run with Max." Lindsey stopped still. She could hear the tension in her husband's voice.

"Honey, I need you to get here as soon as you can find someone to take care of Max and get a flight out to Zurich. We'll pick you up at the airport."

"What happened Rich, what's going on?"

"Someone clubbed me while Ari was showing me around the lab. When I woke up, she was missing and the mice are running loose. Ari and I must have surprised whoever decided to steal Liisa's research. Hank is—well, you can imagine how he is." Grabbing a nearby chair to steady himself, "There's a letter from Liisa's kidnappers. We need you to figure out how to meet their demands, and we don't have a lot of time."

"Are you okay?" Lindsey was on her phone searching for flights to Zurich as she waited for his answer.

Rich swayed from another wave of dizziness and nausea, then gulped and replied, "Other than a mega lump on the back of my skull, yeah, I'm fine.. Looks like they just wanted me out of commission for a few minutes. Ari and I must have interrupted something."

Rich surveyed the disarray in the lab. Cages were over-turned and he could still hear the squeals of mice and the scrabbling of their feet on the tiled floor. That had been the noise he had heard when he was coming to. He was way too old for this crap and knew just who he'd call once he got off the phone with his wife.

"I can get there faster from San Francisco. I'm calling Kate to make sure she can take Max. I'll try to be in Zurich by this time tomorrow, I'll call you when I know the time I'll get in. Be careful Rich, please." But there was only dead air, he was long gone.

"Hey, McAllister, Rich Jansen here. Are you and Baron still roaming around the country, free and easy?

"Yo, Rich!" Jansen could hear the smile in his voice.

"Gabe, are you still looking to work for Zach and me?"

"You mean like as a private investigator?"

"Probably a little more than just investigation, Gabe."

"What do you mean?"

"This one could get dicey. Two women have been kidnapped. Reardon has a note threatening to kill the head of research at Andrews, Sacks, and Levine—his pharmaceutical company—if he brings in the police or the feds. She also happens to be his daughter. I managed to get attacked within my first hour here." Scanning the space once again, hoping that Ariana would materialize, Jansen added, "Looks like they grabbed the head of the animal research labs, too. She was showing me around when we were assaulted, and now is nowhere to be found. From the looks of what they've pulled off so far, these threats don't seem empty. Has to be an inside job."

He took a shaky breath, trying to think past the excruciating pain in this head. "In other words, we'll be working solo. No safety net. No backup."

"Jansen, this is by far the best thing that has happened to me in the last three months. Baron and I are sick of the life of leisure down here in Baja. Where do I go and when?"

"Can you get to Switzerland? Like head to straight to Zurich on the next flight out of whatever airport you're closest to?

"Sure, but I'm bringing Baron with me, Rich."

"Good, we can use him."

"Call me when you get your flight confirmed and I or

somebody will pick you up at Zurich Airport."

Dialing his law partner in Mustang, Oklahoma, Jansen closed his eyes in relief when Zach answered on the second ring.

"Hi Zach, I think we need Toni out here in Lausanne. But you need to know this looks bad, really bad. If you don't want her to take the risk, I'll understand."

Jansen smiled when he heard the reply.

"They've taken Ariana too, haven't they?"

Jansen looked over his shoulder to see Hank Reardon standing behind him. Uncharacteristically looking every one of his sixty-eight years, the slight billionaire CEO needed no reply to his rhetorical question. As he looked around the research lab at the scattered cages, still scurrying mice and small pools of blood on the otherwise immaculate floor, the story told itself.

They stood in their driveway watching the white Ford truck towing a fifth wheel drive slowly down the dirt road to the highway, with one head leaning out of the driver's window and a second on the other side. The head of the driver belonged to Gabe McAllister, former Marine Captain and veteran of four Afghanistan tours; former Texas State Trooper, and acquitted Huntsville Prison inmate. The passenger's head belonged to Baron, a black and tan Doberman. "I'll miss Gabe, won't you?"

Lindsey looked over at Jansen and grinned. "And our boy here will miss Baron. Maybe we should adopt another Dobie, what do you think?"

"Maybe, if you really want to. We can talk about it, Linds, but right now, I'd like to get some sleep in our own bed. Can I interest you in some rest?"

They had been in the air on a flight from Switzerland to Houston for close to fourteen hours and were both exhausted. Although it was three in the afternoon Houston time, it was eleven at night Swiss time, and they had begun their day at four that morning.

Watching his wife's bright eyes and listening to her

uncharacteristic chatter, he realized that she was just as tired; she just didn't know it yet. Rich extended his arm to grab her hand, and literally pulled her up the stairs to their bedroom where he trusted she would conk out as soon as her head hit the pillow.

Two hours later, Lindsey was sound asleep, but Rich was wide awake, exhausted but unable to sleep. Very quietly, he slipped out of the sheets and stood at the side of the bed, trying not to wake up his wife or his dog. Lindsey had not stirred, but Max sat on his bed, watching warily on alert, not wanting to be left behind again. Rich grabbed a pair of pants and T-shirt on the way out of the bedroom, signaling to the dog to follow.

Max and Rich stood on the porch together. Max was pacing nervously, and Rich was restless. This was one of the rare times that Rich Jansen wished he smoked. It would be dumb to drink coffee now and alcohol held no interest for him. He yearned for something to do with his hands, something to stop his mind; a run would be just the ticket, but he didn't want Lindsey to wake up and find them gone.

After five minutes of silence, the Doberman managed to insinuate himself between the porch railing and Rich. He sat, whined quietly and lifted his paw up to Rich.

"Okay Max, I know. You've been abandoned and ignored, I know," he said, smiling at the almost human personality of his dog. Sitting on the floor of the porch, he sat there with Max's paw in his hand, stroking the dog's head. Little by little, he was calming down and beginning to analyze the reasons he felt so wired.

They had just returned from a two-week Christmas trip to Switzerland where their good friends Kate Townsend and Steve Cooper were married at a medieval castle. They had stayed at the home of one of the wealthiest men on the planet, and he had received an invitation to partner with one of the best defense lawyers in the country. Stories of which movies are made, but not typically the reality of ordinary people like Rich Jansen, but all true nonetheless.

Sighing, Jansen stretched out on the porch next to his dog, relishing the hard, unyielding wood surface under his cramped back after all those hours on the airplane. Within minutes, they were both asleep.

In the very early morning hours of the next day, Jansen opened his eyes at the feel of Max's nose on his face and the sound of Lindsey calling them. "We're out here, babe—fell asleep on the porch." Rich sat up, got to his feet and opened the door to the house, stopping before he ran right into his wife. Lindsey was in her scrubs and looked to be leaving.

"I thought you weren't going in until next week?"

"I wasn't, but Monica called about thirty minutes ago. Then Bob called right after I hung up with her. There is a 'situation' at the prison." Lindsey's generally sensual mouth was compressed into a thin line. She was stressed and unhappy.

"Do you need some help?"

"I'd love some, but you no longer work at Huntsville, husband dear, so I'm not sure that would be a really great idea." Sarcastic, almost caustic even, not her usual style. She seemed frightened and tried to hide it, mostly from herself.

Jansen grabbed her by the shoulders and forced her to look up at him. "What's going on there, Linds, what happened?"

"There is a riot between the Texas Syndicate, Mexikanemi, the Aryan Brotherhood and others that I cannot think of right now. Inmates are wounded, and the prison is on lockdown. To say that things are out of control is a bit of an understatement."

"There's something else. Come on, what is it?"

Lindsey took a deep breath, and closing her eyes, said, "They got Devon Preston again. That's why Monica called; she knew I would want to know." When she opened them again, she could no longer suppress the grief, and tears stood glistening in her eyes.

"Okay, let's go. I'll drive."

"Honey, it's no longer your job, you have no authority there."

"Right. Come on Max, let's go."

More relieved than she could express, Lindsey managed a smile, then reached up to touch his cheek and whispered, "This is one of the millions of reasons I love you, Rich Jansen." She took his hand, profoundly comforted by the feel of her hand in his as they climbed into her new SUV. Max scrambled up and into the back of the vehicle, then settled on the bed she kept there.

Within fifteen minutes, they pulled up to the Walls. Despite the fact that Jansen had worked at the main Huntsville Prison for over two years, he remained impressed with its ominous appearance, well deserving of its nickname. Particularly on this early morning when he knew there were prisoners rioting inside.

The prison itself was completely hidden behind a well-fortified, ten or twelve-foot brick wall. The wall was dark, with razor wire running between the guard towers at each corner; easily spanning the distance of a city block in each direction. Rich had seen his share of prisons, but the Walls seemed to emanate menace. It was a little before seven in the morning, but the rising sun did nothing to dispel this feeling as Rich slowly drove around the block, seeking the parking space reserved for Dr. McCall, the Medical Director.

"Man, you two are a welcome sight!" Bob Cleary stood beside the armed guard at the employee entrance. His welcoming smile was real enough, but his eyes were darting all over the parking lot as if he half expected to see a fusillade of armed prisoners any minute.

Lindsey started to move past the two men, but Rich placed a hand on her gently, and she stopped at the restraint. "What happened, Bob?" Jansen spoke so softly that Cleary and Lindsey had to strain to hear him.

The Doberman was on a leash and stood to the right of Jansen, ears straight up and eyes wide open; watching, sensing the tenseness and seeming to know there was danger in the air.

"Lindsey, I don't know what happened exactly. Devon Preston came back a few days after you guys left on vacation." The tall, lean, and troubled Warden sighed deeply. "I missed it. I didn't find out he was here until early this morning, just a few minutes before all hell broke loose."

Jansen suppressed a smile at Bob's reply to Lindsey. The guy was better than he had hoped when he'd selected him to be Warden just a few months ago. No excuses, shouldering all blame and responsibility squarely on those wide shoulders.

"Had I known he was back, we'd have put him in administrative segregation of course..." Cleary's voice trailed off, anguish evident in his eyes and expression. "I don't know if he was set up again by La Emi or what, but Lindsey, Monica just called me as I was on the way out here to meet you guys. Devon died on the way to the Emergency Center. This time, they succeeded."

Rich watched Lindsey's shoulders slump, head drop, and her slight body turn away from him and Cleary while she regained control. He knew what she was thinking.

Jansen asked again, "Bob, what's happened so far?"

"At," Cleary looked at his watch, "O-six-thirty—thirty-five minutes ago—three prisoners in G2 began a ruckus.

Within a few seconds, the whole floor was involved, and someone either ignited a smoke bomb or managed to start a fire that emitted a helluva lot of smoke, making breathing very unpleasant."

Cleary glanced quickly at Lindsey, lowered his voice and practically mumbled, "Devon was in G2 and was one of the ten inmates who was first wounded. Only Devon has died...so far."

The Texas Judicial System classifies prison inmates into five custody levels. The levels rank each prisoner's threat to society if he escaped, with G1 representing the least threat and, therefore, can be housed outside the prison with periodic observation. While G5 requires that the prisoner is housed in a cell during most, if not all, of his waking hours, and allowed outside only under armed supervision. Level G2 is dormitory housing with groups of twenty to fifty prisoners together.

"How many are involved? Are they armed?" Jansen was watching his dog while keeping an eye on Lindsey, then he turned back to the warden.

"If you mean do they have guns, no. Thank God, no guns, at least none that we've seen or heard so far. But they have plenty of shivs and may have some explosive devices, we're not sure."

Although weapons are prohibited in prisons, the creativity of inmates can provide them with a most effective arsenal of weapons. Each prisoner is provided a toothbrush and a razor when they are checked in. The razor can be easily removed from its package and once embedded in the plastic handle of the toothbrush, a most efficient knife can result.

Texas prison system inmates not deemed to be threats can work in a variety of industries; from carpentry to textiles, furniture to metal work, all under the rubric of Texas Correctional Industries. The items are sold in showrooms and are available for purchase online; with the proceeds returning to the prison system since the inmates are unpaid. Incendiary devices can be created from flammable materials obtained in the many workplaces on the premises—such as the carpentry or metal shops—and then smuggled into the prison with surprising ease.

"Have you called the governor?"

Cleary stared evenly at his former boss. "Rich, if you're asking if I think we need the guard out here, then no, I believe that we can quiet this down ourselves."

Like Jansen, Bob Cleary was a former Marine. Although he was the youngest of all the Wardens, barely thirty, Rich trusted his judgment implicitly.

Lindsey turned back toward the two men and her dog. The smile on her face was more like a grimace, and the expression in her green eyes could be described only as fierce. "Well, gentlemen, shall we go in?"

Cleary began to object, "Dr. McCall, I'm not sure this is a good idea..."

Cutting him off, her voice cold and imperious, her expression completely flat, "Bob, if you weren't going to let me in, why did you call me?"

There were times, Jansen thought, as he watched Lindsey intimidate the hell out of Bob Cleary, that she almost scared him. She could be as warmly feminine and loving as a nurturing mother, and one second later turn into an automaton. Like now. During times like this, she reminded him of some of the Marine Recons he had worked with while in the Corps. Sure of their authority and ability, they oozed command. Rich had never known another woman like her, and at times like this, he wondered if he actually *knew* his own wife.

To his credit, Cleary stood his ground. "Because I needed

to tell you what is happening in there. But we've already had one death. I'm not interested in causing the death of my medical director as well." Cleary's usually expressive eyes were dark and hard.

Rich stood back and watched, sympathizing with both people. Idly, he wondered what he would do with this aggressive medical director if he were Cleary, and also if he would be interested in help from someone who no longer carried any authority in the prison system. Like him.

While he waited for the standoff to end, Jansen considered the possibilities. Most likely, this was gang related, exactly as Lindsey had guessed. Probably La Emi or the Mexican Mafia battling the Texas Syndicate or the growing Tango Blast gang. Gang membership within prisons in Texas is estimated at over one hundred thousand and climbing.

Back when Jansen was the captain of the homicide department for Harris County, the gangs were becoming a serious threat to Houston. But now, close to fifteen years later, the menace of gangs to Houston, along with many other major American cities, had worsened for several reasons. Uppermost among them was that gang organization and leadership had improved significantly; the structural reality of these twenty-first-century criminals belied the public image of chaos, ignorance, and ineptitude. Effective gangs like the La Emi or the Mexican Mafia, the Texas Syndicate and Aryan Brotherhood were organized either like Fortune 500 companies, or paramilitary with distinct hierarchies and clear allocation of decision-making authority, along with detailed membership policies and procedures. Once a member, always a member was the rule. Attempts to leave were punished severely, often by death. Turnover in these organizations was negligible, and recruitment problems existed only with the occasional exception, like Devon Preston, who is most likely dead due to his refusal to join the gang. In fact, even describing them as gangs now was misleading, implying disorganization and adolescent behavior, when the truth is far more dangerous.

The men at the top rarely get their hands dirty; are dignified in appearance, behavior, and conduct; and are in charge of drug and money laundering businesses worth ever multiplying millions of dollars. In Houston and other southwestern cities, the Texas Syndicate and La Emi were increasingly tied to the Mexican drug cartels like Sinaloa and had expanded into human trafficking for sex as well as drug transport.

Gang membership was estimated to be over fifty percent of the prison population and responsible for an estimated fifty to eighty percent of prison homicides. Young or old, vulnerable inmates were prime recruitment fodder for gangs. The appeal of belonging to influential groups for protection and contraband like drugs, liquor and cigarettes became irresistible.

Jansen's thoughts were interrupted by a command from Cleary. "Okay then, Dr. McCall, but my guys will lead the way." The stalemate had ended, and once again, Rich suppressed a smile. Lindsey had won. Big surprise.

Warden Cleary signaled a group of guards to proceed through the doorway. Lindsey went through next, then two guards with nightsticks and tasers at the ready.

Just as Rich and his dog stepped forward, Cleary whispered, "Rich Jansen, you have no business being here, but I am thanking the good Lord that you are!" With teeth starkly white against his black face, Bob grinned at Max, as he crouched down on one knee. "And you, big boy, what a splendid addition you make to my troops. Rich, with Marine dog here, we'll get this thing calmed down!"

Obediently following the contingent of guards, Lindsey took a deep breath and tried to suppress her resentment at being called in several days early from what could be best described as a magical vacation. She began to explore it, gingerly at first, as if it were a wound. *Okay, who wouldn't be annoyed? Less than forty-eight hours ago, we were in Lausanne, one of the most stunning cities in the entire world. Pristine views of Lake Geneva surrounded by the Swiss Alps, covered in snow and wrapped in air that feels hyper-oxygenated. Now, back in another Houston 'winter' where the average temperature is in the high eighties, and a rare week she'd anticipated spending in the hammock reading novels had been hijacked.*

Lindsey smiled to herself, but had anyone been paying attention, it would have looked more like a scowl. She knew she was lying. Lindsey McCall had lived in Houston her entire life and was used to the absence of seasons. And the loss of a few vacation days was hardly enough to evoke this level of antipathy. She had spent too many years working through holidays and weekends to mind the loss of five days. No, her problem was far deeper and was one she had been suppressing ever since she and Rich had left Switzerland. She knew she would need to deal with it, and soon. *Grow up McCall, in another year, you'll be forty...old enough to choose a career and stick with it.*

They were passing through the third set of automatic doors, and her world lay minutes away. With state of the art technology and the very best of trauma equipment, the Huntsville Prison Emergency Center rivaled any trauma center in the Texas Medical Center sixty miles north of the seven Huntsville prisons. Just a year before, Lindsey had personally funded the rebuild of the shabby infirmary, making extensive use of suggestions from former colleagues at the Texas Medical Center. Easily able to afford a multi-million dollar renovation, Dr. Lindsey McCall was a wealthy woman several times over. Aside from her family inheritance, McCall had created an alteration of the digitalis molecule, one that eliminated the dangerous side effects in the body. Her drug—Digipro, had revolutionized the treatment of acute heart failure worldwide, and in the process was making both her and ASL, the pharmaceutical company, billions.

Suddenly they were there. Moving quickly from behind the contingent of guards standing motionless in front of the closed doors to the emergency center, Lindsey surveyed the chaotic scene confronting her as she used her ID to open the sliding glass doors. Drawing on her years of experience in interventional cardiology, and more recently in emergency medicine, McCall's practiced eye took in ten patients, plus three techs and Monica Bradbury admitting an eleventh—who looked seriously injured. Alerted by the sound of the automatic doors opening, Monica looked up and smiled at her boss. Relief was apparent in her expression.

Rich watched while Lindsey transformed herself instantly. All expression left her face, leaving an appearance of calm and confidence. He recognized the drill—the same one he had used through the years as a Marine, then later as Captain of the Homicide Division of Harris County. The readiness for combat was universal and apparent to all who had been there, whether in Beirut, the city streets of Houston, or an emergency room, the need for an almost inhuman self-discipline was critical.

Nodding to Bob, he whispered, "Let's go."

CHAPTER TWO
Huntsville Prison

Cleary had left four guards in the Emergency Center with Lindsey, her staff and the eleven injured inmates. At the first sign of trouble early that morning, Bob had called for help from the other wardens in the Huntsville Prison System. Each of the six prisons had sent four guards within ten minutes of receiving the request, and would send more if the riot at the Walls was not contained by ten in the morning.

When he was appointed Chief Warden, one of the very first things Rich Jansen did was to write a protocol enumerating the response to a riot, both within the affected prison and addressing reciprocal responsibilities with the adjacent seven prisons which made up the Huntsville Prison System. Calling the Governor for National Guard reinforcements was unavoidable for stand-alone prisons where there was no trained help nearby. But the consequence of releasing untrained National Guardsmen inside a prison to quell a riot was almost always catastrophic. A series of prison riots in the late 1970s resulted in the carnage at San Quentin, Attica, and Huntsville. No governor wanted that blight on their record, and now the expectations of wardens regarding containment ran high, perhaps too high.

Not surprisingly, there had been resistance to Jansen's expectation of shared responsibility from some of the wardens when he instituted the new protocol. Chiefly from those with the most seniority. This was why Jansen had asked Bob Cleary if he had called the governor when he first arrived; what he really wanted to know was if the other wardens had done their job.

They were walking slowly and carefully through the five levels of the prison. The first two floors were under control. The smoke had thinned out, and they were heading up to the third level when Max stopped dead. The hair along his spine raised like a brush and a low rumbling growl sounded from his throat. His back legs were quivering, he liked nothing of what he was sensing.

Turning, Jansen was relieved to see Warden Cleary raise his hand to stop the forward motion of the guards behind them. There were four of them, and they were talking quietly. Bob motioned once again with his hand, and the talking immediately ceased.

Watching Max carefully, Rich unclipped the leash to see what the dog would do. They had approached a corner and could smell smoke, but the air was clear. The Dobie suddenly dropped to his haunches and began to creep along the floor, a constant low growl emanating from his throat. At that, Cleary turned to the guards in the rear and harshly whispered, "Get down!"

A bottle filled with some kind of liquid came flying around the corner and exploded as it hit the wall. Fortunately, one of the guards had thought to bring along a fire extinguisher, so within minutes, the fire was out.

Jansen and Cleary were on the smoke-filled cement floor following the dog. When Rich pulled out his Glock, he saw Cleary's eyes widen, and he reached into the back of his trousers and pulled out his Judge. At that, Jansen gave a thumbs up.

They were approaching the turn in the corridor. Obviously, whoever was waiting there was well aware of their presence. Completely blind, Jansen and Cleary had no idea of who the combatants were, how many there were and what they possessed for arms. Max was just starting to creep around the corner when an arrow came flying toward them.

An arrow? What the...?

Jansen and Cleary saw the razor blades affixed to the projectile at the same time. It had missed Max's chest by less than two inches.

"Max, stay," Jansen hissed. The dog looked at him, fearful that he had done something wrong. Jansen said it again, and the big dog hugged the floor, motionless.

There were security cameras and mirrors in the hallways and at each angle of the corridors for incidents such as this, but they were too high up on the walls for Cleary and Jansen to see. Since they didn't know for sure what all had been compromised and controlled by the inmates, they didn't have the benefit of input from the control center via radio on what activity the cameras were picking up.

Just then, one of the guards from behind came crawling toward them. Before Jansen could order the man back, he saw who it was. "Luke!" he whispered, none too softly. The surprise combined with both delight and deep sadness at the sight of Devon Preston's older brother resulted in an awkward grimace.

Pulling out a long flexible tube, Luke silently nodded at Rich and Cleary, then passed the scope up to Bob, who was closest to the corner.

Watching Bob configure the device, Jansen wondered where on earth a Huntsville prison guard could get his hands on a piece of sophisticated military equipment such as a fiberoptic photonic scope. Once the implement was threaded around the corner, they could clearly see three men crouched about a third of the way down the hall.

Preston had been devoted to Lindsey, even before she saved the life of his little brother Devon by operating on him without a license the first time La Emi had tried to kill the boy. The huge man's face was a mask of grief, rage, and determination.

Wordlessly, the three men pointed at the ceiling. The grille to the entrance to the ventilation system was down the hall about twenty-five feet, and the entrance vent in the next hall was directly over the heads of the three inmates.

Creeping back the way they had come, Rich, Bob, and Luke, along with the remaining three men, quickly decided on a plan. Within thirty seconds, they were implementing it. The smallest of the six men, a guard from nearby Ellis prison, and a buddy of Cleary's stood on Luke's shoulders and was easily able to remove the grate.

Luke Preston was a massive man, easily six feet ten inches tall and close to three hundred pounds. The prison guard had been a tight end for Texas A&M University, and although it had been more than a couple years since Preston played football, he was in surprisingly good shape.

Watching Preston take the smaller guard's weight on his shoulders without batting an eye, Jansen thought again of the scope and wondered what Preston had done before becoming a guard at Huntsville.

Preston caught Jansen's gaze on him and held it. The expression of grief remained in his eyes, but now there was something else, Rich thought, as he stared back at the bigger man.

The toughest part was still to come. When the small guard got to the vent which opened directly above the heads of the three inmates who appeared to be running this thing, he would yell, "Ooh-Rah!"

At that signal, all six men would rush the three prisoners. Jansen insisted on being in front and would have Max with him, unleashed. It was risky—for both him and the dog—but with the combined chaos of the surprise attack, the dog, and the guy jumping down on them from overhead, he thought they could overwhelm these guys. Or so he hoped.

All hell had broken loose. The smoke was so thick that Rich's eyes were streaming, and he could hear screams, but could not see.

"Luke! No, Stop!"

The shouts were Bob Cleary's, and he was obviously hollering at Preston.

"Max, here." Although he could not see him, Rich suddenly felt the cold nose of his dog in his right hand, the one which was groping along the wall as he moved in a rapid semi-crouched crawl, and breathed a sigh of relief at the touch. Suddenly, there was a pocket of clearer air, and he could see a pile-up of bodies on the floor. The skinny guard who had climbed through the ventilation ducts had one inmate in cuffs and another meekly standing against the wall away from the melee formed by the other seven bodies.

Luke Preston was on the floor, his body crossways on one of the rioting inmates, his formidable legs in a scissor kick that was slowly asphyxiating the prisoner. The downed prisoner was a member of the Texas Syndicate, the TS tattoo readily apparent on the skin under the throat currently being crushed. His eyes were bulging, his skin slowly turning blue. Jansen crawled up behind Luke, ignoring all the other guards, and pulling out his Glock, placed the business end of the revolver on the side of his head.

"Luke, let him go. Now." Jansen's voice was low, menacing. He guessed that Preston knew this creep and had figured him for the murder of his little brother, Devon.

The massive guard looked up and stared at Jansen. His eyes were enormous and filled with rage. Jansen kept his revolver on Preston's head and stared back. He didn't move. Or blink.

Cleary and the other two guards were scrambling to get two other prisoners under control. Cleary was pretending he didn't see what was taking place on the floor.

Still staring at Jansen, Luke's face collapsed and contorted into a grimace which combined the worst kind of sorrow, remorse, and shame. Nodding, he relaxed his legs, then swung around and sat up.

The prisoner, released from Preston's death grip sat up, still in distress. A bald Hispanic, he was somewhere between thirty-five and fifty, with over-developed upper body muscles and black-inked tattoos so dense they were illegible. He was coughing, choking and trying to breathe while still managing to spew epithets, vomit, and spittle all around him.

Now that the other two were under control, Cleary calmly walked over to the spitting, sputtering, screaming man and pulled both arms behind him to apply plastic cuffs which he pulled tight around both wrists.

"Sure Martinez, after you get out of 3 months in solitary, you can sue all of us niggers, feel free."

The smoke was clearing rapidly, Cleary had given the approval to turn on the ventilation system, now that the leaders had been subdued.

The skinny guy who had crawled through the air ducts

turned to Cleary and drawled sardonically. "Well Boss, it's only eight-thirty, what else you got for us to do before lunch?"

The guard was dark, with a thin face and a military haircut. He was Italian-looking and about thirty, Cleary's age. Jansen bet they had served together.

"Mission accomplished," Cleary said, as the two men high-fived one another. At an unspoken signal between them, Bob's wiry friend gathered up guards and prisoners alike, and took off down the hall, leaving Rich, Preston, Cleary and the dog standing alone in the hallway.

Preston was standing apart from them, still immersed in a riot of conflicting emotions. He was staring at Max, but looked as if he did not see the dog or anything else, his eyes were vacant.

Reaching down to stroke his four-legged partner, Rich murmured what a good boy he had been and watched the stubby tail wag in appreciation. Profoundly relieved that none of them had been wounded or killed, Rich was happy to stand there quietly and wait to see what Cleary would do. What he would say. This was his show, after all. Rich and Max had merely been invited guests.

After what seemed like five minutes, although it most likely was less than one, Bob Cleary approached Luke.

"Why don't you take the rest of the day off, Luke?" Cleary's voice was gentle and kind. "Your mom will need you at home today."

Preston looked dazed as he regarded his boss. Shaking his head, he asked quietly, "You mean you're not going to fire me?"

Placing a hand on the shoulder of the much bigger man, Cleary chuckled, "For helping to quell a riot between the Syndicate, La Emi and probably Tango Blast? Are you kidding? You'll get a commendation for this." Left unsaid was the very personal motive behind Luke's actions, as well as the fact that he would have killed Martinez had he not been stopped.

"So much for La Emi and the Texas Syndicate were being arch enemies. What's up with that?" Rich asked as he and Luke were walking slowly down the corridor.

"They were sworn enemies up until the last couple years. Then, we started to see some changes and suddenly, on some topics, they act like best friends. Amazing what money can buy." Preston was talking about a coalition plainly animated by the lure of gigantic profits from Cartel controlled trafficking. The big guard walked sluggishly as if each leg weighed a ton. Jansen understood and wanted to try to help, which was why he'd asked the question in the first place. He hadn't been out of the game that long and still knew the affiliations very well, but he needed to get the big guy talking.

Rich was confident that Lindsey would need to spend the next couple of days there, if not the whole week. He and Lindsey had planned only relaxing things to do for the rest of their vacation. Stuff like watching movies, and daily runs in the woods at their house that they and Max loved. Oh well. He was still very curious about where Luke had gotten his hands on that scope. Without that scope, Jansen shuddered to think of what could have happened.

He had an idea and used the two-way radio to call Bob.

"Hey Bob, are you heading to the Emergency Center with those guys?"

"Yeah, Rich, we're almost there. What's up?"

"Can you tell Lindsey I'll be back in a couple of hours, and will bring her a chicken burger and fries when I get back? Tell her that Luke and I are headed to The Texan for breakfast. Oh, and Max too, of course."

There was an answering chuckle, "Sure Rich, I'll tell her."

Seated across from Preston at The Texan Cafe in the center

of Huntsville, Rich laughed inwardly when he saw the waitress approach. She was the same woman who had brought him and Lindsey the Texan lunch of grilled chicken breast sandwiches and fries on the day she was released from prison. It had only been two years, but it felt like three lifetimes to Jansen.

The heavy-set redhead smiled at them and in a thick East Texas drawl asked, "What I can get for y'all this mornin? She looked down at Max then at Rich.

"I've seen you in here before." Looking down at Max, who was seated uncomfortably on the hard floor, she said, "You wait right here." She disappeared through a door in the back, returning right away with a large square dog bed. They were seated in the empty inner room near the wall of the restaurant, there were fewer than ten people in the entire place. She plopped the bed down against the wall and pointed to it.

Max looked at Rich and back to her, then sighed and stepped onto the bed, turning three times before laying down.

"Thank you very much, you must know how Dobie's hate sitting on hard floors. Most people are afraid of these guys."

Smiling, the waitress held her pad and observed, "These boys and girls are lovers, all of 'em, Me, I've had four of my own."

"Now, what are we having?"

After they had ordered and were comfortably settled and drinking coffee, Luke looked at Rich. "I don't know how to thank you," his chin trembled with emotion. "If you hadn't been there, I would have killed Martinez, I know it." Tears were shining in Preston's obsidian eyes.

Speaking truthfully, Rich said, "Luke, I understand. Bob does too. Had we been in your shoes, we would have felt the exact same way. We're all capable of murder. After a few years in the Corps, I finally figured out that was what we were.

Murderers sanctioned by the government."

Preston was hanging on every word.

Jansen took a sip of the steaming coffee, "Man, this is good coffee." Completing his thought, "Back in the days when I was in combat, and then later as a homicide detective—which often felt exactly like combat—I did some things I'm not proud of." Taking a bigger swallow of the brew, he went on, "The reason more people aren't killers is that most of us are never given sufficient cause like you just were." He put down the cup to look directly at Preston. "That's one of the main things that keeps me from leaving the church...I *know* what I am capable of doing."

Nodding, the big man exhaled slowly as if he'd been holding his breath, and his features slowly began to relax. Luke picked up the coffee creamer, stirred it into his cup of coffee and drank a long swallow.

Smiling now, "You're right, it is good. Superb. And so is this." Preston's big hand unclenched and gestured back and forth, signaling the connection between the two men, the understanding of failures and disappointments, and the need for something or someone greater.

"But, I do have an agenda, Luke. I am really curious about where and how you got your hands on that scope. Had you not had it, this story could have a very different ending."

Preston merely nodded.

Jansen regarded Luke inquisitively. "Tools like that just don't appear in the toolkit of the average Joe. What were you? Delta? Ranger? Marine Recon?"

Shaking his head in amusement, Preston started to answer, but then their breakfast appeared.

The redhead set a pecan waffle with three strips of burned bacon, exactly the way he liked it, in front of Rich, and the grilled pork chop breakfast in front of Luke.

Standing back, she smiled. "Anything else I can get you, boys?" Looking down at the Doberman, she asked, "Okay if I give him a bone?"

"Sure," both Luke and Rich answered simultaneously, "We've all had quite a morning." Rich told her, "If you have two, he earned them!"

Reaching into the pocket of her wraparound apron, the waitress brought out two large milk bones. Immediately Max sat up and stared at the bones. When the waitress gave them to him, he was salivating, but stared at Rich until he heard the okay, then grabbing the ends of the bones, he settled back down to eat them.

"What a gentleman you are, Mr. Doberman!" Then looking around at their table, she said, "I'll bring you fresh coffee in just a sec, we're just brewing a new pot."

The next few minutes were consumed with the sounds of contented chewing.

"Man, this waffle just melts in my mouth," Rich said to the redhead as she filled their coffee cups. "I'll need to run an extra two miles tonight, but this is worth it."

Once she left the table, Luke swallowed and said, "Seal. I was a Navy Seal," then quietly continued eating his breakfast.

Swallowing a thousand questions that were crowding his mind for answers, Jansen suppressed his curiosity and concentrated on his food. Thinking as he did so about how we tend to underestimate some people and overestimate others. It was comical really, how profound our ignorance of one another really could be. And then he filed the information away. Rich had found that a coincidence like this was never mere happenstance, there was always a reason. There would come a time, he sensed strongly, when the conversation would happen.

Within ten minutes after dropping Luke off at his car, Rich and Max were back down at the Emergency Center where things seemed less chaotic. Over half of the beds were full, but there looked to be plenty of help. Looking around to locate Lindsey, Rich saw her on the phone at the end of the open unit, out of earshot of the patients and staff.

"Sure, I'll hold, thanks." Her face lit up when she saw Rich and Max coming toward her and whispered to him, "Man, are you two ever a welcome sight!"

Rich knew what she meant, it had been less than four hours since they had arrived at the prison, but it felt more like twenty-four.

"Well, yes. I'm not due back from vacation for another week, and we've had an uprising here resulting in injuries. I have ten patients here in the Center who need medical supervision," Lindsey had closed her eyes as she completed her sentence, a sign that she was working hard to be patient with whoever was on the other end of the phone.

All medical directors in the state of Texas served under the direction of the University of Texas Medical Center Branch at Galveston. Responsible for providing medical treatment for eighty-three Texas prisons, infirmaries, and clinics; a total of one hundred and sixty-eight thousand, two hundred and eighty inmates, a number equal to twenty-five per cent of the total of prisoners from all other forty-nine states combined. The practical result in routine matters like staffing was bureaucratic complexity of a Byzantine nature, or in English, "It's not my job, it's Joe's, and he's not here today."

Rich had listened to Lindsey's laments about the maze of approvals necessary for trivial matters and guessed what the outcome of this conversation would be.

He watched his wife's tired shoulders sag when she uttered the words he knew she would say. "No, forget it, it's okay, I'll just come back from vacation early. Thanks anyway."

CHAPTER FOUR
I-45 South to Houston

Lindsey had taken the day off. Things at work had finally settled down, and the center had only a few patients; the usual assortment of flu's, minor work-related injuries and the Martinez complaint, which had been resolved, finally. As she pulled onto I-45 to take the long way to downtown Houston, she reflected back on the last ten days and began to enumerate the reasons she was feeling trapped and unhappy.

She was driving into Houston alone for the first time since before she'd been indicted for murder. And it felt great to be alone. When Lindsey left the house, she had just told Rich and Max that she would be gone for most of the day and that she'd return by five or before.

Both of her boys were happy. Max, because the three of them had been on a long run in the woods; and Rich, because he and his new partner Zach were working on a new case that was taking all of his time and energy. Her husband was happiest when he was busy.

Her analytical mind began to list the problems. The first of the top ten highest priority was the bureaucracy and the attitude that seemed prevalent among many—even most—of the people who worked in the prison. The first people who came to mind were the team from the Institutional Effectiveness and Institutional Compliance Departments, called to examine the response to the long list of complaints that Martinez had claimed.

Admittedly, Lindsey was not the most compliant individual on the face of the earth, but even the department names conjured up images of bureaucracy upon red tape, wrapped in procedure. She knew her laughter was a stupid reaction, but honestly, when they introduced themselves along with their titles, she had thought they were joking—Kafkaesque to the extreme.

Thank God for Monica, because she had spoken and filled the painfully chilly silence following Lindsey's most inappropriate response to the two officials. From then on, Lindsey had needed only to reply when Monica directed specific questions at her.

And then on the heels of these two, came a visit from the Senior Medical Director. He was, Lindsey thought, a pompous ass. More so than even Lance Pettigrew, the medical director who had initiated a class action suit against her, and everyone else in the Texas Judicial System. Because she had practiced medicine without a license when she saved Devon Preston's life. At least Pettigrew had an excuse. He was a Harvard medical school graduate, and he was an addict.

She had spent two hours with Dr. Stanley Nixon, DO, as he exhaustively picked apart both Martinez's complaints and the written responses of Monica and Lindsey. From the moment Nixon walked into the center, Lindsey knew this would be trouble. His manner was condescending, referring to her and Monica by their first names, and himself either as Dr. Nixon or Senior Medical Director.

Because the man was a graduate of an osteopathic program somewhere in Minnesota and had most likely barely made it through the program, he was probably cripplingly insecure around physicians like Lindsey. At least that was Monica's theory, it was as good as any.

Lindsey was not a snob, far from it. She could care less whether other doctors were trained in medical or osteopathic schools or foreign medical schools. What mattered was his or her competence, nothing more. But the Osteopaths she had worked with in the past, frequently had a chip on their shoulders. Almost without exception, the man or woman seemed determined to prove themselves superior to her and everyone else as they competed with their medical school colleagues. A futile exercise, Lindsey believed, but some of these insecure people could be very dangerous, particularly if they had a title. Dr. Stanley Nixon could be very dangerous indeed. So for two hours, she kept her mouth shut while the man picked at, criticized and questioned the most trivial details. When he began to grill her and Monica on the basics of emergency medicine, she almost lost it but blessed Monica made sure that her foot was always only an inch from Lindsey's so that she could stomp on Lindsey's toes when needed.

And then there were the patients, the prisoners. In the year and a half or so that Lindsey had been Medical Director at the Huntsville Prisons, she had cared for maybe twenty men with real medical problems. The rest—and there had been hundreds—merely knew enough to claim chest pain, induce vomiting or any of countless other methods to feign the symptoms of acute illness. There was absolutely nothing wrong with any of them. More and more, McCall found herself exhausted, and from the worst kind of fatigue, because it emanates from endurance rather than the challenges of problems and their solutions.

Since it was a Saturday morning, the traffic was light enough for her to reach the 610 cutoff within a little over thirty minutes. Lindsey was still getting used to her new car, a Ford Escape. Her yellow jeep she'd had since her Cardiology Fellowship had finally bitten the dust and she and Rich wanted a car which would be roomy enough for Max. He loved it, mainly because they had bought him a new bed for it. And he loved new beds.

Lindsey was turning off the 610 loop onto Bellaire Boulevard by a quarter to ten. Turning left, she drove slowly toward the medical center. She knew how tempting red cars were for the police, particularly down Bellaire where more than one incorporated township made their budgets handing out speeding tickets to those drivers caught at only one or two miles over the speed limit. Red cars were not her favorite, but this color was more rose than red and surprisingly appealing. The longer she drove the car, the better she liked it.

After driving another ten minutes or so, Lindsey turned left onto Bissonnet and then right onto Edloe where she stopped the car. She sat staring at a chocolate-brown wood-shingle house on the corner of Edloe and Bissonnet.

It looked the same. Except there was landscaping now, the new owners had put money and time into the small yard. And they had torn down the trellis around the corner from the driveway to put in a patio.

Lindsey had bought the house when she had been accepted on staff at Houston Medical and was finally making decent money after close to twelve years in training. Strangely, she felt nothing as she sat looking at the place. No emotion at all. At times like this, she wondered if something was lacking in her emotional makeup. Shouldn't she feel something about a house she had called home for over ten years?

Ah, that's it, isn't it? This wasn't home...I'd never had a home before now.

Smiling, McCall continued down Bissonnet and then

turned left on Fannin to drive by the medical center. Checking the time again, she decided to drive through the medical center for old times' sake and turned right onto Ross Sterling, driving by Houston Medical on her left.

The TMC was like Texas—huge. With over sixty independent medical institutions and eighty or ninety thousand physicians, researchers, and employees in the sprawling twelve miles of incorporated TMC prime real estate. Located within a single block from one another were two nationally known medical schools, and seven of the finest hospitals in the nation, perhaps the world.

Driving slowly along the central strip, she passed St. Luke's and the Houston Methodist Hospital on her right. Lindsey slowed to a crawl as she gazed at the hospitals made internationally famous by the medical warfare between Denton Cooley and Michael DeBakey during the latter half of the last century. Smiling once again, she thought with deep affection about these two giants of cardiovascular surgery. Without warning, she began to cry.

Pulling over in front of the large Methodist Hospital, Lindsey laughed and cried at the same time.

Is this the kid who thought she had no feelings? Ha!

The emotions were like a tsunami, carrying her and throwing her around as if she had no will of her own. Sobbing into her hands, she was mortified when an off-duty Houston cop stopped at her car and knocked on the passenger window.

Quickly drying her face, she rolled down the window to see a concerned male face. "Miss, are you all right? Do you need help?"

Shaking her head and smiling, she said, "No, Officer, I'm good." Taking a deep breath, this time, the smile was almost genuine.

"I've been gone a long time. It's good to be back here."

The cop nodded, but still he stood there, waiting.

"Honest, I really am fine," she said. When she got out of the car, she pointed down the street at the University of Houston Medical School. "I used to work down there...I've not been down here since..." she cut herself off from verbalizing the thought *since you guys arrested me for murder.*

CHAPTER FIVE

Forty-five minutes later. Downtown Houston

I guess today is my day for sitting in my car and staring at buildings. But the last two have washed away all my makeup. Tears were once again pouring down her face because she was looking up at the stained glass window and thinking of the way Rich had described it late one evening.

The searchlights illuminated the majestic bell tower, but high up and beyond the bell tower soared the crowning achievement of the Co-Cathedral of the Sacred Heart. As they had gazed up at the over fifty-foot, illuminated stained glass window of the resurrected Christ, Rich had told Lindsey how awed he felt by the magnificence of the artist's depiction. Rather than the weakened and pitiful representation of the Savior favored by artists of the last several hundred years, the Italian who had created this Christ had designed a hero, a warrior. A God-man whose humanity was perfected by the spectacular blood-red sacred heart residing in the massive and muscular torso from which power, strength and love seemed to flood the city of Houston.

Her husband had explained the controversy when the window had appeared during the construction of the new

Co-Cathedral; traditionalists from all walks of Christianity complained about the unorthodox nature of this Jesus. All unnoticed by Lindsey, whose sole focus had been her work at the medical center.

Rich loved the window—had treasured it from the first few shots he had seen on television. He had even taken to driving downtown at night so that he could see the brilliant colors illuminated by the bright light within the church, and reflected through that crimson, sacred, heart. Each time Jansen viewed this Lord, he thought of the old Christian hymn, "Onward Christian Soldiers." This was a general he could follow into hell.

Smiling through tears once again, Lindsey winged a simple prayer of thanks to this God who had, for reasons she would never understand, graced her with this man, Rich Jansen; this faith; and this astounding priest, who was now approaching her car.

"I've been watching you sit here and wondered if you knew where to park?"

"In fact, I have forgotten, it's been too long!"

Nodding, Father John Tobin motioned for her to follow him as he walked rapidly around the block long footprint of the Co-Cathedral, to the Rectory on Louisiana Street. He gestured at an enclosed parking area with an open gate, waited for her to park the car and catch up with him, then closed the gate.

Together, they walked up the stairs to the Rectory. Once in, they headed down the hall and around the corner to the huge kitchen shared by four priests, an archbishop, and the cardinal. Lindsey and Father John ambled slowly down the hallway to the kitchen where there were a few long and several smaller tables, couches, and a formally outfitted dining table with seating capacity for twenty.

Looking over at the table sitting in the corner by a window facing out on Jefferson Street, Lindsey saw two thick ham-and-cheese sandwiches with a side of macaroni salad and chips sitting there alongside two glasses of red wine. Her stomach began to rumble loudly at the sight.

Lindsey took a seat and a sip of wine and waited for John to say the blessing. He did so, and soon, only sounds of contented chewing could be heard in the spacious room.

Half of her sandwich devoured, Lindsey leaned back, drank more of the good Cab, and said, "You are a lifesaver; that was the best sandwich I've ever had."

John nodded. "I do make a great sandwich. Not much else, but sandwiches I can do." Fixing his keen gray eyes on Lindsey, he took note of the shadows under her eyes, the residue of mascara on her cheeks indicative of recent tears, and her thin frame. It had been only a couple of months since he had last seen her, yet she looked like she'd dropped ten pounds that she didn't need to lose.

"What's wrong, Lindsey?"

With a Ph.D. in clinical psychology from the University of Michigan and a Ph.D. in philosophy from Rice University here in Houston, the priest had been a successful psychotherapist in Southern California with a thriving practice. Until he decided he could no longer say no to the 'hound of heaven,' a reference to a little-known poem by that name, and a favorite of John's. He had been brought up as a Catholic but had stopped attending church in his undergraduate years while at Berkeley and had not entered the seminary until he was thirty-five.

One of the first methods that the Lord had introduced to teach him humility, John had once observed wryly to Lindsey, was when he joined his class of fellow seminarians. He, a thirty-five-year-old double doctorate, with forty-three other seminarians age twenty-four or younger.

"It's complicated, Father." Lindsey opened her mouth to continue but was suddenly stuck. Her thoughts seemed jumbled and chaotic, and suddenly embarrassed, she wished she hadn't come here, and didn't quite understand why she had.

"Of course, it is."

"I don't know where to start."

"At the beginning might be a good spot."

And she began to cry for the third time in less than two hours. This time, it took a good ten minutes for her to stop.

While she cried, the priest sat there calmly as if this were the most normal thing in the world, and perhaps, for him, it was.

Lindsey stared at John, absorbing the kindness, patience, and gentleness which were so evident in the long, angular face. A face which mapped the battles he had fought to achieve those virtues; his cheekbones were very prominent, almost gaunt- the look of an ascetic. Father John's long arms ended in big wiry hands with long skeletal fingers which were clasped loosely in front of him.

"I want to quit."

Without a change in expression, the priest merely echoed her. "I want to quit..." then asked, "quit anything in particular or everything in general?"

Laughing in delight at this man whom she trusted as deeply as her husband, her eyes lit up.

"My job."

John said nothing. He just sat there waiting.

Lindsey described the events of the last three weeks in detail. Father John listened, asking a question now and then only to clarify the people and timing so that he could understand. She talked for close to an hour before finally admitting what bothered her the most.

"I no longer know why I became a doctor." Staring at the remainder of her sandwich as if it contained the mysteries of the entire universe, the physician continued speaking, her voice now subdued. "I've tried to talk myself into going back to the medical school, to Cardiology. At least there I'd see real patients rather than these guys who have become experts at faking all kinds of ailments. But I know it would be a mistake." The priest had to lean forward across the table to hear, her voice was almost muffled. Father Tobin suspected Lindsey was not talking with him but with herself, now that she was in a place where she felt safe. Rather than interrupt that interior monologue by asking that she speak up, he merely strained to hear. "It would be like trying to recapture the past, days when I was convinced I knew exactly what I was doing and why."

Suddenly the screech of a siren sounded close enough to startle them both. Lindsey laughed as they both jumped a bit. Then she wryly asked, "Confirmation, maybe?"

Now gazing directly at Tobin, Lindsey declared, "I have never liked taking care of sick people. In med school, we all used to joke about it because none of us wanted general internal medicine. We all wanted to be specialists; it was far more interesting than the monotonous litany of GI, pulmonary or joint problems." Her voice dropped to almost a whisper, and her tone changed to one of self -disgust. "I left the care of my dying mother to my sister, and even refused to take care of my own baby...I gave her up to my best friend to raise!"

There it was, the priest thought. Finally dealing with these burdens suppressed for so many years. But the priest knew that this was not the time to delve into the birth of a baby he had not known she had, nor her decision to give the child to her friend to raise. Perhaps one day, but not today.

"So why don't you just quit your job as Medical Director

at Huntsville Prisons, Lindsey? What do you think is keeping you in a job you dislike so much?"

She mumbled something.

"I'm sorry, I didn't hear what you just said." John leaned over the cushioned armrest of his chair to get closer to her. She was staring fixedly at some point on the carpeted floor. He doubted that it was the carpet that held her rapt attention.

During her outburst, Father John had led them to a corner where they could speak more privately, should one of the other priests or a member of the staff come in for a bite to eat.

"To atone," she repeated.

Father John reached around, took Lindsey's chin in his hand, gently lifting it up so that he could see into her eyes; thinking as he did so, that she had been given one of the larger crosses to bear. For so many of us, our unhappiness and misery were chiefly due to our own choices. But not for this gal, she'd been given a heavy load when she hit the planet, and precious little of her burdens were due to her own ignorance or poor choices.

"Atone for what?"

"My mother, Paula, my child...and all of this money that Digipro is bringing in...and it keeps increasing but Mother and Paula are still dead." This time, the tears were silent as they tracked down the familiar terrain of her face.

"You can add famine, drought, and poverty to that list, while you are at it, Lindsey."

The droll comment had its intended effect. Startled, Lindsey blinked and stared at him.

The priest got up, retrieved the opened bottle of Cabernet and topped off her glass, though she'd only had a few sips. Father John poured a generous amount into his own. Then he waited until she brought the glass to her lips to drink. When she did, he said, "Have more, it's splendid, don't you think?" Smiling at her, John said, "It's the same Cabernet we drank back in Beaumont, remember?"

She did. She remembered very well because she had figured out what had been missing in her life, other than Rich and had decided to become Catholic. After decades of agnosticism, sure that neither faith nor religion was relevant, to anything or anyone.

They sat in companionable silence for a few moments. He was right, Lindsey thought, the wine was delicious.

"Atonement." The word was said carefully, cautiously. Father John held his half-filled wine glass in his hand and was tilting it one way and another. "Some say the more 'legs' one sees in red wine, the better the wine is."

He was talking about the viscous transparent tears left by the wine as it clung to the sides of the glass. "Others say that the legs reflect only the percentage of alcohol; that thicker, slower legs are indicative only of a higher alcohol content. While still others claim the legs mean nothing because they have no relationship to the quality of the wine. All the focus on legs is rubbish. Wine is good, they say because it tastes good to the palate.

"Atonement is like that." The priest peered at Lindsey over the rim of the glass he was twirling about. "Most of the conversation about atonement is said by people who know nothing about it... because there is so little to be said on the subject. There was one act of atonement Lindsey, only one." The intense gray gaze of the priest focused on the crucifix on the wall beside him.

"Your sins, my sins, and those of every being ever born until the end of the world are nailed on that cross with Him. In His wisdom, He has given you intellectual gifts of immense proportion. Your discovery of a drug too late to help your mother, now relieving the suffering of untold millions is resulting in a tsunami of cash." Father John shrugged. "So what?"

Mildly, Father John asked, "Would you feel better if you drove a ratty old car that broke down all the time, or lived in a ramshackle house in a fourth world country? Would that change any of the mistakes you think you've made in the past?"

Studying this gifted woman who needed desperately to leave the stultifying environment she was in, the priest thought of Blaise whom he'd not seen since they had taught together, years ago. He smiled.

Catching the smile and more, she asked, "What? What nefarious plot are you cooking up for me?" This time, the twinkle was back in those intensely green eyes of hers, and so was the light.

"I was in grad school with a Jesuit, who tried to persuade me to come into the Jesuits and to switch from clinical psychology to organic chemistry, like him." The corners of his thin lips turned up at the memory. "And I came very close to joining the Jesuits and switching to science." Father John's smile broadened. "Perhaps if my quantitative skills had been better, I would have done it, but science isn't how I roll."

Lindsey laughed, this time, the humor mixed with relief. She could actually feel the tension of the last week disappearing and understood why she had felt so impelled to come here for counsel.

"Blaise Roderick is one forceful, compelling man who now runs the animal clinical research lab at California Polytechnic State University in San Luis Obispo. Blaise is looking for a new researcher, one with experience, guts, and money."

The priest regarded Lindsey thoughtfully, thinking as he did so, that these two would be perfect for one another. She with her extensive medical research knowledge, Blaise with his deep comprehension of hard science. *Imagine what two brains like these two could concoct to improve the health of Americans?*

"He is looking for someone just like you. He fired the last of the five who were in the department when he took it over. I'll give you his contact info and let him know he may be hearing from you."

CHAPTER SIX

Corporate Headquarters, Adams and Adams Pharmaceuticals,
Chicago, Illinois

Glancing quickly at his watch, Matt Adams flinched. *Oh, no, I've done it again…for like the third time. Late on Friday night and here I am, perched on the horns of a dilemma worthy of a game theory case discussion at Wharton. Or is it a trilemma? I've never avoided risks before, but here I am, alone with my gut…but by God, this acquisition will not happen, not on my watch. I drew a line in the sand at this morning's board meeting that will never be erased. But this is my company, I own fifty-one percent of the stock, and I'm not selling to some German who wants to create who knows what kind of evils with my business.*

He had promised his wife that he'd not miss yet another of her galas at the prestigious Driehaus Museum, but the show had started over two hours ago. A successful artist in her own right, Carolyn Adams had built a trust fund for the support of fledgling artists which had become the darling of movers and shakers in the city. Tonight's show featured the work of a young woman from the projects. Just eighteen, the girl was, in Carolyn's words, 'insanely gifted.'

Matt's wife was a patient woman and for over thirty years

had been incredibly supportive of the unreasonable working hours of the CEO of one of the few remaining privately owned pharmaceutical companies in the world. But she would be more than slightly unhappy that Matt had missed the first show for her protégé. And rightly so.

It was already close to ten at night, so he may as well keep working on this third rebuttal to the latest missive from the very aggressive lawyers from Germany. When their offer first appeared, Matt was excited, even relieved. This mega corporation looked like the perfect solution to the problems created by extraordinary success. Matt's small company was at a critical junction in its development. Adams and Adams lacked the firepower to compete on the new global playing field. If the company was not infused with many billions more for research and development, within ten years, Adams and Adams would be just one of the long list of pharmaceutical companies that could not keep up in the cutthroat business culture of the twenty-first century.

Everyone was for the acquisition. Adams' son and partner, his thirty member board, and his wife. Everyone except, of course, the twenty-five hundred employees of Adams and Adams in danger of losing their jobs if the company was taken over by the German conglomerate. The rationale of his son, board and wife were compelling, and in truth, Matt agreed with them. He was sixty-eight years old, had worked pretty much non-stop since he started in the pharmaceutical business at the age of fourteen. He was tired. These people looked perfect on paper, too perfect. Matt had learned long ago that when something looked too good to be true, it generally was.

The intensified offers from Diedrich Gruppe in Germany made him nervous. They felt wrong, somehow obscene. The offer had been increased by a few billion with each approach. And when Matt or any of his people tried to learn about the

CEO, Diedrich Braun, they could uncover only the most superficial facts about his multiple corporations. Merely sketchy summaries revealing hardly anything about the actual products. And there was scant information about Braun himself, other than the indisputable wealth that his corporations had at their disposal.

When Matt told Carolyn that he had turned down Braun's offer in a way that could not be misunderstood, his absence at the museum gala would pale in comparison. He understood she was worried about him. She wanted a life with her husband while they were both healthy enough to enjoy one another. But there was something that was so off-putting with this offer, knowledge that was too profound to ignore. The hell of it was that Matt had no hard evidence to buttress his animosity toward Braun and Diedrich Gruppe. He had only his gut feeling that he had learned to trust through the years.

So engrossed was Matt Adams in his musings about the enormity of the conflict with his board and the disappointment he would cause his family when he told them that he had rejected the last offer, he did not see the shadow of the assassin. The man was tall, clad completely in black and had entered the corporate offices of Adams and Adams the way anyone would. But none of Matt Adams' visitors had been prepared with the skills of this man. Years of experience with Force Recon—the elite Marine special forces outfit—had created an efficient killing machine. One which left no tracks.

Matt's office was located in the heart of downtown Chicago. On the fifty-fifth floor of the Chrysler building, the view was panoramic. All four walls were glass, each revealing the lights of the city in all directions. Lights which he would never see again.

Sensing a presence only at the last moment, Matt had time only to gasp when the sharp needle penetrated his jugular, injecting enough ketamine to paralyze a horse. His eyes were mere slits when the gloved hand placed the thirty-eight revolver, the one Matt kept in his desk drawer, in Matt's left hand, and then forced his hand to close around the gun with two fingers on the trigger to propel the bullet into his temple.

Wishing he had used his own silenced Glock, the assassin knew that the noise from the shots could alert someone else working in the building. Adams' offices were empty, he had made sure of that when he entered the suite. But there were other suites and other floors.

Working rapidly, he erased all the narrative Matt Adams had painstakingly written in his written refusal of the Diedrich Gruppe offer. In its place, the tall assassin wrote an apologetic suicide note to Carolyn Adams and their son, Matthew Junior.

Within five minutes, he was on the elevator and heading down to the first floor, looking just like any other fit, forty-something-year-old man, in search of a night on the town.

CHAPTER SEVEN

Hesse, Germany, Diedrich Braun's Villa

Braun sat alone on Sunday evening in the garden of his magnificent estate, sipping Glenmorangie Pride on the rocks as he watched the sun slowly set. It was a lovely June evening in the 'spa city' of Konigstein um Taunus. The name was derived from the days before WWII when Konigstein um Taunus was known as the 'Jewish Spa,' because of the numerous Jewish artists and musicians who had summered in the spa-like atmosphere of the small but charming town in the Taunus mountains of western Germany.

Inhaling the forty-two hundred-dollar single malt scotch, the German billionaire breathed a sigh of immense relief. His idea to combine business with a weekend at his mountain estate had been an instant success with the mainly Frankfurt and Berlin guests and members of his Board for Diedrich Gruppe.

The risk was immense because everything needed to happen in a tight time frame. There was no margin for error, imperative that each action be executed precisely.

A prominent Chicago city official with almost a million dollar gambling debt had fallen all over himself to grab the money offered anaonymously via a secure untraceable linc.

The man agreed instantly to reveal the confidential details of the mounting dispute between the Adams and Adams Board Members and CEO Matt Adams over the acquisition. Friday morning in Chicago, the dispute culminated in an explosive meeting where the Board Chairman presented Adams with a unanimous statement signed and notarized by the entire Board, which commanded that Matt Adams accept the fifteen billion dollar sale price. All thirty members had been in attendance. The three-hour meeting had ended in a stalemate, where the Board Chair and Matt Adams were each threatening litigation. The Board for executive malfeasance, Adams for unlawful coercion, a charge which even Matt Adams knew would not stick. But a gift for Braun and just in time. That board meeting easily established a credible reason for the unfortunate suicide of Matt Adams.

He had received the call at a little after ten, US time, on Friday night. It was done, his plan would work.

The board members of Diedrich Gruppe were influential political and business leaders in Germany and Austria and were not fools. Had the Adams 'purchase' taken any more time to achieve, Braun would have been in serious trouble. The twenty-four member Board of his company, Diedrich Gruppe, had spent the weekend meeting discussing the third quarter earnings which were far below predicted. CEO and Chairman of the Board Diedrich Braun had run his company into the red, deeply in the red. Braun decided he would open the books and demonstrate why. Transparency was in, after all. Fancy footwork, rhetoric, and gourmet food would appease, but only for a time.

The meetings had begun at seven sharp on Saturday morning and ended at five Sunday afternoon. Breakfasts, lunches, cocktails and dinners had been the finest cuisine available in Germany. Excepting the Glenmorangie Pride of course. Single malt aficionados had twenty-four-year-old Macallan and Bunnahabhain to choose from, happily so, since the group had consumed ten bottles of each over the weekend.

Braun's detailed explanations of the research and development debt carried over from the acquisition of Adams and Adams had been mostly fancy footwork because the company had not been in debt at all. But the board members were all aware of the 'creative accounting' methods of the twenty-first century because most made use of them themselves. Therefore, aside from standard questions, the presentations all went well. And since none had any experience with the lifeblood of the pharmaceutical industry—research, and development—they were fascinated by that presentation.

After a good bit of deliberation, Braun had asked his new CEO of Adams and Adams to do the talk about the emerging battle for life-extending medications. Dr. Viktor Dragovik was a ruthlessly ambitious Serbian scientist. But one with extraordinary charm and brilliance. Within the first ten minutes of Viktor's talk, they were eating out of his hand. Especially the women.

Braun had hoped this bit of theater would work, and it had. Following Viktor's hour long presentation on epigenetics and the work being done by competitors on life-extending research, Braun had cut short the discussion and claimed a need for another two hours on the next quarter R&D budget. He had feigned surprise when the group had unanimously asked to spend the two hours with Dragovik. Viktor was tall, olive-skinned with black hair and deep blue eyes, and the features befitting movie stars or gods. Fluent in six languages in addition to his native Serbian, he had asked the board if they would prefer German or English before he started to speak. Startled by the question, there had been a few seconds of heavy silence until Heddy Schmidt, the German Finance

Minister replied that English would be fine. And then followed with one of her rarely seen smiles.

As Braun had expected, the majority of the questions were aimed at the race for development of the life-extending drug. 'What companies were furthest along,' and 'where did Diedrich Gruppe rank among the contenders,' were questions asked in several different ways by various board members. None was satisfied with the truth that the research of other companies was confidential and therefore protected. Braun came close to divulging his plan to steal Longevive, because it was clear that the majority of the board was interested in getting the drug out before anyone else. But of course, he said nothing, and just let the conversation ebb and flow under the skillful baton of Dragovik.

"I quit my job today. Actually, I resigned three weeks ago; this was my last day." Rich stared at his wife, Lindsey.

"Are you surprised?" She stood in the doorway of their log home in the Sam Houston State Forest with the setting sun lighting up her blonde hair, an expectant expression on her beautiful face.

Rich laughed, as he walked toward her to wrap her in his arms. "Seems no one in this family can hold down a job for more than two years. Let me guess, you're going back into research."

"That is *exactly* what I want to do, but I feel as if I've deserted Bob, Luke, and Monica." Gnawing her lower lip, she stared solemnly at her husband.

Only a year ago, Jansen had witnessed the grueling hours of study that his wife put into passing the Emergency Medicine Boards, adding the specialty of Emergency Medicine to her impressive medical credentials.

"While regular people enjoy the benefits of a stable job where they know what to expect when they get to work, you and I lose interest if we spend a day without a crisis!" Grinning at his wife, Rich took a couple of steps backward, only to stop suddenly when he ran into an immovable object.

"Hey Max, did all this commotion wake you up?"

The big red Doberman stood in the hallway, nervously looking from Rich to Lindsey, then back again. His stub of a tail wagging slightly, his ears at right angles to his long face and his beautiful amber eyes directing the classic Doberman stare, as he regarded each of them. A sure sign that he knew something was up. Lindsey approached the dog, got down on one knee and murmured.

"This is nothing for you to worry about baby, nothing at all. We'll never ever leave our boy. I was going to suggest we eat out to celebrate—or maybe mourn—but our psychic boy can sense a change in the air, so it's not the time to go out for dinner. Let's grill those sirloins you bought last weekend and have a bottle of wine or two. I'll make the salad after I change clothes, sound good?"

"Sounds great, Lindsey. I'll turn on the grill, blacken the steaks and open the Silver Oak to breathe."

Rich brought the seasoned steaks and a glass of wine out to the sizzling hot grill on their outside porch to sear. Neither he nor his wife could abide overcooked beef. Jansen had learned the elemental rule for cooking an excellent steak. Never leave the grill until the steak is done. Rich sipped his wine while he reflected on Lindsey's resignation. Despite all the effort and money she had expended in the total rebuild of the Huntsville Prison Emergency Center, and the fact that she was now credentialed as an Emergency Medicine physician, his wife had been restless. Jansen knew the signs well.

Prisons were not populated by the best and the brightest. Mostly, the law enforcement and justice systems got it right, those in prison needed to be there. The injustice which had landed Lindsey in jail for murder, and within a year following her release, Gabe McAllister, who had been wrongfully convicted of sexually molesting a little girl, was very rare. The majority of the Huntsville inmates was of a singular nature; one that claimed he was a victim and totally uninterested in accepting responsibility for his actions. His imprisonment was unfair, in fact, each of the bad things that happened to him was unfair, the fault of someone else. Over time, cynicism almost invariably began to invade the personality of even the most optimistic of people working with prison inmates.

Taking a healthy sip of the excellent Cabernet, Jansen flipped the steaks with tongs, careful not to lose the simmering juices of the meat by using a fork to turn it. It was a pet peeve of his that most chefs could not correctly grill a steak. Although Rich did not consider himself a gourmand, he knew how to cook and expected the food consumed at Houston's best restaurants to meet his standards. Frequently, he was disappointed. Most of his friends preferred to skip the scrutiny with which Jansen examined a dish prepared by one of the Chefs currently celebrated by the media. It was far more enjoyable to dine with Rich at home and enjoy food that met his standards because he had cooked it.

Rich had not regretted his decision to leave the Chief Warden position and return to his first career as a criminal defense attorney. On the contrary, he had relished the intense challenges of the trial attorney. His reentry had been a tumultuous one, taking the case of an inmate, a man convicted of raping and sodomizing a little girl. Shaking his head as he thought about the three months of preparing for and facing one of the best and fiercest prosecutors in the country, Rich smiled at the memory.

Those weeks were among the roughest of my life. Including those under fire in Beirut. The whole appeal was impossible, we didn't have a chance. And yet we did it, between Cunningham and me, we won an acquittal for Gabe McAllister.

His smile faded as he thought about the recent conversations with his former law partner, Todd Kensington. Todd had been nothing but gracious and understanding when Jansen told him that he was going to accept the partnership offer made by Zach Cunningham. But he knew exactly how Lindsey felt. Leaving people who were far more than colleagues hurt mostly because of the stark truth of it; they remained behind while you moved on.

Comparing the feel of the skin beneath the palm under his thumb with the feel of the steak when he touched it with his opposite forefinger, the meat felt soft and a little bouncy… perfect.

With the tongs, Rich grabbed both steaks and carefully placed them on the plate. Then he balanced the platter, wine glass, and the front door as he waited for Max to go back into the house. The dog's olfactory senses were on overdrive, having inhaled the irresistible scent of the beef. Placing the sizzling steaks on the table to sit for a few minutes, Rich grabbed a couple of cups of kibble and fresh hamburger and put it in the dog's bowl.

"Sit boy."

The Doberman sat, both ears straight up and his eyes focused on the food, as small streams of saliva dribbled out of both sides of his mouth. Rich placed the bowl on the raised platform where he ate. Remaining motionless while waiting for permission to eat, those amber eyes were like a laser beam on Rich.

"Good boy, go ahead, Max."

In seconds, the stubby tail was wagging so fast it was almost a blur while the food was joyfully consumed. Dobermans love to eat.

Lindsey and Rich smiled at one another as they watched the dog. "How about seeing how the Patriots are doing in the

Playoffs, Linds, are you up for watching the Sunday night game? It should be starting right about now."

Although Rich Jansen was a native and loved all things Texan, he had received his undergraduate degree at Harvard University in Boston. While at the college, he had developed an affection for the New England Patriots, an affection which had been boosted by the remarkable Super Bowl achievements of the Belichick-Brady duo. Lindsey had never paid any attention to football before she had met Rich, but had caught some of his enthusiasm for these two men and had begun to enjoy the games almost as much as he did.

"So why do I feel excited, sad, disloyal and selfish all at the same time? And you don't seem surprised at all."

"Honey, I remember the look on your face as you were describing Liisa's new drug, are you kidding? Frankly, if anything, I'm surprised it took you this long to quit!" Jansen was discussing Longevive, a new drug currently in phase one studies in Liisa Reardon's research lab in Lausanne, Switzerland.

Lindsey was lying on the large dark brown leather couch in their living room, her head in Jansen's lap. Rich was seated with his feet propped up on the coffee table in front of the couch, has hands were immersed in his wife's hair, alternately stroking and rubbing her scalp. A February norther had blown in bringing with it a cold rain, rare for the mostly tropical and humid climate surrounding Houston. There was a fire going in the floor to ceiling fireplace of the great room, the dancing flames providing the only light. Max was stretched out in front of the fire, gently snoring.

Surprised at the lack of a reply, Rich stopped the motion of his hands, earning an immediate complaint.

"Oh, don't stop, that feels too good! Please?"

Sighing, his wife mumbled something inaudible.

"I'll stop again if you don't talk loud enough for me to hear you!"

"I had to do battle with the self who believes that quitting is weakness and failure. You know that part of yourself, right Rich?"

Jansen smiled and returned to his primary task of massaging the good doctor's scalp. "I do know him, very well."

"What did Bob say when you told him?"

"Exactly what you just said… why has it taken you so long?

"He is such a good guy, as are Luke and Monica…very special people who were astoundingly generous to me, back when I was an inmate…" Rich could hear and feel the sadness and deep sense of obligation in her voice, but he said nothing, knowing there was more.

For a while, the only sounds in the room were the steady, comforting sounds of rain thrumming on the roof, the crackles and pops of the burning wood, and the light snores of the dog. Rich thought of the still new year and all the changes it was bringing.

Telling Todd that I was going to leave his law firm yet again was something like what she is feeling now. Except that Todd and his partners had never functioned as my lifeline like these people did for Lindsey.

Occasionally, as a finger touched her cheek, he could feel wetness where the silent tears had fallen. He had no doubt that this was a great move for his wife. Though had he known what would transpire over the next several weeks, he might have had very different thoughts.

CHAPTER NINE
Southwest Airlines Flight 348 to San Francisco

"I could get real accustomed to flying first class." Taking a sip of the Freixenet Cordon Negro Brut Cava she had discovered of late, Lindsey enjoyed the light celebratory taste of the dry Spanish sparkling wine. She had never liked champagne until Kate and Steve's wedding, where Lindsey had discovered the other European sparkling wines of Prosecco and Cava. And there found a brand new addiction.

Rich smiled and nodded. He took a sip or two of the bubbly occasionally but preferred red wines to whites of any modification.

They were celebrating several events. Worthy of a McAllen on the rocks, Rich thought as he sipped the smooth amber malt liquor. He looked over at Lindsey to take in once again, the remarkable sight of her reading a novel.

They were heading to Palo Alto where they would see their good friends, Dr. Steve Cooper, Chief of Cardiology at Stanford, Kate Townsend, his wife and investigative journalist, now staying home to care for their new baby boy. After spending a few days with them, they would continue south where they just might buy a house in Pismo Beach.

His wife looked happy and relaxed for the first time since

their first few months of marriage close to two years ago. Feeling the weight of his stare, Lindsey looked up from her new Kyle Mills novel with a question in her eyes.

Jansen smiled. "Just enjoying watching you read for fun!"

"It's a really great story, you'll like it when I'm done. His characters feel like people we know or would like to know...all too human with glaring but loveable flaws." Taking a sip of Cava, she lifted her glass, waited for him to do the same with his drink and touched glasses. "To our new life, my husband. Who would have ever dreamed we would be moving to California?"

The last two months had been crammed with activity. Lindsey had taken Father John Tobin's suggestion and contacted his Jesuit priest friend, Father Blaise Roderick, who headed up the Animal Research Center at California Polytechnic State University, along with a veterinarian named Jodi Tamarack. After several conversations with the priest, she had decided to take Father Roderick up on his invitation to fly out to Cal Poly for an interview in late March. Planning to stay only a weekend, Lindsey had called Rich to explain how taken she was by the charming college town of San Luis Obispo, and the Central Coast of California.

Jodi, the Co-Chair of the Department, was an added plus; Jodi was tremendously excited about the prospect of Lindsey joining the team. In fact, she had insisted on taking Lindsey to dinner at one of the many charming restaurants in San Luis Obispo. The only other vet Lindsey had ever worked with had headed up the Animal Welfare Committee at Houston General; he was a man who seemed to savor his bureaucratic authority and relish the obstacles in the path created by the absence of a document. A total opposite of Tamarack. Jodi was a researcher at heart and had even dabbled in epigenetics, and had listened avidly to Lindsey's plans for her joint research with Liisa Reardon.

Lindsey was not given to superlatives about most things, except Rich and Max. After listening to her keenness on the job and this part of California, Rich had suggested that she stay a few more days to look for a house. Adding that he'd love to fly out there to join her, but was in the middle of a case that had rapidly become more than he and Zach had bargained for. Rich had sounded enthusiastic but tired. Excitedly, she had agreed with his idea and had looked around Pismo Beach and what was called the five cities of Avila, Pismo and Shell Beach, Grover Beach and Arroyo Grande area for houses.

Lindsey had sent him pictures of Pismo and the Oceano dunes from her phone. He had to agree with her that these beaches were stunning, equaling Cannes, and the Greek islands. Each time she had called, Rich ended up laughing because the list of attributes kept growing with each subsequent conversation.

But when Rich opened the link to the house she had found at Pismo Beach, his jaw dropped. More than a McMansion, the seven thousand square foot house was situated in a gated community located high on Route 101—the main road hugging the entire California coast—and boasted astonishing ocean views from almost every room.

This house, however, required a herculean psychic shift for Jansen.

First, because he had mentally always belittled those who needed large homes, members of the elite, a class in which he felt he did not belong; and did not want to belong for that matter. Jansen had assumed Lindsey felt the same since she seemed to care nothing for things like jewelry or clothes, and the house she had lived in before she was arrested had been very modest.

He felt the same regarding the whole notion of a gated

community; there was something about the phrase that did not fit with him.

A gated community – huh! What snobs reside in palaces like this? Privilege, superiority, and entitlement that's who he expected to find. And the rules... After years in the Marines – Rich soundly hated rules. *Why...rules got you killed!*

It felt awkward, and he did not know how to talk to his wife about it, she was so excited about these next two weeks, the new house and the new life. Rich chuckled to himself as he thought the words again: *new life.* That was it exactly.

Get over it bud, Lindsey has a chance to start over: a new job, one that fits her this time. A new state and so what if the house costs many millions? Millions that belong to her, not you, and if anyone deserves a new start in a beautiful place, it's Dr. Lindsey McCall.

This time chuckling out loud, he answered Lindsey's inquisitive look. "Can't wait to take Max to the Dobie rescue place to choose his new friend."

At Lindsey's suggestion, Rich had cut off Highway 101 to take the more scenic Route 1, which hugged the California coastline as it meandered through Monterrey, Carmel, and miles of some of the most beautiful coastline in the world.

The couple had rented a Porsche convertible, for the simple reason that they had always loved the Queen of sports cars but had never driven one. Every hundred miles, they switched drivers so that each of them had the opportunity to experience the fine engineering of Porsche, and the efficiency of the way the car handled the narrow winding highway.

Sitting at one of the many lookouts along the way, Lindsey declared, "If this Pismo house is just too kitschy for you, Rich, we can walk away from the deal. The deposit only secured genuine interest, not a commitment to purchase."

She was staring at the crashing ocean breaking on the rocks below but after a moment turned to look at her husband. He was laughing.

"What's so funny?"

Her long blonde hair was blowing in the wind, and despite the sunglasses hiding the intensity of her stare, Rich could easily see the laser focus of those intensely green eyes.

"Kitschy...what does that mean exactly?"

Shaking her head, Lindsey assumed an exasperated pose and remained silent.

Reaching over, Rich took off her sunglasses so that he could see her eyes, and whispered huskily, "Do you have *any* idea of how much I love you, Dr. McCall? Do you have even a clue?"

Staring back at this man who was sometimes a complete mystery to her, Lindsey felt that familiar thrill, the tingling and trembling in her abdomen that turned to heat and desire.

"You know what you do to me when you talk like that, right?" She could see the answer in his dark eyes.

Simultaneously, they turned around to look at the back seat of the compact little Porsche and laughed, shaking their heads to cool off the sudden heat between them.

There were parked cars on either side of them also enjoying the view. "Maybe they know where we could get a room for an hour?"

Jansen opened his door and walked around to the passenger door, where he opened it, bowed gallantly, extended both arms and gently drew his wife up and out of the Porsche. Putting his arm around her, he walked her to the lookout point where he tipped up her head, looked into her eyes and kissed her, first gently then with increasing hunger. Whispering into her ear, "Lindsey, love of my life, you deserve this place in Pismo Beach if it's what you want. Me, Max and whoever else joins our family will love being there, so long as we have you."

Lindsey stared up at her husband conscious only of her suddenly watery knees, the desire coursing through her body and the sheer *want* of him.

"Let's delay the trip to San Luis Obispo a few days, shall we?" Rich's dark eyes were dancing. "Steve gave me the name of a place which will suit two people who want nothing more than one another and an occasional meal."

CHAPTER ELEVEN
Big Sur California

"This feels like another world, as if Houston and Huntsville exist, but in a parallel universe." Lindsey stretched her lithe body and turned over on her side to gaze at Rich. It was a little after five in the morning, but already dawn, a bit late for Lindsey who was an incurably early riser. While they had stayed with Kate and Steve, she and Steve had been up for an hour or two before they were joined by their spouses. Occupational hazards of medicine, all those years of little or no sleep coupled with ordinary days which began before six in the morning. Habit.

He was lying on his back, eyes closed, but she knew he was awake, she could tell by his breathing. Finally, he opened his eyes and grinned.

"Pretty nice place isn't it? We owe Steve for this one, Linds."

Smiling wryly, Rich remarked, "Guess we must have been shedding pheromones all over the place while we were with Kate and Steve.

"It was kind of a non-sequitur as we were leaving their house. You and Kate were talking off by yourselves, and Steve was thanking me for my advice. He told me that he thought

Kate would want to include Reardon in on the discussion about his namesake and Godson, so most likely, it would be a few weeks before they got back to us. Suddenly, Steve said, 'You know Rich, the drive from here to the central coast is quite stunning. You and Lindsey may want to take more time than you had planned to drive it. One of my patients is an artist and rents out his place in Big Sur to people he knows or who have been referred by him. I saw him in the clinic last week and asked him about the availability in case you guys were interested and he told me he's been in the city all month so here is his card. Just call him and use my name and you'll be good to go.'

"Then Steve had grinned and said something like, trust me Bud, you will not be sorry you stayed there...there is a magical feel to his small cottage, and the views are spectacular."

Lindsey nodded her head because Steve had so understated this lovely place. Although they had been so wrapped up in one another that many of the aesthetics had completely gone unnoticed for the first sixteen hours, when she had come up for air, the energy, peace and tasteful elegance of the cabin seemed to seep into her pores.

Neither Rich nor Lindsey could get cell phone reception or get online. Perhaps it was the absence of that worldwide connection, or more likely, it was the constant pounding of the surf far below the rocky coastline which made this a unique place, a healing place. Perhaps there was something to the claim that negative ions promoted health and restoration of the body after all.

There were small patios outside the bedroom and front door with chaise lounges, a built-in wooden table and bench on the rock wall out on the cottage stone patio. The kitchen was redwood with concrete counters and stainless steel appliances, a veritable surfeit of accommodations for cooking excellent meals.

"I'll go make coffee if you want to get some more sleep."

"You don't mean that."

"You're right, I don't, but that's what a loving wife would say, wouldn't she?" Dodging the pillow coming her way, Lindsey pulled on one of Rich's shirts as she padded into the kitchen to make the coffee.

A few minutes later, she was sitting in one of the Adirondack chairs holding a cup of hot coffee in the cool, almost cold early morning air.

"Thanks for this retreat, Rich. I think we had no idea how much we needed something like this." Lindsey heard him behind her, but she had not turned around, she was mesmerized by this ocean. The majesty and ferocity of it, so different from the tame and tepid Gulf of Mexico she had grown up with.

When Rich leaned down to kiss her, he yelped. "Your face is freezing! Get in here and get some clothes on....or then again, maybe off again..."

That night after a satisfying dinner, they sat on the sofa in front of the roaring wood stove drinking the bottle of Jordan that Steve and Kate had insisted they take with them.

"Are you ready to rejoin civilization, or should we see if Steve's friend will sell his place to us?" Rich's legs were stretched out on the long ottoman in front of the sofa.

"If I were a cat, I'd be purring," Lindsey sighed. She was lying down on the couch with her head in Rich's lap. "How long have we been here? Three days? Three months?"

Chuckling, Jansen nodded. "Somewhere between three days and three months, I think.

"Did you set up times to meet with the people at Cal Poly or the realtor in Pismo?" Rich had asked the question out of idle interest, but when he saw the abrupt widening of the green eyes in his lap, he laughed. "Forget an appointment, Dr. McCall?"

Lindsey was a stickler for meetings starting on time, deadlines, and all that accompanied a perfectionistic personality like hers. Curiously, Rich watched her, intrigued by this uncharacteristic lapse of hers.

"It's Wednesday, right?"

"Nope, it's Thursday."

A small smile, "I knew that."

"Right."

"I was supposed to meet with all of them yesterday."

"All of them."

"Right. Father Roderick, Jodi the vet and the Realtor."

"Okay."

Lindsey giggled.

Good for her. This is a side of her I have never seen.

"Is it alright with you if we leave tomorrow?" She was fondling the hand that had just been playing in her hair.

"We can leave tomorrow or the next day either one, Linds. This is your journey from now on in, I'm just along for the ride.

"Gotta admit though, I miss our Max and want to get him out here with us as soon as we can."

"This is exhausting, let's just flip a coin, Lindsey."

They had looked at seven or maybe ten houses over the last few days and were back at the motel staring at each other.

"You didn't seem all that psyched about the 37 Bluff Drive property, so I asked Eileen to show us some others."

Rich stood up from the chair where he had dropped, then walked over and sat beside his wife on the king size bed. "How many times do I have to tell you that the palace is fine with me? And stop wincing every time I call it a palace. That's what it is...at least in this or the last century. From what I've seen of real castles, none of us would have liked to live there, including Max."

Standing up, Rich started to pace the small motel room. "I think you've wanted to buy this place and have from the very beginning, but somehow you don't think you deserve a beautiful place like that, or you're afraid I'm intimidated by the price. Of all of the houses we've looked at, 37 Bluff Drive is superior in every way. But before we discuss why, let's talk about me and your money."

Jansen stopped his pacing to rub his chin, "Man, I need to shave, remind me to do that, will you please?"

"Well alright then, are you bothered by the fact that I am a wealthy woman?"

Rich threw his head back and laughed. "Honey, you are not merely wealthy, you are rich, immensely rich, and will continue to live in the upper minuscule percentage of humans on this planet who rank among the most moneyed of us, for the rest of your life!"

Squinting at the look on Lindsey's face, one between embarrassment and shame, Jansen quickly sat down. "Here is what I know. Honestly, I believe that no one *deserves* wealth, just like no one deserves beauty or intellect." He took her chin in his hands and looked into her eyes. "But God in His infinite wisdom has given you all of them. And he knew what he was doing when he gave those gifts to you.

"Are you sitting around getting fat and happy off the estate of your family or the money rolling in from Digipro?" Staring at her with intensity, he answered his own question. "No, you understand intuitively that money is a tool, that you are the steward of a gift which must be cared for, judiciously. Just a few months ago, you donated a very hefty sum of your Digipro profits to Liisa Reardon's new drug and then invested another percentage as venture capital.

"And the very first thing you did with that several million-dollar estate from your parents was to divide it up into trusts for your sister's kids and for your daughter." Rich waited for the sheen of tears which always appeared when he mentioned the child her best friend Julie had adopted and raised as her own. Lindsey never mentioned the girl.

Only once had Lindsey spoken to him about the child she had never seen. She had gotten pregnant during the last year of her Cardiology fellowship and somehow managed a pregnancy, completion of her training and worked out an adoption to her best friend and new husband. Countless times,

Rich had wondered why Lindsey had not aborted the baby like so many women did back then, in the mid-nineties and still today. And how on earth had she managed all that, alone, for she had most definitely been alone? The heroic, super-human reservoirs of strength she had to have plumbed to manage all of that were unimaginable to him each time he thought about it.

But Lindsey merely sat at the edge of the bed and chewed on her cheek, deep in thought, and seemed to have traveled a long distance away. But there were no tears. He didn't know if that was good or bad.

After a few minutes of silence, Lindsey looked up at him and smiled, saying, "Let's go buy that house!"

Looking at his watch to note that it was close to five, Jansen slipped his loafers back on and said, "Well, this should make Eileen's day."

Arriving at the Central Coast Realty office at five-thirty the Friday afternoon of a holiday weekend was dicey, but when they got there, Eileen was in her office working on her computer. Spying Rich and Lindsey as they walked in through the glass foyer, she came out of her office to meet them.

Eileen Simmons was the opposite of the quintessential California coastal realtor. Short, chubby and with a broad New York accent despite thirty years in California, Eileen managed to combine her aggressive Brooklyn upbringing and a blunt, almost forceful way of speaking with an overlay of California ease that was sincere and went deeper than veneer. From the very first conversation Lindsey had with the woman, she had liked her style and appreciated her honesty.

Standing in the hallway, Eileen regarded Rich and Lindsey. Dressed for the upcoming Memorial weekend, she wore blue jeans with a sparkly American Flag sweater and matching flag earrings. Fingering the shirt and earrings, she grinned and said, "A little bling is expected with California Realtors, isn't it?" Her brown hair was short and styled in an adaptation of a pixie, befitting her small, almost pug nose.

"Torrie said she was dead on her feet after showing you ten properties today.

"Excuse my manners, you must be Rich. I am delighted to meet you and welcome you both to our paradise here on the central coast!" Gazing at Lindsey, she said, "Why, you are even prettier live!" Then after studying the two of them, "You two belong here, you will definitely intrigue the local gossip mongers as they try to figure out who you are…it will be most interesting, I think."

Watching this perky lady, Rich was charmed. The flattery should have felt ingratiating, but it didn't at all, not in the least.

Jansen smiled broadly as he shook the small hand.

Eileen checked her watch and said, "It's five- thirty, can I buy you a drink after you tell me what you've decided? There is a lovely wine bar that opened up a couple of years ago that I'd love to show you."

Rich tried, but could not suppress his laughter and Lindsey was chuckling as well.

Eileen got it. "Look, I know you've made your decision, it's fairly obvious, should we get to it now and get the details out of the way?"

Like two little kids, they followed the small powerhouse into her office and sat down.

Taking out the paperwork for the 37 Bluff Drive property, Eileen stared at them. "What do you want to offer?"

The smile still on his face, Rich said, "Wish she'd been with us this morning Linds, we could have saved ourselves a lot of time."

"No, Rich." Suddenly, the realtor was all business. "You

needed to do exactly what you did. Although the process is exhausting, it's essential to assure yourselves that the house you are drawn to at first is, in fact, the right one.

"Unfortunately, the only way to do that is by trudging through all the other options. That way, once you move in, you'll not be second guessing your decision."

Nodding at her comment, he surprised himself by agreeing with her. This Eileen Simmons was a class act, and he was extremely impressed. But this was Lindsey's deal so he sat back and watched to see how she'd handle it.

The ever vigilant Ms. Simmons took note and switched her gaze to Lindsey. She waited patiently in silence.

"We'll write a check for four million nine hundred and five thousand as soon as the inspections all come in."

Eileen nodded in approval and remarked, as if to an able student, "Ten percent off the asking price and a cash deal. I suspect the owners will be quite pleased."

After the documents were signed, Eileen once again eyed the two of them soberly, "Before we leave the office and go sample Ventana Grill's array of California wines, is there anything you want to discuss about this purchase you are making? Last minute questions about anything at all?"

There was silence for a moment or two and then, "How did you know it would be 37 Bluff?" Lindsey had tilted her head at Eileen. "We just figured out that was the one an hour before we came in here?"

"None of the others fit what you were looking for." She reached into her desk drawer and removed a student type lined notebook with a rueful look. "I love computers for almost everything. But for important notes about potential clients, these notebooks just work for me."

Paging back to find it, she read from a long list. "Clear ocean views from the majority of the rooms," "library," "wine cellar," "large gourmet kitchen," "office space for two," "separate living area for guests," "patios overlooking the ocean with built-in cooking grills" and "dog runs big enough for two large dogs."

Lindsey looked stunned.

"Did I say all of that? I don't remember having a list like that!"

"You didn't have a list exactly, but remember our early talks about a dream house?"

Smiling now, Lindsey nodded. "I do! Of course, you took notes!"

Later that night at dinner, Rich and Lindsey were discussing the details of the move. "What do you think Greg will say about his cabin?"

Greg Bell was Governor of Texas, had been for three terms and gave his 'cabin' in the Sam Houston State Forest to Rich and Lindsey as a wedding present.

"He's happy to take it back, especially since we added the guest cottage in back. Says he's looking forward to having some retreats down there. As soon as we are out, he'll take it back over."

Lindsey took a bite of her halibut, and swallowing, said, "Between us, we have just enough furniture to fill about half a room in that place."

"Right," Rich agreed, "But we'll be able to fill up the library shelves!"

CHAPTER THIRTEEN

*Two days later, California Polytechnic Institute Animal
Research Lab San Luis Obispo*

Lindsey had driven Rich to the tiny airport at San Luis
Obispo to catch a flight to Oklahoma City. There he'd meet
and stay with his law partner, Zach Cunningham. Their long
distance law partnership worked surprisingly well, but occasionally they needed some face to face time.

On a whim, Lindsey had called Jodi Tamarack after she
dropped off Rich to see if she was in on this last day of a long
holiday weekend, and been delighted when she answered her
office phone.

"Another workaholic I see, Dr. Tamarack."

"Hey Lindsey, what are you up to? I'd assumed you'd
probably left by now."

"Actually, I just dropped off Rich at the airport and
wondered if I could impose on you and Father Roderick before
I head back to Texas. Do you have any time today or
tomorrow?"

"Come on up now, I'd love to see you again. I'm just
babysitting some brand new lambs born just last night to
make sure their moms will decide to feed them. Father Blaise
is out of town, but I would love some company!

"Do you remember the way to my office?"

Fifteen minutes later, Lindsey was turning off the 101 Highway onto Grant Drive ascending up a few hundred feet to the university. Driving the Porsche slowly up the road to Cal Poly, she stopped at a kiosk to pick up a parking pass Jodi had left. Searching for building 10, Lindsey drove slowly up the main road through the campus. Small, sad white signs were placed in front of each building explaining that the withered, golden brown lawns and empty planters were due to the drought, now in its fourth year.

Jodi had told her to park in any of the staff parking lots and then to find her way to Building 10. The campus was small but packed with a variety of buildings which weren't clearly marked. Jodi stood in the doorway of the building with her keys dangling from her hand watching Lindsey approach.

"Feel like feeding some babies?" Clad in jeans and a sweatshirt, the vet looked more like one of the students than a department head.

At Lindsey's answering smile, Jodi motioned to Lindsey to follow her. Clicking her key fob to unlock the big black truck, Jodi climbed up and in, laughing as Lindsey fumbled with the hand-holds to pull herself up into the high seat.

"Yikes, I take it you don't wear tight skirts to work, girl. We rented a Porsche in San Francisco and drove it down the coast. Compared to that, this feels like I'm climbing up onto a horse."

"You don't want to take that Porsche where we're going, believe me." Within less than ten minutes, they were on dirt roads leading to the barn where there were seven brand new reluctant moms.

Jodi stopped the truck in front of a large old barn from which could be heard bleats and cries that sounded almost like human babies. Lindsey followed Jodi, who had rapidly sat down among the enclosed small herd of about ten to fifteen tiny baby lambs and ewes.

"They sound just like human infants," Lindsey exclaimed as she dropped down beside the vet. "I had no idea." The bleats of the sheep suddenly became raucous, and Jodi motioned to Lindsey to follow her out of the enclosure and to the back of the barn where several short white lab coats hung on hooks.

"Here, Lindsey put one of these on and then they'll accept you. They'll recognize the scent from one of the students who come down almost every day."

Donning the coat, Lindsey followed Jodi back into the enclosure and adopted the same position as earlier. This time, there was no reaction. Lindsey watched as Jodi guided a tiny lamb over to a sheep who seemed skittish, dancing around a bit as Jodi brought over the baby to nurse.

The vet's movements were slow and measured. Soon the little guy was happily nursing. Two more baby lambs needed the same kind of help and one ewe finally surrendered to the gentle persistence of the vet but the third did not. The irascible animal became more and more irritable with each attempt to get her baby to suckle. After another five minutes, Jodi picked up the lamb, smiled at Lindsey and asked rhetorically, "Ever feed a brand new lamb?"

Stepping out of the enclosure, Jodi called over her shoulder, "Hang on, I'll go get some colostrum for him—be back in a second. Then you can go ahead and let him drink as much as he wants."

After the little thing had finished all of two bottles, along with the colostrum the baby needed soon after birth, everyone in the enclosure settled down. Sighing, Jodi stood and motioned for Lindsey to follow her out.

Grinning at Jodi, "Wow, I had never even seen a baby

lamb this small, never mind fed one! How often will you need to feed him?"

"Every two hours until Mom decides to give in."

Lindsey stared at Jodi, "Like all day and all night long?"

"Yep," Jodi replied with a nod, "but I've checked her out pretty well and don't think she's got mastitis, her teats aren't inflamed at all, and this is her only baby, so she's got plenty of milk. I think she's so skittish because she's pretty young herself. She should come around sometime today I think." Jodi tried and failed to stifle a yawn.

"When did they start having the babies?" Lindsey was staring at the miniature animals in amazement.

"Bertha there started around ten Sunday night, then everyone else followed suit, but were kind enough to wait for their sister to finish."

"So you handle all this by yourself? I thought there were students assigned here to help...No?"

Shrugging tiredly, Jodi replied, "There are. But its Memorial Day weekend..." she rolled her eyes, "But I need to get this last little guy fed."

Taking note of the dark circles under Jodi's eyes, Lindsey offered, "Let me do it, Jodi. I'll go with you, and you can show me where to get the colostrum and bottles for our little guy, then you can go home and get some sleep." Looking at her watch, "I don't want to see you until at least four this afternoon, and by then, hopefully, all will be under control, and we can get an early dinner somewhere. This time, I'm buying to celebrate our new house in Pismo...assuming the owners accept our offer, that is."

Jodi's eyes widened, "Are you for real? If you're serious, I'll take off now and be back after a shower, change of clothes and some sleep." Eyeing Lindsey's jeans and shirt, "You might want to change into scrubs so we can go to dinner directly from here—we do have showers here." Yawning again, she smiled, "Okay, I'm gone, thanks for this Lindsey, I owe you!"

Five minutes later, Lindsey had changed into scrubs and was back in the enclosure, happy to wait here until time for the next feeding. She could feel the smile on her lips as she sat cross-legged among the ewes and their babies. The ewes were concentrating on the grass spread liberally among them, their babies, a minuscule copy standing right by their side. It was mostly quiet aside from an occasional bleat from one of the ewes.

Wonder what Monica and the gang are doing now...I'm so grateful they listened to my pleas for no going away party. I do hate those things, and enough tears have been shed in that center already. I wonder if that new Senior Medical Director will implant a clone of himself for Medical Director...

Her smile broadened as Lindsey recalled the last conversation with Monica.

"We are *not* going to say goodbye, Lindsey McCall. I have some vacation time coming, and I plan to get on a plane and come out to visit you in your new digs. We'll have a better party there in California. So just give me a hug and walk out that door as if you'll return tomorrow." Monica's eyes were a bit too bright, and Lindsey could see the sheen of unshed tears as she leaned in to hug her as hard as she possibly could.

"We'll make that a promise then Miss Monica, a promise."

Then for the last time, she had turned to walk out of the Center that she had designed and paid for with her estate money. She never looked back.

Later, stroking the flank of the frightened animal in long, deliberate movements, Lindsey talked to her, crooning to her exactly the way she did to Max when he was anxious. Under her fingers, she could feel the young mother relax, and could see the rate of her breathing drop and her eyes narrow down from the deer in the headlights look they had had all morning.

She hadn't worn a watch when she and Rich had left their room for the airport, but Lindsey estimated she'd been here for five, maybe six hours. And was certain, this time, the young mom would let her baby nurse. She just knew it.

Lindsey had taken some time to explore the surrounding area when her charges appeared content. Finding the rest of the herd about half a mile away from the barn, she breathed in the cool coastal air and received the calming, invigorating energy of the peaceful sloping hills. The silence was absolute. The herd, close to one hundred head of sheep she guessed, quietly grazed, staying very close to one another as they did. Watching the quiet animals, Lindsey could feel her psyche soaking in the serenity and calm of the creatures. She had never before even seen a herd of sheep, much less fed a baby lamb; so the scene before her seemed timeless.

It was disorienting to consider that a mere two months ago, her twelve hour days were spent in windowless rooms, walking on concrete among people with mostly fictitious ailments. The beauty, peace, and silence of this place were intoxicating.

I am so psyched to be back in research that I almost don't know what to do with myself! Isn't it a sin to be this happy? To have more than you dreamed? The best husband in the world, and now the best job?One that is stress-free? Is that even legal?

Although she'd not said anything to Rich, the move from Texas had cost her many sleepless nights. Texas had been her home for her entire life, and she loved the place, the people and all things Texan. The central coast of California was undeniably beautiful—but Lindsey had worried that maybe it was more of a vacation resort area, one where the focus was on play rather than serious work. But now that she had spent time with Jodi Tamarack, Lindsey understood that the beauty and peace of this place did not endanger serious workaholics.

Wandering back into the barn, Lindsey took her place among the lambs once again.

"There, baby, there you go." She had been serenading these and other nonsense words for at least the last forty minutes and decided it was time. Picking up the baby, she guided him slowly to his mom with her left hand while keeping her right hand on the ewe's side and constantly crooning to her in that same soft cadence.

Finally, *yes!*

Straightening up was not easy. After a couple of hours on the floor, her butt was numb and legs stiff, but Lindsey felt great.

Just as Lindsey had finished showering, dried her hair and applied a smidge of makeup from what looked like a group supply, she heard, "You did it! Lindsey McCall, you are hired!!"

"I'm a One Health Vet." Jodi's last comment about the exciting potential Lindsey would bring on board had ended with a descriptor Lindsey had never heard of.

Putting down the glass of an excellent Californian cab she'd been about to sip, Lindsey cocked her head at Jodi and repeated, "One health, what does that mean?"

"I think the One Health Initiative may end up saving the world," Jodi declared, deftly articulating her words without spewing out any of the contents from her mouth.

Over the course of the last few months, Lindsey had spoken with Jodi numerous times and did not consider her a drama queen, the image of which her last statement evoked.

Watching Jodi, Lindsey's thoughts split along two tracks. One, how different she was from either Kate or Julie, her two best friends. Jodi could be attractive if she just took a little time with her hair and applied some makeup. And lost about twenty-five pounds. Her eyes were an unusual shade of light green, so light they looked faded. That second, the words, 'saving the world,' echoed in her head. Just then, Jodi looked up from her salad and chuckled. "You're wondering if I'm a closet psycho or maybe a conspiracy nut." Her expression was merry, and the laugh lines around her eyes deepened, making them a deeper shade of green. Then all trace of amusement left her face.

"The One Health Initiative is our best and perhaps our only chance to save ourselves, the animals, and this earth. Formed somewhere around 2004 by a small group of savvy vets, a very few medical and public health docs, and some environmentalists, One Health is dedicated to improving the health of all the species on our planet. I wasn't joking when I said I thought it may end up saving the world. I'm actually dead serious when I say it.

"Want to hear more or am I boring you?" The vet's expression was neutral. Almost convincing Lindsey that her reply didn't matter. In just that second, Lindsey could see the passion simmering under the façade of detachment.

"Jodi, you could not bore me if you tried, please continue. I was staring at you because you're different; different in a good way." She was smiling widely now as she reflected on the numerous times that she and her best friend, Julie Grayson, had discussed the burdens of 'being different.' And she was excited because she knew that she and Jodi were destined to be the best of friends.

Shrugging off the quasi-compliment, Jodi looked intently at Lindsey. "You know the worst fear of the World Health

Organization, right?"

"Sure, a pandemic which will end the era of antibiotics. Because the organism will be resistant to every antibiotic, we have. Some are predicting it will be the end of medicine." Lindsey stared at Jodi. "Which may be just what the doctor ordered."

At that provocative statement, Jodi raised her eyebrows in an unspoken invitation to explain. But Lindsey said nothing more, she just picked up her wine to take a large swallow, thinking as she did that she'd best not sound too radical this early in the game.

A broad array of factors was contributing to what Lindsey was referring to. Over-utilization of antibiotics worldwide has been a problem for several decades. Combined with the widespread use of low-level antibiotics in feed used by the large animal feeding operations, the evolution of 'superbugs' or organisms resistant to all antibiotics was rising at an alarming rate. Death from infectious organisms resistant to antibiotics ranged from about twenty to twenty-five thousand per year and was increasing. The Centers for Disease Control estimated that over three hundred thousand people could die from antibiotic-resistant disease by the year 2030. By the middle of this century, there could be rates of mortality to rival the 1918 Swine Flu epidemic. During that appalling plague, one out of three of the planet's population was infected with the deadliest strain of influenza that had ever been seen. Fifty million people were killed, more than the total losses of the 'Great War.' With superbugs and the globalization of travel, a repeat of that catastrophe was far too possible; and the new numbers of deaths could make 1918 seem like child's play.

Lindsey studied her new partner and recalled the Google search she did on Jodi. Over one hundred articles in journals like Nature, Biology, and Epidemiology. She was not only trained in Veterinary Medicine but also in Public Health with a specialty in Epidemiology.

"You're right Lindsey, but I'm talking about a zoonotic disease on the scale of the AIDS virus, only worse."

Transmission of bacteria and viruses from animals to humans is not a new threat to public health. Rabies, brucellosis, psittacosis, and of course, the plague, are only a few of the diseases which can be contracted from animals. Fortunately, understanding disease transmission, as well as the development of prevention and treatment options, have prevented major outbreaks. However, Jodi's flat statement about AIDS as a zoonotic disease was terrifying. In med school, Lindsey had been taught by the infection control faculty at Houston Medical that AIDS was not of zoonotic origin because direct evidence of monkey to human disease could never be proved. Medical researchers were unanimous in their belief that none had occurred. Watching the casual certainty on Jodi's face now, Lindsey wondered if the physicians had merely taken the safest path.

The alternative was too terrifying to contemplate—a really cunning, deadly disease of primate origin that is smart enough to adapt. Horrifying. It could pave the way to an apocalypse, for real.

CHAPTER FOURTEEN
Present Time, Lausanne Switzerland

"Do we need to get you to the ER, to have you checked out at least?"

Reardon was looking at Jansen, and saw the blood drip from the back of his head, as if for the first time.

"My God, man. I'm sorry, I should never have asked you to come."

Reardon looked dazed, exhausted and scared.

"Hank, I'm okay I think," Jansen replied, leaning down to pick up the ransom letter he had dropped on the linoleum floor of the ASL research lab. He was immediately sorry when the six cups of coffee he'd had on the red-eye flight from California to Zurich threatened to make their way back up, and he staggered a bit. Thankfully, Hank Reardon didn't notice as he looked around the lab.

"Let's leave this exactly the way it is, Hank. It's a crime scene." Regaining his balance, Rich reached out to Reardon. "We're going to have to decide what to do and figure out a sequence. I need some air, anyway. Come on, let's step outside."

A few minutes later, Rich was squinting in the bright June sunshine and walking slowly along the pathway from the labs to the main building of Andrews, Sacks, and Levine; with the befuddled and frightened CEO at his side.

As they walked, he struggled to ignore a throbbing headache which amplified with each step. Slowly his jumbled thoughts began to settle, and Rich began to recall what had happened to him in the few short hours he had been in Switzerland.

George, Reardon's live-in chauffeur, butler and anything else Reardon needed, had met him at Zurich International Airport.

George was not a young man—about Reardon's age, Rich had guessed when he met both he and his wife Stella back in January. But George had easily aged ten years as he stood in the airport pick up area next to Reardon's black Bentley. Smiling warmly, George said, "Good to see you again, Rich," and extended his hand. Although the smile did nothing to lighten the somberness of his dark gray eyes, the handshake was firm.

"That's all you have for luggage?"

Without waiting for a reply, George opened the passenger side of the car, grabbed the bag with his right hand and tossed it into the back seat. Watching him as he briskly walked around the back of the car to take the driver's seat, Rich wondered about him. Rich remembered a pleasant man with ruddy cheeks and a ready laugh, but today he looked drawn and tense. There were many possible explanations under the circumstances, of course. Seated in the passenger seat of the luxurious car, Rich said, "George, it's going to be a mighty long drive if you don't talk to me."

They had left the airport behind a good thirty minutes ago. Initially, Jansen thought his silence was due to the traffic in the busy city of Zurich. But with the tone of Hank's frantic call still echoing in his ears, Jansen's cop instincts were firing on all cylinders. Everyone was a suspect, even George.

He and Lindsey had been just about to turn in. It was only ten at night, Pacific time. They had been unpacking book cartons; lugging the heavy containers from the foyer, where the movers had left them, to the library on the far side of their new house, when the phone rang. The Texas house had been furnished by the Governor and his wife, making their move to Pismo Beach quite simple...except for the tons of medical and legal texts, most of them heavy tomes. Moving furniture would have been easier.

"They'll kill her if I call the police. Sorry to disturb you guys—but Rich, I need your help!"

At the expression on Rich's face, Lindsey had raced to pick up the extension and was listening, motioning for Rich to take the lead. Reardon sounded as if he were about to come apart.

"Hank, who do you mean? They will kill who?"

"It's—uh, L-Liisa, she's gone. I got a note but no request for ransom, just the letter telling me not to call the police."

Looking at Lindsey standing across the large room, Jansen could see the expression on his wife's face. And, he could read her mind.

Last January, after Liisa Reardon had shown her the results of the first stage tests on the experimental mice, Lindsey had been really excited about the promise of ASL's new drug, Longevive. Excited too, about the almost serendipitous findings in a small cohort of the Digipro patients who were demonstrating early and electrifying results after three months on a dietary regimen. She could barely contain herself and was, for Lindsey, quite effusive about her prediction of the impact that the drug may have on medicine as it is practiced in the twenty-first century. But Rich recalled her anxiety as well. Lindsey had emphatically stated that the drug was alchemy, only this time, it actually *could* turn into gold. Her expression had looked exactly like the one she wore now, but tonight sorrow had overwritten the pleasure of being proved right.

She was shaking her head slowly back and forth—tears flowing soundlessly, as she listened to Hank Reardon explain to Rich that his daughter had been kidnaped.

Lindsey quietly put down the phone and padded back into their bedroom where she grabbed a pad of paper and scrawled out a message, then handed it to Rich who read it and nodded.

"Hank, I'll get headed to you on the next plane—we're in San Luis Obispo, so it'll be after midnight over there before I get in. Lindsey will call you with the flight and arrival time as soon as we get it confirmed."

Lindsey had dropped him off at the airport at five-thirty the next morning, just an hour before the departure of the first leg of his arduous sixteen-hour flight from SLO to Zurich. These were the times when the cost of living in paradise seemed ridiculous. Had he left from Houston, he could get to Zurich in eight hours on a non-stop flight, rather than taking all day.

"So, you and Stella have worked for Hank for quite a while, right George?"

"That we have, Rich; that we have." His Scottish burr was noticeably more pronounced, it seemed, and his broad stubby fingers holding the wheel of the Bentley were white from his grasp.

Turning on to the toll road at Baden, Rich was surprised when George greeted the toll collector in German.

"Guess it helps to be fluent in all three languages if you live in Switzerland, huh?" Reardon made the comment more to himself and was not really expecting a response from the driver. He was surprised when George laughed heartily.

Was the laugh a little too hearty?

Rich could not get the comments Lindsey had made as

she had driven him to the airport out of his mind.

"You know I hate this, right?"

Rich had been lost in his own thoughts when he realized she'd said something. "Sorry, Linds, say again?"

"The very last thing in the world I want to see is you getting on that plane."

Startled, he'd twisted his head to look at her. Just then, a passing set of headlights illuminated her worried and penetrating gaze as she quickly turned to glance at him, then back to the road.

"I'm frightened, Rich. Petrified. For you, for Hank, of course for Liisa."

There was silence in the car while he tried to come up with something reassuring. A moment or two passed while he realized he had nothing, nothing at all to offer her. He was scared, too.

"There's only one way this could have happened the way it did, Rich, only one way." Her statement hung in the air, an ominous declaration.

"Hank, I've been looking for you all morning. Where have you been and who is this?"

Jerked back to the present, Rich stood still in the bright sunlight, trying to get a clear focus on the guy. But his vision was blurred. Forgetting for a moment, he shook his head and regretted the motion instantly. The nausea and dizziness were almost overwhelming.

"You must be Rich Jansen from California. Hi, I'm Joe Cairns." The man had offered to shake his hand, but once he drew closer to him and Reardon, said, "Good God, man, that head wound looks serious." Turning to Reardon, the guy said "Hank, I'll take Rich down to the University Hospital. Be back as soon as we can."

Too out of it to argue, Jansen allowed himself to be led by Cairns to a black SUV in the parking lot. Cairns helped him up and into the seat, and there were quickly headed down the mountain to downtown Lausanne at a healthy clip.

Two hours of testing later, Rich was delivered back to the emergency center to listen to a pleasant French physician—a woman who looked to be about eighteen—explain that he had a concussion and should remain overnight in the observation area, just to make sure there were no other complications.

Just as he was about to protest, in walked Cairns with Hank Reardon in tow. Reardon looked anxious, worried and exhausted. Cairns looked like...a cop.

"Hello Dr. Badeau, how is he?"

Simultaneously, the doctor and Jansen replied with opposing statements.

"He should stay here overnight so we can observe him since he has a relatively severe concussion."

"Hank, I'm all right. I'd like to get my clothes and get out of here."

Cairns slowly looked from the young doctor to Jansen, and then to Reardon.

Then he turned with a smile, "Thank you, Doctor. May we have a minute with your patient, please?" The young physician looked nonplussed, then adopted a classic Gallic shrug as she turned and pulled the curtain closed behind her.

Staring at this guy whom he had never seen before, Jansen asked mildly, "And you are here why exactly?"

Reardon started to reply, but Cairns beat him to it. "Liisa and Hank hired me to head up security at ASL."

Before he could stop himself, Rich asked the same question he had asked Luke Preston during the riot at Huntsville. Only this time, he knew he'd get an answer because it was gushing out of every pore. So, this time, it was more of a statement than a question. "Force Recon, huh."

The only tell was the slightest widening of Cairns' eyes and the flash of a quick smile. There and then gone as if it had been imagined. But it wasn't.

Rich had enlisted in the Corps after graduating from Harvard. Turning down a full tuition scholarship to Harvard Law, he was just in time for Beirut, and to develop a love-hate relationship with the Marines Corps.

His Parris Island training was arduous; due more to the psychological games played by the drill instructors than to the extreme physical training. Most of the guys in his platoon were right out of high school and, therefore, a lot more vulnerable to the brainwashing, the relentless razing by experts with a simple goal—transformation. Taking young boys and pushing them past the limits of their physical and mental thresholds; only the few, the proud. Despite Jansen's resistance and his understanding that this was mostly bullshit, his sense of the brotherhood of the Corps was deep, profound and undeniable. After only six months in the Marine Corps, Jansen had achieved the rank of Lieutenant, and his CO was privately recommending that Jansen attend the Basic Recon course.

Only the few...the proud...

The memories flooded back as Jansen gazed at Cairns, awaiting a response. He'd been flattered. Which was, of course, the goal. But the Captain who had interviewed him for Recon had the exact same stare as Cairns: flat, opaque, dead. Reardon recognized that if he accepted the complimentary invitation to Force Recon, he would lose what these men had lost, a deficit that Rich feared could never be recovered.

After a few minutes of awkward silence, Hank explained further, "Joe came on board a couple of months ago, Rich. He has been conducting an analysis of our vulnerabilities to cyber-attack." Trying and failing to cover the break in his voice with a cough, Reardon pushed on. "Liisa was convinced that was where we were most vulnerable." He moved closer to Rich so that he stood partially between Jansen and Cairns, "Liisa was so excited to find him..." Visibly trying to collect himself, Hank further explained, "Joe had been working out of the Cyber Warfare Center at Omaha."

That seems strange somehow, this dude switches from Recon to geek squad?

Keeping his thoughts to himself, Rich nodded at Cairns with what he hoped was an admiring expression on his face, then smiled at Hank Reardon.

"Hank, can you please hand me my clothes so we can get out of here and do some planning, please? We have a lot of work to do and not a whole lot of time to get going on it."

CHAPTER FIFTEEN
Same time, Swiss Air, somewhere over the Atlantic Ocean

Lindsey smiled as she accepted the Macallan on the rocks from the friendly steward. She was both exhausted and wired, an unpleasant combination. Closing her eyes at the burn of the scotch from the first sip that was more like a gulp, Lindsey could feel a few of her rigid muscles start to loosen. Finally, there was nothing more she had to do...physically, anyway.

When she'd hung up from her abbreviated conversation with Rich, Lindsey had booked a two-thirty flight to Zurich from San Francisco, fully aware she had less than a thirty percent chance of making that plane. A little over seven and a half hours to get back home, throw clothes in a bag, grab Max and his food and get to Palo Alto with enough time to make it to the airport. It was impossible, but here she was. She'd be on the ground at just before eleven in the morning, Swiss time. Lindsey leaned her head back against the plush headrest of the first class Swiss cabin and allowed the effect of the liquor to wash over her. She made no attempt to control her thoughts as they flashed through her mind. But one thought predominated: Rich's plea, echoed, incessantly, *I need you to get out here as soon as you can.* He was scared, Lindsey could hear the alarm as his voice replayed in her head. This man who seemed to fear nothing had sounded close to panic-stricken, affirming the black thoughts she'd had while driving Rich to the airport. She thought about that, his fear and how she felt about walking into a morass which scared even Rich Jansen. The pace of her thinking was slowing down now both because of the scotch and a meditation technique Lindsey had learned during the crazy days of her two years as Chief Cardiology Resident. Fifteen minutes of watching your thoughts as if they were clouds—making no attempt to judge, control or react— provided profound relaxation and peace of mind. At times, as much as several hours of sleep. She began to analyze her feelings now, picking them apart now that there was time.

Am I scared too? Yes, for Liisa and Ariana absolutely, I'm terrified. But for me? No. Maybe that's what I heard in Rich's voice, fear for them and for Hank. That would make more sense...and also explain his desperate need for me to get out there. Neither Hank nor Rich could know where to find Liisa's research notebook or the formula for Longevive. So that's it then. We, no I, need to figure out how to do what the crazed brain behind this scheme wants enough to kill for it.

Just as Lindsey was reflecting on her last thought, that a single individual, a man, was behind all of this, she sensed his regard rather than hearing any sound. And Lindsey opened her eyes to look directly into the gaze of the steward who had noticed her empty glass.

Did I really drink all that? In less than ten minutes?

"Can I get you another?" Another smile. Then he gently suggested, "Maybe, if you do have another, you can sleep a few hours of this flight."

Lindsey looked appraisingly at the man who regarded her so earnestly. Rather plain, almost nondescript, except eyes which made him appear attractive, even intriguing. They were a dark, smoky, gray-blue, widely spaced and large. Noticing his wedding ring, she said without thinking, "I'll bet you have a bunch of kids. Three, or maybe four?"

The steward blinked, surprised at the personal comment, then smiled slightly at the rightness of her guess. "Five...with a sixth on the way. It's a good thing I travel so much, or we would probably have eight by now." Then, cocking his head to the side, he asked again about the drink.

"Sure, maybe it *will* help me get some sleep."

This time, she sipped more slowly and returned to her internal dialogue, specifically the thought about a crazed brain wanting the data and the formula so bad that he would kill for it. And realized her conviction that this was corporate espionage, coming from another pharmaceutical company. All it would take was a few hundred thousand dollars offered to the right person at the wrong time, and all loyalty to the Reardons would evaporate with the money.

Unhappily, Lindsey recalled her stunned reaction to what Liisa Reardon had created back in January. Sure, Liisa was keeping all the information in a locked safe in her office at ASL, but any hacker could access her computer site. When she had told Hank the size of the investment she was making in Liisa's drug research, she remembered the intensity with which she had tried to explain the need for pulling out all the stops to protect the data.

Exactly what I feared would happen when I looked at Liisa's data...the lifespan of her experimental mice had doubled, a few of the test animals were living close to three times their life expectancy. Far too precious a breakthrough to trust with even her closest associate. If similar results occurred in higher mammals, there would be no ceiling on the money to be made on this drug.

Now that she knew exactly what needed to be done when she landed, Lindsey thought about the providential series of events which had lined everything up in such a miraculous way. Closing her eyes again, Lindsey considered the eight or so hours which had preceded her making this flight.

Both Kate and Max had been wonderfully cooperative. Despite the fact that the dog had never before met an infant, Max acted as if he thought JH to be a new type of cool animal. And almost forgave Lindsey for leaving him with strangers. The dog had been on his best behavior from the moment they left the track until arriving at Kate and Steve's house in Palo Alto, seeming to sense the urgency in the air.

Kate had talked Lindsey into a cup of coffee since the airport was a mere thirty-minute drive from her house, and Kate had already covered the two-hundred-fifty-mile drive in just four hours. They had a little time, and Kate knew the Reardons well. She was also gravely worried. Handing her friend a freshly brewed cup of coffee, Kate smiled. "Well, despite these awful circumstances, it's great to see you again so soon, Linds. Looks as if the housewarming party will be postponed for the foreseeable future."

"Oh, good lord! I've got to call and let everyone know it's off. Hope they haven't made reservations yet."

"No worries, I'll be happy to do that for you. Make a list and I'll get everyone called once I drop you off at the airport. Even if they have reservations, they can ask the airline to keep the money but make the flight open-ended. Most of the airlines are happy to do that—they have their money after all."

Lindsey and Rich had planned a housewarming event— kind of an excuse to see their Texas friends —for the following weekend. The Pismo house was large enough to accommodate most of them, they figured. But when more than thirty people had called to say they would come, Rich and Lindsey also had rented a suite of rooms at one of the nearby inns on the beach. Among those planning to attend was Lindsey's oldest and closest friend, Julie Grayson, her husband Ted, and their four kids, the oldest of whom was Lindsey's biological daughter, now eighteen. A contingent from Huntsville Prisons was also coming. To Lindsey's delight, Monica Bradbury, the head nurse from the Huntsville Prisons Emergency Center and Luke Preston, the prison guard who had stopped a vicious beating by prison gang members had said they could come. Luke had undoubtedly saved Gabe McAllister's life with that intervention. Father John Tobin, their dear friend from the Sacred Heart Co-Cathedral, had promised he would adjust his schedule so that he could fly out for the weekend as well. Father John had laughingly informed Lindsey that Eleanor Philbin had already called to tell him about a command performance in Pismo Beach. Eleanor and her sister Marguerite were co-owners of the Houston Tribune, the paper Kate worked for.

Sipping her coffee, Lindsey said. "Thanks, Kate. Yes, I'd appreciate any insight you have."

Starting at the sound of her cell phone ringing in her purse, Lindsey jumped up and grabbed it.

"Hi. Yes, I'm at Kate and Steve's now. Kate's going to get me to the airport for a flight which should get me there by eleven tomorrow morning, your time." She listened for several minutes while her husband explained what had transpired since he'd arrived.

For Kate's benefit, she repeated his words, "So you're there now with Toni and Gabe McAllister?"Mirroring Kate's anxious expression, she asked, "And a new guy? Hired to be head of security?" Lindsey met Kate's frown with one of her own while she listened to Rich explain about this new director of security at ASL, Joe Cairns. Rich thought he was former military.

A little more than an hour later, Kate's van pulled up to the passenger departure area of Terminal Three at San Francisco International Airport. Hurriedly grabbing her bag, Lindsey kissed Kate, and thanked her again for taking care of Max." Kate hugged Lindsey back hard as she exclaimed, "I dearly love Hank and Liisa Reardon, and would do anything possible to help find the creeps who have done this to them. You call me Lindsey, if there is anything I can do to help, anything at all!" Kate gulped audibly, "And Ariana? That little lady is one of the more delightful people I've ever had the privilege of being around. I know you, Rich, Gabe and Toni will get Liisa and Ariana back." Her brown eyes glistened with tears, but her jaw lifted defiantly. I just know you will…Don't worry about Max, we'll love having him around for a few days. Our neighborhood needs to see a real dog, anyway. Most everyone has these little toy dogs out here...they seem more like stuffed animals than dogs."

Enjoying the buzz from the Macallan, Lindsey reflected on the last Click Meeting conversation she'd had with Liisa Reardon. Lindsey was at her home office in Texas, Liisa was finishing up her day at her ASL office in Lausanne. They had talked sometime in March or April. Lindsey had decided to quit her Medical Director job at Huntsville and was considering the move to California to accept the new job at Cal Poly in their animal research center. Liisa had been ecstatic when Lindsey shared her possible plans. The two women had excitedly talked about working together again, brainstorming about Lindsey setting up a second research site for Longevive, this time with Cal Poly dogs.

Lindsey had laughed out loud when Liisa had asked if she would mind playing second fiddle this time around. She had thought the question ridiculous. But when Lindsey noticed Liisa's unsmiling expression on the computer screen, she had snapped a question at her. "Liisa, do I need to apologize again?"

Her expression was grim with annoyance. *Really hope we're not going to play these silly games, Liisa. If that's the case, we'll never be partners, and I'll retreat to a position of financial investor only.*

The look of shock faded to anger, now evident on Liisa's face. A face now colored a deepening shade of red as she barked back, "Lindsey, you are an internationally known medical researcher, while I am a lowly basic scientist. I would think you of all people would understand why I am asking the question. And no, I'm merely making sure there will not be problems as we get further down the road." Liisa had practically spat out her words, but now with the emotional storm ended, her face cleared and relaxed. She said nothing more. And waited.

Regarding Liisa's now composed face, Lindsey chuckled. Then laughed, hard, relieved because she knew they could work together. Flare-ups were normal, natural, even necessary. Soon, Liisa was laughing too. And quickly returned to their favorite subject: research.

This was not their first conflict, far from it. During the early research with Lindsey's drug Digipro, Lindsey had cost Liisa and ASL money and time with her insistence that her drug be tested against a control group of patients already on Digitalis, rather than the far cheaper method of using a control group on placebo. Back during their Christmas vacation when they had met in Liisa's office in Lausanne, Lindsey had apologized profusely for her pigheadedness about the methodology. Liisa had deflected the apology and insisted that the final Digipro trial had been far stronger because of the unusually tight clinical trial.

After a few minutes, Liisa's enthusiasm had returned with gusto, the dissension was now forgotten. The scientist had been talking so fast that Lindsey had to ask her to slow down because she wanted to jot down some notes to herself for later study. But between the erratic internet connection and the pace of Liisa's conversation, Lindsey missed some key components of what Liisa had been talking about when she had switched their discussion away from Longevive. The gist was a new program that she and one of the techs had developed to handle the massive amounts of data coming in from the millions of people now on Digipro.

There was something about a subset of women, about a finding that Liisa had first thought were merely black swan events, but that after more analysis, a pattern had emerged. Something that Liisa thought could point the way to a dietary regime and maybe drug which could prevent or, at least, diminish the symptoms of cardiomyopathy. The group was identified by the inactive x chromosome of a subset of women; strangely, women who had developed the disease at a relatively young age. Due to the poor connection, Liisa's words were choppy so that only one out of two or three words could be understood, but Lindsey lay there wondering about that data, where Liisa was storing it and who she may have told about the finding. The potential value of this observation was incalculable. So there were two almost irresistible discoveries for an enterprising thief. This must be the reason Liisa had decided she needed a new head of security—to build a failsafe firewall around that subset of Digipro women.

Closing her eyes again, Lindsey thought back to the care Liisa had taken with the data for her new drug. While in Liisa's office at Christmas, Lindsey had watched Liisa return her files on Longevive to a safe under her desk. She bet that no one knew that safe was there. Lindsey had helped Liisa move her massive desk to retrieve the ledger and then once they were back in the safe, to replace it once again. She was reasonably confident that Liisa had recovered the Digipro data on a thumb drive and hid it in the safe as well. Those data were far too valuable to risk keeping them on one of her computer programs. Concentrating now, Lindsey's photographic mind could see the combination to Liisa's safe. It was the formula for Pi 3.14159.

CHAPTER SIXTEEN
Reardon's Home in the Jura Mountains North of Lausanne
48 Hours Later

The young Swiss emergency medicine physician had unhappily released Rich from the hospital after enumerating a series of symptoms which would require a return trip. Thankfully, after about twelve hours of sleep in one of the guest houses with his personal physician and wife, Rich was almost feeling back to normal. Although a slight headache and dizziness appeared now and then, the symptoms of the concussion were kept at bay so long as Jansen moved slowly. Very slowly.

Rich stood in front of a whiteboard writing names and associated tasks. Seated on the love seat and two upholstered chairs beside him were the members of the team who would get to the bottom of Liisa's kidnapping. He hoped. It was early in the morning, Swiss time, not yet seven, but everyone's biological clocks were off due to jet lag.

George had more than earned his salary in the last forty-eight hours. He had made three more trips to Zurich International Airport to retrieve the group. McAllister flew in from San Diego, Toni from Oklahoma City and then Lindsey from San Francisco.

The team had hit the ground running. Within hours of

getting off the airplane, each person had been assigned specific responsibilities, which he or she would report on at this morning's meeting.

Gabe McAllister sat close to the edge of his seat, looking every bit the former Marine and Texas State Trooper he had once been. Toni Martinez had chosen a seat next to Gabe, surprising Rich because immediately to her right, lay Baron, McAllister's black and tan Doberman. Toni was no fan of Dobermans, at least not of Max, his red male Doberman. Ignoring Rich's raised eyebrows, Toni's sleeved arm of pastel tattoos was comfortably resting on Baron, occasionally stroking the dog's glossy black coat. Lindsey perched on the loveseat next to Toni and murmured to Baron. She was surprised and delighted to see the dog again. The stubby tail wagged in rhythm to the cadence of her voice, his dark brown eyes closed in contentment with each stroke from Toni's hand.

"Morning everyone." Despite dark shadows under his eyes, Reardon acted every inch the CEO he was, with two men in tow as he strode through the open doors of his library. He motioned for Cairns and the other man to take a seat and then he did the same. "Sorry, we're late." Jansen was relieved to see the amused twinkle back in Reardon's eyes as he spoke. The night before, they had agreed to meet at eight sharp; it was now five after seven.

"Rich, please add Dimitri Vlasov here to your list there on the whiteboard." As Jansen added the name, Reardon continued. "The folks at the Federal Office of Police in Berne were outstanding yesterday. I met with the Director and his two top people for over two hours. Director Pierre has more than a little experience with cases of corporate espionage, and since our case has the additional dimension of kidnapping, Pierre has assigned Dimitri here to our group."

As one of the three founding companies of the International Criminal Police Organization, or Interpol, in 1923, Switzerland boasted leadership to much of the world in effective international police cooperation. Switzerland's police jurisdictions among the twenty-three cantons and the Federal Police tended to be far freer of the internal turf wars seen throughout the rest of the world, particularly in America. Each member country of the one hundred ninety member countries of Interpol is required to designate a National Central Bureau or NCB, Fedpol was the NCB for Switzerland and functioned as the sole federal-wide police force, as opposed to the sixty-five federal police agencies in the US. But in 2009, the revelation of the fourteen member TIGRIS unit, or Supercops, galvanized extensive controversy in the Swiss legislature, similar to that seen in the US. Dimitri was a member of the TIGRIS unit.

"Dimitri was Captain of Homicide for the canton of Berne, and then transferred to the criminal investigative division of Fedpol where he serves as a member of their special ops group, TIGRIS." Turning to Dimitri, Reardon asked politely, "Is there anything else these people should know about you at this point?"

The cop leaned forward, regarding each member of the small group individually, while both hands hung loosely between his knees, a failed attempt to look relaxed. Turning back to Reardon, he spoke.

"I mean no offense by this Mr. Reardon, none at all, but I must tell you all that I don't like this setup. A civilian-run team with me as the obligatory legit cop is stupid and dangerous. I told Pierre that I was wholeheartedly opposed to doing this, that we should be running this whole operation on our own." Despite the aggressive words, Dimitri's tone was neutral, free of emotion. He worked in a bureaucracy, probably accustomed to reporting to idiots, he would do what he was told. But he would say what he thought, respectfully. "Nothing more right now than that, Mr. Reardon. Thank you."

Still standing by the whiteboard, Rich studied Vlasov. Hank Reardon was the top employer in Lausanne, most likely in the top one or two percent in the entire country. This was politics, pure and simple. Rich had been where this cop was and hadn't handled it as graciously as this guy. He had guts, Rich thought and was no game-player. Surprised at his observations, Rich decided he liked him, and that Dimitri could undoubtedly help them, a lot.

All eyes were on the policeman. Lindsey, though, darted her gaze to Rich for just long enough to convey a message. *Take control, this could get out of hand. Fast.*

From his slight accent, Rich guessed the guy was Russian. Maybe Ukranian, for he was very dark-skinned, which made the contrast of the skin with his very blue eyes quite startling.

Nodding slowly, Rich spoke quietly, respectfully. "I'd feel the same way if I were you, Dimitri—is it okay if I call you by your first name? " He waited for the tight nod of agreement before continuing. "For all you know, we're a group of American yahoos without a clue about what we're doing in your country." Rich dismissed a fleeting idea to introduce everyone, to demonstrate who they were but decided to let the cop discover for himself. He started with Lindsey, "Why don't you start by letting everyone know what you found yesterday in Liisa's office?"

"Sure. It actually looks like one drug and a Protocol grabbed the interest of an enemy mogul. The first is an anti-aging drug called Longevive that Liisa created about a year ago. When Rich and I were here last Christmas, Liisa showed me her data from two groups of mice." Despite her fatigue and anxiety, Lindsey could feel her speech speed up as she explained the effects of Longevive on the test group of mice. Standing now at the huge whiteboard which also functioned as a massive tablet, Lindsey wrote the two names of the stolen drugs under the column Jansen had named Lindsey. Then over her shoulder, she asked.

"Hank, what is your username and password?" Quickly entering the login info on the keyboard sitting next to the board, Lindsey touched the bottom of the electronic board. Fiddling with the keyboard for a few seconds, she moved the columns around on the now online whiteboard, and within seconds had created a Gantt chart marching colorfully across the board. "These dates are fictitious of course, but at least this provides us some structure." Smiling at the amazement on almost every face, Lindsey chuckled and said, "Bet you make use of these super helpful charts all the time, right Dimitri?"

Without waiting for his reply, she minimized the chart, tapped at the keyboard once again and then stepped back so people could read the quote shown in bold. "The human genetic potential includes a disease-free life with a programmed longevity potential of longer than 140 years." Dr. Joel Wallach.

"Dr. Lindsey, I know you're a genius, I get that—but no way did you just put all this together in the seconds we've been watching you."

The coarse gravelly voice belonged to Toni Martinez, the only person in the room who was not laughing. Even Dimitri could not control the smile contorting his practiced deadpan expression. Toni merely waited, expectantly.

"You're right, Toni. Once Rich was sound asleep last night, I came back into the main house to put my thoughts together for this morning and saw this electronic whiteboard. It is so much easier for me to talk from an outline, especially if the material is kind of complicated." No one missed the amused, affectionate looks passed between Hank Reardon and Lindsey; similar to that between a father and daughter.

All trace of weariness now gone, Lindsey's energy and excitement seemed to fill the room."So, do you get that, guys? 140 years average lifespan? If Longevive works in mammals anywhere near the way it works in mice, we're talking about a minimum of 140 year median age for humans…a minimum!

"My new partner and quasi-boss at Cal Poly studied under Joel Wallach. Jodi took every course he taught at UC Davis School of Veterinary Medicine because she said she knew this guy was one of the rare few: A researcher looking for truth rather than profits." Flipping through a series of slides on the board, Lindsey seemed like the professor of medicine she once was, despite the jeans and T-shirt.

"I know we have a ton of work to do but some background will help everyone get a handle on just what is at stake here. Why it is worth kidnapping Liisa and Ariana." Scanning the room quickly, Lindsey's gaze stayed on Toni for just a beat. "I promise I'll be brief."

"The term epigenetics had been coined during the mid-twentieth century by scientists beginning to understand that genetics and developmental biology were not, in fact, separate disciplines. But it was not until the nineties and the early twenty-first century that the area of epigenetics was taken seriously by scientists. What had been understood to be fixed genetic growth and development was found to be inheritable." Lindsey watched a few pair of eyes begin to glaze over. Quickly she explained. "We used to think that the genetic profile we are born with predetermined our risk of disease in measurable ways, we've found that the tops of genes-epi meaning top-can be so affected by the individual's environment that the mutation can be passed on. The alteration is called methyla-tion. Hypomethylation of DNA has been found to activate cancer cells or oncogenes, cancer cells while hypermethylation of DNA results in silencing of tumor suppression cells. Primarily, epigenetics can be viewed as a set of adaptations to human genetic material that alters the way genes are switched on and off.

"One of the classic experiments demonstrating this heritable trait of altered genes was an unplanned event during the second world war, the Dutch Hunger Winter. In western Holland, a German blockade resulted in twenty thousand deaths from starvation during the bitterly cold months of November 1944 through spring of 1945. This horrific event provided a perfect scientific experiment of the Dutch survivors, one of whom was Audrey Hepburn. Surprising data were revealed by the study of the children who were in the womb at the time. If the mother was malnourished only during the first few months of pregnancy, the baby tended to be normal weight. If the period of starvation took place during the last few months of pregnancy, the baby was underweight at birth. But these effects remained with these people throughout their lives. Small underweight babies grew up to be thin Audrey Hepburn like people. While those babies who had been malnourished only in early pregnancy, tended toward much higher rates of obesity and heart disease in adulthood. These changes were found in the grandchildren of the Dutch Hunger Winter survivors, proving that genetic change caused by the environment could be transmitted to future generations."

Just then, Stella and George appeared. "I know Lindsey and Mr. Reardon are too busy for the meager fare of food, but I'll wager that even you two would like some coffee." Stella was pulling a silver cart with a humungous pot of coffee, while George followed with another cart filled with pastries of all shapes and sizes. The fragrance was divine.

"Okay Lindsey, we get Longevive and its value to whoever is behind this scheme. Thanks for that.." Hank Reardon scanned the room, "But don't ask any of us to repeat what you just said. But TirNan, what is that? You seem persuaded that we're talking about two drugs here."

"I am Hank, I'm certain of it. TirNan is the name Liisa gave to her formula for modification of the Digipro molecule. During our conversation back in May, she told me about a subset of young females among the patients taking Digipro that she was studying. All of them had developed cardiomyopathy before the age of ten. She theorized that the cause may have been related to the inactive x chromosome suddenly activated by methylation.

"Since I was here last January, I've been studying epigenetics through some online classes Liisa has given me. And I've been taking a crash course in developmental biology from one of my new bosses at Cal Poly, Father Blaise Roderick. He explained that about ten or twelve years ago, a master gene, or immortality gene, was discovered in human embryonic stem cells. They call the gene *Nanog*, after a Celtic legend featuring a land off the coast of Ireland in the Realm of the Terrestrial

Fairies. A land where there is no death and is inhabited by two lovers named Oisin and Niamah; notably, immortal Niamah and human Oisin." Lindsey was speaking to Reardon as if he and she were the only two in the room, completely ignoring her husband, McAllister and the others.

"Liisa believes these girls and young women can potentially be cured of their cardiomyopathy, at least of the symptoms—if they agree to a strict nutritional plan." Her tired eyes were bright. "She and I were—" Lindsey stopped herself as her eyes widened, then she said decisively, and emphatically, "She and I *are* Co-Investigators on the TirNan study.

Lindsey's words were a tonic on Reardon. Whether Lindsey's exclusion of the others was intentional or accidental, Reardon's focus on her was absolute. The dullness of his facial expression was gone, and the electricity in his blue gaze was close to full-strength. Like all of them, he still looked exhausted, but vigilant.

Looking at his watch, Rich knew they had to keep pushing. He looked over at Gabe. "You and Toni checked out the route Liisa took to work, what did you find?"

Gabe said, "Looks like they grabbed Liisa from a shortcut Hank told us she takes to work when she's late. And Stella said Liisa was late that morning, wouldn't even eat any breakfast because she was meeting with a couple of new investors. We gave Baron her scent off some clothing Stella provided from her room, and then took off in Reardon's Bentley along the road, getting out and walking to see if Baron could grab a trace of her. After a while he did."

Gabe had been a dog handler while a soldier in Afghanistan. Baron's namesake had been killed in country by an IED. Training the rescue dog in search and find techniques had played an important part of the soldier's recovery, from both war and prison. Now, he and Baron were inseparable.

"Right around where Baron lost her, we saw tire marks at the side of the road. It's been dry so we could see them. Looks as if someone played her, maybe claiming that their car was broken down. Off the side of the road pushed into the forest, we found a car with German plates. Baron got no scent from the car, so our best guess is that they somehow overpowered her and got control of her car: Reardon says she was driving her Jaguar convertible."

"Them." It was a statement, not a question.

But Gabe replied as if it were a question. "Yeah, I figure it would have been a man and woman. Less threatening, early in the morning like that. Making it more likely for Liisa to stop and offer to help. She was in a hurry, so probably figured she could get them as far as her office, where someone else could drive them into town. So one person got in back, sitting behind her, the woman probably, and the man sat beside her. Then the woman would have plenty of time and access to use chloroform or whatever sedation took her out."

It was a theory and a good one. Built on a house of cards, but the logic made sense.

"We need to sum up folks, the clock is ticking." Rich was back in front of the group. "We'll list what we know, or think we know, on Lindsey's magic board.

"A couple, German perhaps, grabbed Liisa on her way to meet with potential investors.

"They are most likely working for another pharmaceutical company.

"They have the test mice for Longevive, maybe the formula and most likely the TirNan data.

"Ariana was most likely grabbed by accident. She and I entered the Animal Research Building together. We surprised the inside guy or gal since only a very few researchers have access to the data. The person who attacked me grabbed her because he had no choice.

"Any other ideas or anyone see this differently?

"Dimitri?

"Yes." The Swiss cop stood and regarded each person in the room exactly as he did before. But his manner was completely different. "I apologize for implying..." glancing over at Rich, "what did you call yourselves, American yahoos?" The piercing blue gaze was somber as he said, "I would be proud to work with any of you people, at any time, on any case. This is a good plan." But Dimitri's gaze returned to Joe Cairns. Rich followed it. The man had said nothing for close to three hours.

Now that the discussion was open, the team agreed that the motive for the crime had to be the oldest: Money. Also that the inside person or persons doing the work had to be working for someone that already had a lot of it.

But the perpetrators? Unfortunately, the range of possibilities was daunting, and ranged from business competitors, like other pharmaceuticals, to someone crazy enough to risk almost everything to extend his own life. The attention to longevity by several multimillionaire CEOs had been discussed extensively by Toni, who had taken copious notes on the subject while researching the topic on the plane and again, last night. Once she completed her report, she asked, "Could one of the investors Liisa was planning to meet that morning be involved in this?"

"That is possible I suppose. Anything is possible, at this point. The investors could view the researchers as they worked for sure. But not any data. Liisa shared data only with the ASL scientists involved in the study. And the results of the experiments were not recorded on the computer but were kept in logs, like the old days."

Reardon's muted comment about the unlikelihood of an outsider being involved quieted down the discussion.

But later during the summary, it was Reardon who brought the subject back up, thinking as he did so that Toni's idea had merit. One of the project's angel investors could have talked to someone- if that someone told the right person, then...

Aware of the time elapsing, Rich called the meeting to an end and divided the team into groups assigned to specific tasks.

Lindsey would return to Liisa's office to scrutinize the data, attempting to discover any lapses in dates or times.

Dimitri and Toni were to interview the scientists. McAllister and Baron were to go over the area where Jansen had been attacked and Ariana taken with a fine-toothed comb, looking for clues. Jansen and Cairns would interview as many of the technicians in the animal research labs as possible, while Reardon would search the investor records to see if anything popped out. They would meet back in the library at six that evening to compare notes.

Each team member was provided with earpieces connecting the six of them, in case there was an urgent need to meet sooner or something critical occurred.

Hank looked curiously at Rich and Joe as they walked out of the library together. Rich hesitated for a moment to see if Hank wanted to ask or say anything, but the moment passed, and Reardon headed to his office to pore over donor records.

Glancing to his right at Cairns, Rich noted the tense expression on Cairns' face. A slight grimace had replaced the studied neutrality of his face. *Good, he's not happy...maybe the veneer is starting to crack. It may be something as innocent as resenting my coming in to take over, or suggest something far more ominous... like he's in on this. But there is something disturbing about this man. Dimitri senses it too. And Reardon is well aware of the way I feel. I just can't get a grip on a guy who is into hugely extreme stuff, then suddenly retreats to a desk. It doesn't make sense.*

CHAPTER EIGHTEEN
Somewhere dark and hot

Liisa Reardon had to work to open her eyes. The lids were stuck together, she wondered at the goop accumulated along her eyelids, and why she could see nothing. Nothing at all. And why her tongue was sticking to the roof of her mouth as if she were so dehydrated there was no saliva at all.

Cautiously, she experimented with her body. Yes, hands, feet, legs and arms worked, albeit slowly, and a bit reluctantly. Feeling the strange texture of the cotton pants and top she wore, Liisa realized that someone had changed her clothes. She had left the house early Friday morning in a business suit, prepared to meet with a team of potential investors, she'd had her gray pantsuit and heels, with a white cami. She'd been on the road to corporate headquarters by seven.

Did she make the presentation?

Or had someone grabbed her on the way?

Narrowing her eyes to a squint, Liisa began to see some shapes in the blackness… and breathed a silent sigh of relief. At least she wasn't blind.

Liisa Reardon was a scientist. With a doctorate in developmental biology and another in inorganic chemistry, she had trained her mind to think in linear and systematic ways.

That training was paying off in a most unexpected way now.

Almost by default, rather than succumb to panic or paralysis, Liisa's mind began to analyze her current predicament as if it were an experiment gone awry.

Think! Did you make it to the presentation? You spoke with Ames and Marconi several times on the phone. Did you meet them?

Slowly, fractions of images and memories began to assault her. There had been someone at the side of the road, flagging her down on the back road she took as a shortcut to work. The road was hardly ever used. Her dad had expressed his concern about that shortcut, but it shaved off fifteen minutes from her commute, and she'd left later than she'd planned that Friday morning.

She had stopped to help a couple who had broken down on the side of the road. They had raised the hood of a late model sedan and were standing by the side of the car. Traffic was infrequent and cell phone reception spotty along that road, which was why she'd stopped, even though she was short on time.

Hi, I'm running late for a meeting, but I'd be happy to give you a lift to my office, then we can get someone to help you find someone to repair your car.

Since the license plate on the car was from Germany, Liisa had figured they were far from home, and maybe even lost. She'd been driving the Jaguar convertible, so the woman had scrunched into the small back seat, and the man had taken the seat next to her. They were average looking she recalled. Medium height, no outstanding features. Overweight by thirty to fifty pounds. Like most westerners, except the French who seemed to avoid the epidemic of obesity afflicting much of the civilized world. Since her childhood, she had repeatedly heard her Dad claim that the sole reason people were too fat was the tastelessness of the food they ate. French food could be described in many ways, but blandness would not be included.

What did they say when they got in the car? Did I even start the car once they got in?

She could recall no conversation with either the man or the woman, but could visualize them clearly as they got in. Liisa knew she never met with either Ames or Marconi, investors she had hoped to interest in her new drug, Longevive. She had never made it to the office.

Stupid, stupid, stupid girl.

Liisa realized she had never started her car—and that this ordinary-looking couple had taken her to God knows where; after drugging her with something potent. She was sure of it.

Dad must be crazy with worry. He would have known something had happened almost immediately. The meeting was to start at eight and the two angel investors would have been there right on time since we added the bed and breakfast to the campus. They had flown in from the UK the night before and stayed at the Inn.

ASL was growing at quite a clip due to the success of Liisa's leadership in research, and her father's experienced hand at the helm of the entire corporation. Last year, the Reardons had added a ten room Bed and Breakfast for investors and occasional staff members stranded by a sudden snowstorm. A retired couple from Lausanne lived on site and managed the hostel.

Liisa sat up and extended her arms up and then out to guess at the size of her cell.

So far so good. Maybe I can stand.

Swaying slightly from the effects of whatever sedation she'd been given, Liisa stayed on her feet in the dark and took one tentative step and then another. She realized that her feet were bare, and the floor surface was gritty. She was standing on some kind of dirt floor or sand. More confident now, she took several more steps and then ran into something.

What the hell is that?

Pulling her bare foot back as quickly as if it had been burned, Liisa had felt something—no someone. Lying there.

Now crouching down on her knees, she reached out in the oppressive stale air and felt nothing.

Okay then, let's try it this way.

Now kneeling, Liisa walked on her knees very slowly and felt in front of her until she felt something; hair, lots of hair. Trailing her fingers down to the face, she felt closed eyes, a small nose, and full lips. A woman.

Quickly now, she examined the neck and shoulders of the woman lying motionless on her back. Around the neck, she fingered the tiny crucifix. Realization dawned on Liisa. Though Ariana insisted she was not religious and did not go to church, Liisa had never seen her without the little crucifix.

"Ariana, wake up...come on, wake up. What have they done to you? *Wake up!*"

CHAPTER NINETEEN
Library in Reardon's home, Lausanne Switzerland

The entire team was assembled in the library. They had been at it for three hours and had heard reports, names, opinions and conjecture, but really, they were fundamentally nowhere.

No longer at the whiteboard, Jansen was seated in one of two upholstered chairs next to Hank Reardon, across from Cairns, who sat alone at the far end. On couches on either side of the long coffee table sat Dimitri and Toni; McAllister and Lindsey were seated on the opposite couch, Baron at her feet.

Stella had stuck her head in twice to ask if they wanted dinner. Each time she was ignored. Suddenly, both doors of the library burst open, and George and Stella appeared, pushing carts loaded with plates of fragrant food which smelled divine.

"I know none of you is hungry. I know you all feel sick at what has happened with Liisa, and Ariana, but you'll not be able to help if you don't take care of yourselves. So each of you, take a break now. Take twenty minutes to refresh your body and soul." The speech was delivered in Stella's rapid fire Irish brogue by this caring woman who seemed to be the heart of the place. Her husband George was by her side, setting plates in front of each of the seven tired and dejected members of the group.

In front of each of them was placed a roast chicken dinner, complete with roasted potatoes, a medley of braised carrots, fennel and red peppers accompanied by Stella's freshly baked rolls.

From the seemingly endless supply of food and utensils on the carts, came wine glasses and silverware with napkins which were carefully placed by George in front of each member of the team.

By now, they were all salivating. And, despite themselves, each of the seven faces was wreathed in a grateful smile directed at George and Stella. Especially, Hank Reardon. Rich studied Stella's husband George and decided there was no way the man could be part of this. Too old, he must be in his seventies, and, too loyal to Reardon. His character seemed written among the peaks and valleys of his coarse features. A broad nose which had been broken at least twice. Crevices and furrows in his forehead, cheeks and short neck which looked like a map of service and self-sacrifice. But mostly it was his eyes. Light blue with amber highlights, full of warmth, light, and sincerity. Those eyes caught Jansen's, and George tipped his head forward, in acknowledgment. Then he saluted, so quickly, Rich wondered if he had imagined it. The older man was telling him that he understood Jansen's earlier suspicions, and held no animosity. On the contrary, the signal indicated respect and admiration.

One of those quiet, unsung heroes. A man who has asked little out of life. Expected nothing handed to him. Accepted the harsh realities, including the inherent unfairness of life. A very different generation from those who have followed.

Watching Reardon, Rich thought once again of the depth

of his affection for the man. Without thinking about what he was about to say, Rich stood up, blessed himself and prayed. "Dear Lord, we thank you for this food we have received, we ask your blessing on George and Stella for their kind and gracious hearts in preparing this meal." At that, Rich saw broad smiles on both Stella and George. "We ask too, Lord, for your Spirit to guide us, direct our effort and beg you, Lord, to keep Liisa and Ariana safe until we can rescue them." Taking a deep breath, Jansen added, "We ask your forgiveness on those who have perpetrated these crimes, and we ask that you soften their hearts so that whoever is behind this will admit this crime, and tell us who has paid them to do this thing." Rich doubted that any of the others was religious except Lindsey and maybe George and Stella, but the prayer had been prompted by another dinner, about two years ago, when everything had looked hopeless. Trust.

Opening his eyes, Jansen saw eight people standing, eight people crossing themselves and heard eight Amens. Including Dimitri and Joe Cairns, Rich noticed with wonder.

Later that night, Lindsey, Rich, and Toni met in the guesthouse where McAllister and Baron were staying. Dimitri had begged off, saying he needed to get home to Bern.

"There's a German guy. There's something there..." Toni looked through the notes she had taken during Dimitri's interviews with the researchers. "His name is Eric. Apparently, he and Liisa have dated on and off for the last couple of years.

"Liisa broke it off. At least, that's what a few of the techs seemed to think. Eric is one of five people with the code to the research labs. And he seemed fidgety, edgy during the interview. Definitely knows more than he is saying." Toni looked at Lindsey who was working hard to keep her eyes open. "Eric mentioned you, Lindsey. Liisa brought you around to meet him and his team while you were here over Christmas. That was a big deal to him." Lindsey's eyes snapped open, remembering. "Yes, he's a really tall, kinda lanky guy with dark curly hair, right? " Nodding to herself, "Yeah, I remember him, Toni. Maybe I'll wander over tomorrow and talk with him a little."

Toni named another scientist with the access code but explained he had been out of town with his wife for a week and was not expected back for another full week. "Ariana is the fourth and, of course, Hank and Liisa. We couldn't determine whether Cairns has access or not. A lot of the techs seem uncertain about what he does around here." She looked at Janson waiting for a comment. Rich said nothing, merely nodded.

Rich scanned the small room. The four of them looked spent. As they should, he felt it too. The combination of the long flight, the attack on him in the lab, and the immensity of the task in front of them weighed him down. Suddenly he felt a cold nose on the hand that rested on his knee. Baron was standing only inches from him; once the dog caught his gaze, he sat down and plunked his big paw in Rich's lap. Exactly like Max would be doing right now. Jansen grinned and took the paw.

"Thanks for bringing this guy, Gabe. He brings just a touch of Texas with him to this huge mess; along with a big dollop of that Dobie spirit."

Glad to get his mind off their present situation, Rich explained to the others. "Lindsey has a friend who runs a Dobie rescue ranch in South Texas. Baron here had been abandoned by a couple who'd gotten him as a pup, but decided they could no longer deal with him. Baron was, in the words of Ardis, frantic, at the reality of being kenneled. Ardis thought he could be an excellent dog again if he were with someone who knew Dobies. Someone that could train him, and restore his trust again. Lindsey had Gabe's agreement before she brought him over to the house to live with all of us during the months while Gabe was recovering from his experience at Huntsville, and he also provided great company for Max." Glancing over at McAllister, Rich smiled again. "I'd say you accomplished the task, Gabe. This boy is wonderful."

Jansen swallowed hard. An unexpected surge of emotion engulfed him as he opened his mouth to speak again. "Lindsey and I really don't know how to thank you guys for agreeing to come out here." Looking first at Toni, then Gabe, Jansen's voice cracked, "I can't say I'm really all that surprised that you're here, but I sure appreciate your decision to take the risk with us. This is a damn sight more dangerous than what you were doing back in Oklahoma."

"But not that much different from what I was doing while at Huntsville." Gabe's wry reference to an attack from a gang of other inmates intent on killing him brought tired smiles to everyone.

Obviously uncomfortable with Jansen's sentiment, Toni looked around at Gabe and grinned, her smile splitting her broad face. "After last year, we sort of became a team. You know what they say about saving a life—I think the Chinese say that once you save a life, you are responsible for it. So Gabe, you and I are a team, albeit an unlikely one."

Grabbing a yawning Lindsey by her hand, Rich rose, pulling her up as he did so. "Come on sleepyhead, let's all go get some sleep.

"Dimitri predicts we'll hear from the kidnappers tomorrow, and we'll need all our wits about us to beat them at whatever game is being played here."

CHAPTER TWENTY
Somewhere dark and hot

Liisa could get no response from Ariana. She was sure that riotous mass of curls belonged to her, though. Remembering the features she had felt as she had run her hand over the still form of the woman lying in this horrible place. That tiny crucifix was Ariana's, she was sure of it. Liisa had traced the contours of the pert nose, full lips and high forehead of her Chief Lab Technician at ASL, but was not at all sure she was breathing. She could not feel Ari's breath on her suddenly clammy palm as she held it over her mouth.

Recognizing the accelerating signs of panic; her racing heart rate, shallow and rapid breathing and the sweat drenching her shirt, Liisa knew she had to get a grip on herself. She had no clue about the volume of air in this place but reckoned that the space could be air tight, with, therefore, limited oxygen. Her panicked panting was merely using up precious oxygen and increasing the carbon dioxide level.

She forced herself into her last conversation with Lindsey about Longevive. Initially, parts of her mind were reluctant to give up the terror and crushing sense of doom and despair, leading to negative thoughts. *Give it up... You have no chance... You'll be as dead as Ariana in not very long... They have no idea where you are so no one will find you... not in time... The CO2 will build up and anesthetize you slowly, killing you from CO2 narcosis... These people, whoever they are, will have no problem killing you, just like they killed Ariana.* The thoughts raced through her mind, tumbling one after the other like clouds scuttling across an portentous sky. But Liisa impelled herself to visualize Lindsey and Harvey Cunningham in her lab back in January. At first very slowly, gradually the memories and images began to repel the horror.

Steve and Kate's wedding was over, and Liisa had offered to show them her work on the new drug. It had been the week between Christmas and New Years with only the overachievers at their research stations; and therefore, a great time to tour Lindsey through the production labs of Digipro. On a lark, Liisa had decided to show the initial results of her new drug, Longevive, to Lindsey, just to see what her reaction would be. And risk the startling results of the Digipro subset of young women with idiopathic cardiomyopathy. Maybe also to break through to Lindsey, who seemed to be working hard at maintaining a polite but chilly distance.

Lindsey had spent over forty-five minutes poring over the experimental mice results of Longevive. Then another half-hour with the Digipro data which had been discovered by accident. When Lindsey finally spoke, Liisa had been staggered at her words, her excitement, and most of all, at the inferential leaps made by the physician.

Face glowing, Lindsey regarded Liisa with a look that seemed to penetrate straight through to her core. "Simon Bayer, probably the finest physician of the twentieth century, used to tell me that it was only a matter of time until the biologists took over." Her green gaze now focused somewhere far away, Lindsey had a wistful smile as she recalled the wisdom and foresight of the former Chief of Medicine at the Houston

Medical School where she had trained and practiced as a Cardiologist.

Her voice almost a whisper, Liisa had strained to hear her words. "Simon would tell his Cardiology Fellows that medical ignorance is vast, but our arrogance is growing in exponential proportions to our ignorance. Somehow, he saw this Liisa. Saw what you and others are doing in Developmental Biology...by God, you are revolutionizing the practice of medicine."

Lindsey had interrupted herself, and the intensity of her gaze had increased exponentially. "You understand what you have here, right? You know how badly others would want to lay claim to what you are doing, if only to stomp it out, don't you? And this tiny cohort of patients in the Digipro group? This is astounding, revolutionary stuff. And the glory of what you're revealing here is the suggestion that the cure can be found in the body, assuming proper nutrition, that is. Dangerous stuff, Dr. Reardon, I hope you and all the data are well protected."

She thought she was.

Liisa believed the security systems at ASL to be the best they could be. Now that the memory of that conversation had calmed her, Liisa got it. Like a glaringly bright light. This had happened because of someone inside the company; there was no other way. Someone desperate for money or fame, or both.

In the dark, Liisa heard movement. A rustling. Then a soft moan. *They haven't killed her, thank God!*

Although she and Rich had not gone to sleep until after one in the morning, Lindsey was wide awake just a few hours later. She lay quietly beside her husband, listening to his deep rhythmic breathing, and looking into the blackness of the bedroom. She was thinking about how profoundly grateful she was for this man beside her, so thankful that he had not been seriously injured in the attack which had resulted in Ariana's disappearance. Lindsey smiled as she thought about the spontaneous grace—more like a full-fledged prayer—Rich had said when George and Stella had rolled in that glorious dinner that no one had claimed to want. He was such a mass of contradictions, this husband of hers. While every inch the soldier, cop, and criminal defense lawyer, there was his faith, and he wore it like a comfortable old shirt. A devout Catholic from birth, Rich Jansen's battles were external: enemies of his country, criminals, and injustice; internally, he was clear and very real about who he was and what he stood for. Lindsey had lived much of her life as a loner, certain that she could rely on no one, even God. This growing belief of hers was new, even startling, like their marriage.

She had watched him while he prayed that remarkable

appeal to God. There was no concern about what others would think, just his heartfelt plea to God for the safe return of Liisa and Ariana, plus that extraordinary addition at the end, actually praying for the abductors and the person behind this evil scheme. The energy had changed in that room during the prayer, she saw for herself the change in all of the faces, and the light returning to their countenance, even Dimitri...and Joe Cairns.

Getting back to sleep is impossible, I'm too wired. The best thing for me now is a good run. God bless Hank Reardon and that gym he built for insomniacs like me. Rich is exhausted. He still has severe headaches from the concussion, I can see the pain when he thinks no one is watching. Hopefully, I can slip out of here without waking him up and make use of the running clothes I had on at the Cal Poly track when this thing started—feels like a month ago now, but it's been only two days.

Ten minutes later, Lindsey was running fast on one of the three treadmills in the well-equipped freestanding gymnasium about a five-minute walk from the guesthouse where she and Rich were staying. She was thinking hard. About what Toni and Dimitri had uncovered during their interviews yesterday. Lindsey did not know Toni well but felt like she did because Rich had worked with her and Harvey during Gabe's appeal. His overall assessment of the woman seemed to be that she was prickly, but one of the best investigators he had ever worked with. That's why he'd asked his law partner to send her over here.

Only five people with access to the research labs...seems that the German is an ideal candidate. Cairns could well be involved, but the inside person would need to be a scientist. These data and research notes were too complex for a non-researcher. Okay, Miss Investigative Reporter, hope you meant what you said.

Cooling down now, Lindsey took a towel off the ample

pile next to the showers and glanced at the clock. Early evening, she may be interrupting their dinner, but she said she wanted to help.

"Kate, sorry to interrupt dinn—"

"You're not interrupting anything but feeding time for JH, Steve won't be home until late. I am *so* glad to hear from you! Are Ariana and Liisa okay? Is Rich okay? How is Hank doing? I have been so worried!" Laughing at her non-stop questions, "See Lindsey, this is what it's like when you stay home with a six-month-old. The rules of normal conversation no longer apply because you're so happy to talk with someone, anyone!"

"We don't know yet if they are okay, Kate. No demands have been made yet, but we expect to hear today in fact. Rich is fine, and Hank is—" she stopped so suddenly that Kate thought the connection had been cut.

"Lindsey, are you there?"

"Yes, I'm here," she coughed to hide the lump that had materialized in her throat and took several deep breaths to get control of the surge of emotion. *She and Hank Reardon had known one another for over ten years, maybe fifteen, and the man had been through so much. The death of his wife and now this.*

"You know Hank Reardon, Kate. He is..." embarrassed because of the unexpected flood of love, fear and sadness had her pinned under, Lindsey stopped.

"A rock," Kate finished the sentence. Kate could hear the feeling in Lindsey's voice, and could tell that she was working hard not to cry. Pretending not to notice, she asked, "Lindsey, look, can I call you back in like six minutes? Then the baby will be in bed, and we can talk more easily. Would that work?"

"Perfect." The word was said shakily, but clearly. Lindsey smiled at the insight of Kate, walked into the shower room, stripped and ran ice cold water over her body.

Three minutes later toweling off and teeth chattering, Lindsey had regained control of herself.

"Hi again Lindsey, I'm good to talk if this is okay for you? By the way, Max says hi, he is sitting right beside me, I think somehow he knows I'm talking to you!"

"Hey Kate, yes perfect timing, thanks. Here's what I need if you are up for it." Rapidly, Lindsey summarized the results of their two days and Toni's suspicion that the German researcher Eric knew more than he'd admitted to when interviewed yesterday.

"Wait, Dimitri? Who is he?"

"Right, the players keep changing here, don't they? Hank wielded his influence in Berne to get the head of the Swiss version of the FBI to agree to look like we are following the demands of the kidnappers by not involving the police. Dimitri is some special ops cop within the Federal Police."

"And Cairns? What do you guys know about him?"

Laughing now, Lindsey recognized that the switch from stay-at-home mom to the investigative reporter was now complete. Lindsey had mentioned Cairns' name just once during her brief visit with Kate. Years of training in the details, and recalling all of them, is what had elevated a reporter from the general ranks to a Pulitzer Prize winning one, like Kate Townsend.

"Nothing much, except that I think we all wonder why Liisa hired an ex-military guy to head up security at ASL. I notice that Rich, Toni and Gabe all check him out, thinking they are being discreet, and even the Swiss cop Dimitri was last night. Cairns just sits in the meetings though, saying nothing at all. That's not easy to do, you know?" Following Kate's line of thought, Lindsey explained, "He could be involved in this Kate, but not alone. Whoever has stolen the test mice—we think they've been stolen, by the way—had to know a lot about the Longevive study. They may also have another set of data." Quickly, Lindsey briefed Kate on what Liisa had found with the subset of Digipro patients."

Kate had been taking notes on everything Lindsey had reported, guessing why she had called. "I'm guessing that you're not calling me at 4 in the morning your time just to chat, how can I help?"

"In a hundred different ways. First, you remember Eric, the German researcher?

"Yes, I sure do. He and Liisa were having a thing but didn't want anyone to know about it. She got really flustered when I mentioned it to her."

"That's what some people told Toni and Dimitri yesterday. A couple said the rumor was that Liisa had broken it off...not smart to date employees and all that. A spurned lover...could be a motive, wouldn't be the first time. You still have your notes from your week out here a couple of years ago, right? The time you spent with Ariana and Eric?"

"Sure do."

"If you can pore through the file and tell us anything, anything at all that you saw then that could relate to what is happening now. Like did Eric work for another drug company before here, maybe that company has contacted him, anything like that? Connections, however weird. There's got to be another pharmaceutical company behind this.

"Back to Dimitri for a minute, Kate. He's likely had experience with pharmaceutical crime. Apparently, Switzerland has been successful in uncovering companies that sell fake pills, like fake antibiotics, tuberculosis, malaria, you name it. Anyway, they've been prosecuting and locking them up." Chuckling to herself as she recalled Rich's 'yahoo speech' to the Swiss cop, Lindsey added, "Seems that Dimitri complements our group then, he can help."

Although she knew Lindsey could not see her, Kate was nodding as she scribbled her notes. Good. It was fun to be able to help them all out there. "Got it, Lindsey. I'll have a bunch of material for you within the next six hours, sooner if I can."

Dear Mr. Reardon:

We commend you for your decision not to inform the police, and assure you that your daughter is unharmed. To guarantee her safe return, we require three things:

That you transfer ownership of the Longevive patent now registered to Andrews, Sacks, and Levine, Inc., by filing a Recordation Cover Sheet with the United States Patent Transfer Office, to Worldwide Epigenetics Foundation, Inc.

That you file a patent for Dr. Reardon's modification of Digipro, TirNan, with the USPO for Worldwide Epigenetics Foundation, Inc.

And last, we need 2.5 million dollars wire transferred to our overseas bank in the Canary Islands. The wiring instructions will be provided to you as soon as you have completed the forms for the patent transfers.

We recommend, Mr. Reardon, that you execute the transfers post haste as the available oxygen in Liisa's current residence is limited due to an unplanned guest there with her, Ariana Dumas. Were Liisa, the sole resi-

dent, we could guarantee sufficient air for more than four days. However, with Ms. Dumas there as well, we are quite honestly not sure how long there will be adequate ventilation. You will hear from us soon, Mr. Reardon. One last thing, we expect that you will require proof of life for Dr. Reardon, apropos of that valid request, please visit this online site: http://www.proofoflife/drreardon

The letter had been delivered via a limousine at six thirty-two that morning. Just like the first letter, there were no prints. Dimitri dusted the envelope and single page document for prints and found nothing. The driver claimed he had been paid five hundred dollars to deliver the letter to Reardon at his Lausanne home. Exactly like the delivery of the first letter.

All seven of the team members watched the YouTube video of Liisa squinting in the glare of bright light. Only her face and shoulders could be seen. As the letter had claimed, she looked frightened but unharmed.

Dimitri had returned from Berne very early that morning with taping and tracking devices for the call he was certain would come. The cop was experienced in controlling his facial expressions, which revealed nothing of what he was feeling. But the twitching muscles at the side of his unsmiling mouth showed his frustration at his three-hour round-trip drive for nothing.

Checking her watch for the umpteenth time since they had watched the video, Lindsey spoke into the silence, thinking she should give Kate just a little more time. "I can go to Liisa's office to do the transfers they're asking for. It will take hours because I will be dealing with bureaucratic complexity of a Kafkaesque scale, so I'll get going within the next fifteen minutes or so." She looked over at Hank Reardon's anguished face, "Shall I use your car Hank, or Liisa's?"

Her question startled Reardon. He had been staring at the blank computer screen of the laptop where they had watched the video of Liisa several times, trying to discern some hint of where she was being imprisoned. Blinking several times, the CEO said," What? Oh yes, sorry, cars." More in control now, Reardon explained to the group, "In the main lobby of the research building, you will find a clipboard with a sheet listing the automobiles and license plates belonging to ASL. Anyone who needs one, drive with Lindsey in the Bentley. Feel free to pick one up when you get to the offices. Dimitri, feel free to take one for your use with Toni; Rich and Lindsey, you probably want one each, and Gabe, you and Baron may want to keep the truck you used yesterday. Just if you would, please, write your names next to the vehicle, time of departure and estimated time of return." A tired smile flashed. "We used to do this the twenty-first century way, but learned that no one remembered to sign out. So we returned to paper and pencil. Each vehicle is equipped with a GPS transponder which can be tracked via the corporate site."

"I called Kate early this morning Hank, asking for her help. She is supposed to fax the information she found from her research to your office. Would you mind checking to see if it's there?"

There were six pairs of eyes on Lindsey, surprised. Jansen looked at her with a raised eyebrow, then gave her a thumbs up. Hank Reardon smiled a genuine smile this time at the thought of his young reporter friend, Kate Townsend and said, "On it now, Dr. McCall."

The answering moan determined Ariana's living presence. With an eagerness she had not felt since heading to work on that fateful Friday morning, Liisa scrambled over to her Chief Tech. Just as she reached the awakening woman, Liisa heard a noise outside. "Ariana, pretend you're still unconscious, don't move or make any sound at all."

Acting on pure instinct, Liisa crawled back to her dirt bed hoping and praying—apologizing to the God she wasn't sure she believed in for behaving like all the other agnostics she knew—that Ariana would hear and stay quiet. Somehow, Liisa knew, it was imperative that they not know Ariana was among the living.

A door creaked open at the far end of the enclosure, close to where she had been only a moment ago as she had knelt by Ariana.

More apologies and then, *Dear God, don't let them notice any track marks I made in the dirt going to Ariana and coming back here.* The intensity of the light was blinding, so brilliant Liisa could only close her eyes. Hyper-alert, she strained to listen, to try to figure out what was going on, and then heard whispering in German.

She could speak a little German and deciphered a woman's voice saying something like 'be quick about this.' *Make sure we do it quickly*, speaking again, this time clearly enough for Liisa to understand, the woman's whisper was close to a hiss, almost fierce. Liisa recognized the voice— it was the female of the couple who had flagged her down on the way to work a lifetime ago. Then she heard expletives in harsh German. The light went out with a loud thumping noise. She got it, they were taking a video of her. A video to send to her Dad. Liisa's panic was almost overwhelming, she was breathing so fast now she was close to passing out from her fear. *Dear God, this is bad, really bad. They're filming me so Dad will know I'm still alive. They must figure that Ariana is already dead.*

Her mind a racing jumble of chaotic thoughts, she forced herself to think clearly. To make sense of what was happening. Apparently, the camera had been dropped. Liisa recognized their chance to escape. The door was open, she could hear and sense fresh air, a breeze blowing in. The two were distracted, arguing. But not for long. *But would Ariana be able to move? Would she understand what has to happen if Liisa was able to overpower them?*

Picturing them, Liisa visualized the overweight fifty-something-year-old woman and her stout husband. Neither was in any great shape. Liisa was a marathon runner and trained in Judo and Jujitsu and Ariana was a black belt in Aikido. They could do this—they had to.

Collecting herself, Liisa drew her legs forward into a crouch. Counting quickly but on three, she propelled herself forward toward the crouching form, the overweight guy, praying for all she was worth. She had hissed *Come!* to Ariana loudly as she raced by her moments ago. Liisa was euphoric when she glanced back and saw Ariana up and sprinting toward the heavyset woman who had turned away from them and toward the crouching man so that he could better hear the invectives spewing from her mouth. Together, Ariana and Liisa took down the unsuspecting German couple, then ran out the door to the basement, up the stairs, out into the farmland and vanished into the night.

Fifteen minutes later, Liisa stopped running when she realized that Ariana was no longer beside her. Skidding to a stop, she looked back to see Ariana bent over, close to a crouch, panting with what looked suspiciously like blood pouring from her side.

Jogging back to Ariana, she squatted beside her and confirmed that it was indeed blood pouring from the tech's side.

"Shit, what did they do to you?"

"It wasn't them, it happened back in the lab when…" Ariana was gasping, her face ashen and wet with perspiration. Liisa could read the signs of blood loss, oxygen debt and maybe infection all too clearly.

"Okay… later, stop talking now, let me see if I can get you fixed up enough for us to get to somewhere off the road to rest." Liisa jerked her top off, quickly checked the thin material and found a small tear near the bottom of the shirt. Digging a finger into the hole, she was able to rip off about three inches of the fabric and fold it into a wad, placing it on the wound. Liisa grabbed Ariana's hand and jammed it down onto the wadded fabric, saying, "Hold this as tightly as you can, and let's go."

"This is your fault, you careless, ignorant, pathetic excuse for a man. You couldn't even handle the simple job of taking the camera so we could get the video uploaded onto the site— I had to do it, and if I hadn't been able to get it done, our lives would be worth nothing, nothing at all." Her face was a frightening shade of red, and she was shouting so angrily that spittle was spraying out of both sides of the jowls next to her mouth as they swung from side to side.

He merely said, "We need to call him to let him know they got away."

"No, we are not going to call him to let him know they got away. You are going to find them, now!"

"How, when we have no idea where they went?"

She smiled. Surveying his small close-set eyes, the chins which swayed with each movement of his head, and she hated him.

Swiftly recognizing that look, the smile which was far worse than the ranting, he backed up, turned and ran up the stairs.

They were in a remote farmhouse in a tiny town called Bonvillars about thirty miles north of Lausanne. She was right—they couldn't have gotten that far away.

Liisa had found a copse of trees a short distance from the highway, a short distance if you weren't half dragging, half carrying, almost ninety pounds of dead weight. Ariana was barely conscious, and what should have been a five-minute walk took over thirty minutes. When they got to the shelter of the trees, Ariana collapsed to the ground, forcing Liisa to carry her fireman style to the far edge of the woods. A damn good thing, because the moment after Liisa had finished cleaning Ariana's wound and had packed it with pine cones, leaves, and some dirt then wrapped it as tightly as possible from another strip torn from her rapidly diminishing shirt, Liisa saw the headlights of a pickup truck. The truck was going less than thirty miles an hour. The driver's window was down, and the shadow of a broad arm was extended through it holding an intensely bright mag light roaming both sides of the road.

At the trees, the truck slowed considerably. Liisa could see the beam from the flashlight illuminating the trees close to the road. She was confident that he could not see them, they were too far back. Unless he stopped the car, got out and examined the grove on foot. If he did that, he'd find them for sure. Liisa had no more strength to carry Ariana, who was out, unconscious. Exhausted, she closed her eyes and breathed deeply, willing him to give in to the laziness which made him fifty pounds overweight. There was nothing more she could do, and Liisa felt strangely calm as she waited.

"Slow down, Toni. If we're killed getting there, it'll all be academic." Jansen was watching the speedometer on the Bentley, it was approaching one hundred, and these were mountain roads. Every other curve seemed like a one-eighty and Toni barely blinked as she careened around them, reluctantly dropping the speed to maybe sixty. Sure the roads were clear, it was summer in Switzerland, but Rich was tired, nauseous, and irritable.

The material from Kate Townsend had been bursting with valuable information. There were over fifty pages of solid leads. After scanning it, the group decided to redo assignments. Lindsey's Gantt chart was getting a workout. Because of the information Kate had sent about Eric, the German researcher, Dimitri was paired with Lindsey. What she planned to do was dangerous; she needed a pro to back her up. Reardon was checking on a lead Kate had found in the business news about a surprise acquisition of an American pharmaceutical house by a German conglomerate. Cairns and Gabe McAllister, with Baron, went back to the site of the attack, to see if Baron's nose could give them any more information about what had happened. Maybe with the scent from one of Ariana's lab coats, the dog could provide more info about what had happened to the tech. All of that left Rich with Toni Martinez.

Attempting to figure out the source of his turbulent emotional state, Jansen's mind was crammed with monkey chatter. "Honey, I've got this handled, you don't need to don your Superwoman cape and jump in to save the day."

Was he jealous of his wife? Really? Because she had. There was no way that any of them, including Hank, would have found Liisa's safe under the desk, nevermind the combination to it. Nor would any of them have been capable of deciphering the string of dates and numbers from Liisa's mysterious Digipro modification for women with early onset of cardiomyopathy. But Lindsey did.

And her idea to call Kate Townsend and harness that reporter instinct for intel? Brilliant. There he was sleeping, while Dr. McCall was saving the day. He tried to blame his frustration on the residual effects of his concussion but then had to admit it. Yep, he was irate, fuming, livid...it was humiliating. She'd not even bothered to wake him up, to let him know she was planning to go workout in the gym at some ungodly hour and then call Kate Townsend for help. Nope, she had left so quietly that he'd slept soundly until six-thirty. The limo had already dropped off the second letter by the time he got his rear out of bed, dressed and up to the house. The entire team was there reading the list of new demands when he had walked in.

Rich realized he was gritting his teeth, which sent waves of pain firing up his jaw and radiating throughout his skull. Forcibly, he softened his mouth, relaxing the rigid muscles in his jaw. The pain eased. But only marginally.

Turning his head to his left, he saw Toni observing him out of the corner of her eye with a faint smile. "You know what it's like to be outshined, surpassed, vanquished, beaten, outperformed and outstripped, Toni?"

The fingers of her tattooed sleeved arm tapped on the console of the car between their two seats. She turned to look at him and replied, "Yes, I do, better than you, I'll wager. I have worked with my partner Harvey Cunningham for over five years. I live it. She is infinitely better than I at getting people to talk, open up and trust her. Not to mention her background that seems so weirdly relevant to detective work and making sense out of things that seem entirely unrelated." Toni was referring to Harvey's undergraduate study in anthropology, and graduate work in religious studies at Vanderbilt University. Her hand moved back to the console, tapping it gently as if it were Jansen's hand. He watched the intricate colors of her tattoos pulse with the flexing and relaxing of her muscles.

"You and Lindsey have been married for what, almost two years?" Replacing her hand at the two-o-clock position on the steering wheel, she glanced quickly at Rich and the smile returned. "You'll get used to it."

Despite himself, Jansen laughed. It felt so good that he laughed some more. She was right, he had married a woman who had been one of the leading Cardiologists and cardiovascular researchers in the country, perhaps the world. Eyes wide open. What did he expect? That some magic bolus of wifedom would be infused into Lindsey to transform her upon marriage to him? Empty her head of that fantastic brain of hers? Breathing deeply, slowly, Rich knew; suddenly supremely confident, he was overwhelmingly sure they would find the missing women and unearth the perpetrators of this thing. Largely due to the presence of his wife. The jealousy, frustration, and annoyance were gone in that flash of certainty. Leaving behind a most discomfiting sense of the fragility of his male ego.

CHAPTER TWENTY- FIVE
Farmhouse at Bonvillars

"I'll call him. I've been driving around for over two hours, and there's no sign of either of them."

He was tired, sick of the whole mess. Sick of her, sick of their life, and of their relentless and futile search for big money. Most of all, he was fed up with being scared. Of him.

She stared at him, biting off the insults about to pour out of her mouth. She recognized the surly pig-headed expression in those beady eyes. After dialing the number, she handed him the phone, heaving a massive sigh as she did so.

"Hello Claus, is he in?"

He waited, knowing that the five minutes Claus had told him it would be would likely stretch to ten or maybe fifteen minutes.

Diedrich Braun was the fifth wealthiest man in Germany and thirty-fifth on the list of the Forbes one hundred richest men in the world. His family had been in successful businesses for over three generations, which ranged from custom coffee makers to luxury automobiles and weapons. But it was after Deidrich's bold takeover of one of the top pharmaceutical companies in the world, that he renamed his company at the buyout to Diedrich Gruppe. An acquisition which boosted the family's holdings from mere multimillions, into the double digit billions.

Braun had engineered a hostile takeover of Adams and Adams, a leading pharmaceutical company in the US, during a tumultuous leadership vacuum caused by the sudden death of the CEO of the enterprise. Adams and Adams had pioneered the research on the clot-busting agents in the eighties. Those first patents on lytic enzymes to dissolve clots in the arteries of the heart and brain had revolutionized the treatment of cardiovascular disease. Adams and Adams held the patents until 2005, by which time the financial war chest of the company was estimated in the mega billions.

The oldest son and widow of Adams claimed that he had been murdered, but there had been no evidence of foul play found by the local police. They declared his death a suicide and closed the case.

Braun was in his early sixties but looked fifteen years younger due to a simple diet and rigorous exercise regime. He was divorced with a son whom he publicly claimed was worthless.

"Yes." The wait had indeed been close to twenty-five minutes. The voice was cold, imperious and devoid of all affect.

"They are gone. They escaped from the basement. I spent over three hours looking for them and can find them nowhere."

There was no response. The man held the phone and waited—there was no sound for close to two minutes, a long time when you feel as hollowed out as he was. The temptation to say something, to hang up, to do something other than waiting for more intimidation was overpowering. But he stood holding the phone, and he waited. And then.

"They…are…gone…"

The echo of the three words in his ear sounded evil, and alive with malice. There were unnamed horrors in the ice-filled slivers uttered by Diedrich Braun. His heart rate began to race, far faster than he ever knew it could go, his breathing shallow and rapid. He was terrified. He knew he had just signed their death warrant. He looked over at her and saw she knew what was coming as well; all the rage had wicked away from her face, only shock and panic remained.

Liisa's eyes snapped open. Heart pounding, she opened her eyes expecting only the darkness she had seen for the last two days at the farmhouse. Confused at the thick green canopy she saw all around her, Liisa breathed easier, remembering they were safe, for now. Next to her Ariana lay prone, breathing slowly and quietly.

Moving slowly so as not to awaken Ariana, Liisa moved first to a crouch and then stood, looking around their almost treehouse-like enclosure. Judging by the daylight, Liisa reckoned the time to be midmorning. They must have slept for several hours. She tread gingerly, trying not to make any noise and to avoid any more damage to her bruised and lacerated bare feet. Following the sound of an occasional vehicle, Liisa got to the edge of the copse and peered out at the peaceful village. Looking around, she was relieved at her recognition of this place. She and her dad had come here many times over the last several years. The Bonvillars Truffle Market was known throughout Switzerland, and this meant they were no more than thirty minutes from Lausanne.

Liisa looked around and considered her options, worried about leaving Ari and afraid of running into someone looking for them.

Thinking of Ari, Liisa flashed back to what Ari had been trying to tell her before she lost consciousness for the second time. Liisa asked who had done this to her, and Ari had replied that she had done it to herself using her knife to defend herself from...she had mumbled the name but now, thinking back, Liisa realized that she had been trying to say the name, Eric. It had been Eric who had attacked her or rather defended himself. Maybe it was the other way around...maybe Ari had surprised him in the middle of ...what?

Eric Braun had worked for ASL for over five years, Liisa had been extremely excited to get him. Eric had received his doctoral and post-doc training at one of the top scientific schools in the world, Ruprecht-Karls-Universitat Heidelberg. He and Liisa had even dated for a while. Mind racing, Liisa tried to consider Eric Braun in a plot to steal the patent rights to Longevive. No matter who it was, money had to be what this whole insane escapade was about, though—it had to be.

She continued to think about Eric. About what may have happened at the labs, something which could have resulted in an accidental stabbing of Ari.

One of them was surprised by the other...it had to be Ari who surprised Eric in the lab doing something she thought wrong, so some kind of struggle happened where tiny Ari attempted to defend herself against six foot something Eric...

Eric would have been after the test mice, Liisa decided. Those who had more than doubled their lifespan. Moreover, Ari would have defended her tiny charges with her life. Liisa thought back to the beginnings of her first experiments. Since Ari was so interested in this particular new research project, Liisa had named her as the second principal investigator; she had been thrilled.

To eliminate genetic variation among the mice, they used agouti mice for the Longevive experiments. Ariana had taken some basic courses in caring for the agouti mice and had been the primary caregiver for both the control and test mice.

Hair color in mice is determined by the expression of the agouti gene. Normal mice express the agouti protein at regular intervals which lead to the brown or gray streaked fur with darker stripes or colors because they have two copies of the agouti gene; one inherited from the mother, and one from the father. A mutated version of the gene never switches on and produces mice with black hair while another mutant genetic strand produces mice with yellow hair. Scientists created a strain of mice where both mutant genes are in each cell. Since agouti mice are genetically identical, they should be indistinguishable from one another, but they are not. Some have all yellow fur; some look like normal mice with brindled fur and others are black. Perfect for scientific experiments because all the mice had the exact same genetic make-up, thus eliminating all variables other than the one being studied. In this case, the Longevive drug.

Liisa's doctoral and post-doc work at Stanford's Department of Biology had been in the newly emerging field of epigenetics. One of her favorite professors at Stanford wrote poetry under a pseudonym for the Los Angeles Times. Her favorite was one the professor called 'The Englishman and The Monk." In free verse, the scientist fictionalized a meeting between two contemporaries: the English scientist Charles Darwin and the Czech monk-scientist Gregor Mendel. One made famous with the publication of *The Origin of Species* and his theory of evolution which captured the post-enlightenment minds and swiftly evolved from theory to the truth. The other, confined to his Abbey and virtually unknown. What unique methods could have resulted had Mendel's observations of dominant heritable traits been paired with Darwin's theory of natural selection; how far would science have advanced had such a meeting occurred. Fun and fanciful, Liisa had thought at the time. But she recalled making her decision about her career upon considering the powerful effects of history, culture, and chance on some of the most important scientific discoveries.

The science of epigenetics looks for the reasons why genetically identical individuals are non-identical in measurable ways. There were three hundred agouti mice in the Longevive phase one study; one hundred fifty in the experimental group and one hundred fifty in the control group. Ari knew and had named each of the three hundred small creatures. She had help from the other techs but she watched over them as would a mother; this was exciting, innovative research, the reason that Ariana had gone into the field. And the preliminary results were staggering.

Ari must have surprised Eric, showing up when he did not expect her to be there. Like on a Thursday. Liisa realized that Ari must have already been there when she was thrown down into the basement on Friday morning. Unconscious but there. Which suggested she had been there since the night before. Something must have made Ariana suspicious because Thursdays were the days she went to visit her parents in Geneva. Something Eric had said or done made Ariana cancel her weekly visit home; her mother had married a man fifteen years older than she who was elderly and failing both physically and mentally. Ari's schedule was like clockwork. She always got to her folks early so that she was in time to make them breakfast, lunch, and dinner before she left to return to her Lausanne home.

Liisa visualized the struggle now that her deduction held together more or less logically. Moreover, she thought how comical this would be if their lives were not so obviously now at stake. Her lips compressed grimly; she wondered when, or if, she would ever laugh again, or even smile.

Eric Braun stood staring at the whiteboard in front of him. The formulas written by the youngest member of his team looked like gibberish; he could make no sense of the symbols.

Eric and his team were working in one of the central labs of the ASL compound. The entire second floor of the building consisted of lab nearly the size of a football field. The enormous open space contained at least twenty, maybe thirty, men and women sitting or standing in groups of twos and threes among a variety of cubicles, and others were scattered all over the lab. Despite the presence of over one-hundred-fifty scientists, there was an eerie 'almost silence' in the lab; undercurrents of conversation were audible, but the voices were all muted. There was a reverential feeling in the place.

Stark white walls on one side with the external wall composed almost entirely of glass, permitting the brilliant spring sun to diffuse throughout the cavernous room where artfully landscaped grounds ablaze with marigolds, geraniums, impatiens, and a profusion of blooming plants competed for attention. Although there must have been thirty or so cubicles in the large space, there was absolutely no sense of crowding.

Each work area was spatially defined by S-shaped counters that looked like black marble with a scientist at each of the openings of the S. There were wide rows between the worktops, giving an open, airy feel to the place, with enormous steel sinks at the beginning of each work area.

Eric was aware of none of his surroundings; he felt as if he were in a fugue state. Since his stupid fight with Ari three days ago, he had not slept. The kidnapping of Liisa had been bad enough, but Ari gone too? Because of him? He knew how he was coming across to everyone, his team members had stopped asking questions, they were all just going through the motions, waiting for the other shoe to drop. Those people, Dimitri and Toni, knew he was somehow involved in this insane fiasco. The one with all the tattoos had picked up each hesitation, each subtle change in his expression when they had interviewed him. Interview...right, it was an interrogation, and they had been damn good. Not exactly good cop and bad cop but close enough. His fear for Ariana was growing by the day, by the minute actually.

Thursdays were always Ari's day off. Eric could not recall a Thursday that Ariana Dumas had worked in the five years he had been at ASL. So why had she changed her schedule on the exact day when he had snuck into the lab to grab the test mice?

Eric Braun, like his boss Liisa, was a double doctorate, but in Physics and Chemistry, and had been working at the University of Munich Medical School when Liisa Reardon had recruited him from the cosmopolitan city of Munich to the small hamlet-sized town of Lausanne. But Eric had been happier than he'd ever been in his life. A country away from the agonizing memories of his childhood and his insane father had been invigorating. He'd had no idea of how happiness felt or tasted until he took this job. And then Cairns appeared.

Stupidly, Eric had been happy when he heard that Liisa had hired a supercop to head up security at ASL. Like everyone who worked on the Longevive and new Digipro data associated with cardiomyopathy, Eric was well aware of the market potential, it was mind-boggling. Like most of the other experienced scientists in his field, Eric was well acquainted with corporate espionage. More than once, he had been approached while at the medical school in Munich. It had been a clumsy almost comical attempt at bribery, the money offered had been laughable, and he had done just that, laughed as he walked away. But the trial he'd been working on at the medical school had merely been for a new use of an old drug. Boring.

When Ari told him how she had felt about Cairns, he had trivialized her fear of the man exactly as Liisa had. Eric's cheeks warmed when he thought back to their argument. "Ari, you sound like a superstitious old woman...his eyes are evil. Come on, get your head out of the fifteenth and into the twenty-first century, will you please?"

Her face had flamed, and her retort was in French, so he didn't understand anything after her first exclamation, "Merde." She said it with the classically Gallic intonation and gestures so that even those who spoke no French knew it was some kind of epithet.

That was the last time they had actually spoken until she surprised him in the lab. Ari and Eric had arrived at ASL the same year and had become friends. During the total restructuring of the labs, the institution of radically different methods of conducting experiments and all of the blowback coming at them from all sides, the two had become wonderful friends and had supported one another without reservation. Their deep friendship ended with a whimper with his ignorant dismissals of her eerily prescient impression of Joe Cairns.

"Eric?"

Startled out of his reverie, Eric blinked several times as he tried to orient himself. The headaches were worsening and so were the balance problems. While running up the stairs to his apartment two days ago, Eric had missed a step and tumbled back down the long stairway, crashing into the sharp corners of a table in the foyer. The vision problems were worsening as well. Eric's attempts to attribute these ominous neurological symptoms to MS or insomnia were providing a morbid sense of amusement. Something was wrong, terribly wrong…with his brain.

He was so tired that the face in front of him was distorted. Finally, he recognized Emily, the youngest scientist at ASL. Only twenty-three, she was brilliant but now looked merely annoyed as she stood next to him. The irritation on her face distorted her usually delicate features, Eric noticed with some surprise. Her annoyance pinched her eyes and nose, pulling her mouth into a bitter grimace.

"Sorry, Em, I was somewhere else."

"That was evident, I have been trying to get your thoughts on this latest modification, but you just keep staring at the board. What do you think?" She was pointing at the board which was now crammed with formulas, the others in their group looked occupied, but Eric knew he was being scrutinized. And God knew they had every right to examine him; he'd been useless for days now. Ignoring Emily's question, Eric pointed to Mark, his unofficial backup.

"Mark, sorry to do this but you need to take over for me, please. I'm not well, I need to go." Eric turned to Emily, "Sorry Em, please take it up with Mark and the group. I'll be back."

"When will you be back, Eric?" Eric had turned to leave but stopped at Mark's question. He was a decent guy, not the brightest of the group, by far, but he possessed what most did not: common sense—huge aliquots of the stuff. In Eric's thirty-two years, it was an attribute uncommonly found and rare among scientists. The least he could do was tell him the truth.

"Mark, I don't know when I'll be back." He bit through his tongue before he could say, "Or even *if* I'll be back." Eric strode rapidly out of the research lab, headed down the hall, then took the staircase three steps at a time, easy for the six-foot-four-inch scientist, so long as he could stay upright. He headed for Liisa's office where he figured he would find Lindsey putting the last touches on the patent transfer the kidnappers were demanding.

Slowing his pace down, Eric reflected on Diedrich Braun and for the first time in many years, Eric smiled at the thought of his father, who had harbored a hatred for his only son, the virulence of which was exceeded only by his passion for power. The scientist began to jog—excited, relieved and eager to fix this. And ran headlong into Lindsey McCall and some guy he had never seen before.

Baron had followed the exact same set of behaviors three times. The dog had easily picked up Ariana's scent once he smelled the lab coat he and Cairns had found in a closet in the anteroom of the main lab. Initially, Baron had raced around the large room, sniffing everything. Then had scratched at the locked door leading to the section where the mice were kept. Excited, his stubby tail wagged furiously as he slowly nosed the ground where Jansen had been attacked in ever increasing circles, out to about three feet from the spot.

Baron stopped, looked confused, sniffed the air then trotted a few feet more and sat down in front of Cairns who stood back watching, saying nothing. As usual. But the guy became aware he needed to say something. The dog had parked his butt right in front of him, staring at him.

"I was here for over a week working with Ariana while I was getting my feet on the ground, looking to identify the biggest threats to security here. Baron must be getting traces of her off my clothes."

Nodding in agreement, Gabe said, "Probably." But he thought, *Only if you haven't washed your clothes since you were with her weeks ago.*

The fourth time the Doberman approached Cairns, he stood, back hair raised, head raised and growled.

"What, you think I did something with her boy?" The guy was chuckling, but he looked damned uncomfortable, Gabe reflected. But to be fair, most normal people would be uncomfortable when staring at eighty-five pounds of muscle and a head full of teeth, big and exposed. Joe Cairns was not a dog person. Cairns had never come over to pet the dog and always sat as far away from him as possible. Not that unusual, Gabe knew, especially with Dobermans. They had a reputation.

But from the first time Baron had set eyes on Cairns, he'd acted wary. Unusual for Baron in Gabe's experience. But Baron had been over two years old when Gabe had adopted him, so who knew what the animal had experienced before he came to Gabe. Furthermore, Gabe felt the same way about Cairns and knew his dog could well have acquired his own guardedness. Because the guy was obviously a former soldier, Gabe tried to downplay his suspicions, saying nothing to Rich or Lindsey about how he felt. Besides, it wasn't as if he had any reason to distrust Cairns. Just that the timing of everything seemed awfully convenient. Hence, the first time Baron had stopped in front of Cairns, Gabe had not thought a whole lot about it. But then when Cairns felt pressured to offer that lame explanation, he'd wondered. Now that his dog was acting like he was on alert in front of Cairns, Gabe was puzzled. He murmured "Down" and Baron instantly dropped to his abdomen, but his gaze did not leave Cairns.

When Cairns' cell rang, he glanced at the number, looked at Gabe and said, "Sorry, I've got to take this." And had walked out of the lab. *Saved by the bell, literally.*

Baron whined, asking to be released from the down command, then immediately raced through the hallway and back to the front door, scratching at the door. Obviously wanting to follow Cairns.

Sure, Gabe mused as he watched the dog, *Baron could be wrong. He may merely dislike the scent of Joe Cairns; but why not, let's follow him and see what happens, boy. There's not a whole lot else happening around here right now, anyway.*

Opening the door to the lab, he could see Cairns' black SUV rapidly leaving the complex, but following him was a small silver car driven by, *Toni?*

"Damn it, yes, that was Toni Martinez! Come on boy, I have no clue what she thinks she's doing, but I'm with you in thinking that Cairns is one treacherous dude." Gabe and Baron raced to the truck.

"Dr. McCall? God, I'm so sorry I plowed into you!"

Eric was tall, lanky and there was something off about him. Lindsey squinted into the sun to look at him, but could see only stars.

"Eric, no worries, I'm fine." But she was shaken up and would have slammed to the ground if Dimitri had not caught and steadied her. Lindsey squeezed the cop's hand in a wordless 'thank you' before she let go.

"Eric, this is Dimitri Vlasov from the Swiss Federal Police. He is helping us make sense out of what is happening with Liisa and Ariana, can you join us in Liisa's office please?"

"Yes, of course, we met the other day, and actually, that's exactly where I was headed when I ran you down!"

The voluminous amount of information that Kate Townsend had faxed from her home in Palo Alto contained crucial information about Eric. Like his last name of Braun spelled the same way as Diedrich Braun, CEO of Braun Gruppe Enterprises. And a sister who had died at the age of four from cardiomyopathy followed closely by the suicide of Eric's thirty-two-year-old mother. Eric had been eight when this happened.

And then there was the information about the surprise acquisition of Adams and Adams by Gruppe Enterprises, right on the heels of the suicide of Matthew Adams, CEO of the pharmaceutical company. More than enough material to keep twenty people busy. This was why the group decided to pair Dimitri with Lindsey, in case Eric was his father's son and had adopted Dad's aggressive, perhaps even murderous business tactics.

The three were seated now in Liisa's office. Lindsey had deliberately slowed her pace so she could watch Eric climb the stairs to the foyer of the main building of the corporate offices. He was ataxic, that was what she had picked up outside but had not processed exactly what she had observed. The problem with the muscular coordination of his legs was causing his left leg to drag slightly to his right. And she noticed a tremor in his left hand when he extended his right hand to shake hers. Eric had tried to hide the tremor by instantly shoving the offending hand into his pocket. When they arrived at Liisa's office, Lindsey chose Liisa's chair behind the desk. Leaving two chairs in front of the desk and a small couch for Eric and Dimitri. Dimitri leaned against the closed door of the office while Eric perched on the edge of the couch turned toward Lindsey. Terribly nervous, the scientist apologized again for running into them. Beginning to snap a sharp rebuke, Lindsey stopped herself, startled. *His pupils...they are unequal! His left is larger than the right.*

Noting her start, Dimitri subtly shifted his position and looked at her. The question in his face as clear as if he had spoken, saying, 'Problem? Do we need to act?'

More and more impressed with this quiet, even unassuming cop, Lindsey merely smiled and shook her head.

Frankly, she did not know what to do. It looked to her as if this scientist was in trouble, severe neurologic trouble.

Although she was no neurologist, Lindsey knew that asymmetrical pupils indicated bleeding within the brain. But when she looked at Eric again, because he had shifted position, his eyes looked normal. *Did I imagine that?*

Suddenly, he spoke. "Don't send those documents to the US Patent Office, please, there is no need to do this. I have provided the information they demand, but it is not valid."

Shocked, Lindsey asked, "How did you know about the kidnapper's demands Eric? We just got the letter delivered to Hank's home at six-thirty this morning." Glancing quickly over at Dimitri, Lindsey noticed that he was no longer leaning against the closed door. He was standing straight with one hand in his coat jacket where she bet he had that hand on his gun.

Looking around at the disarray in the office, Eric thought crazily, *Liisa would be really pissed off if she could see what a mess that Dr. McCall has made of her office.* Right on the heels of that thought came this, *what I wouldn't give to see a pissed off Dr. Liisa Reardon hollering at Lindsey for destroying her filing system!*

Lindsey was still operating under the demands stated in the last document Hank had received about Liisa's release, her survival in question because the claim had been made that she was imprisoned in a place with a limited reservoir of oxygen.

Changing the owner of a patent sounded like a relatively straightforward procedure but, in fact, was anything but. The United States Patent Office was a bureaucracy, and like most modern governmental organizations seemed focused on demonstrating its power over those it ostensibly served by establishing a quagmire of red tape. Where a one-page form would suffice, there was a twenty-page document. Although the Patent Office was the place where the ultimate decision of awarding a patent was made, there were myriads of sub-offices who had a toe in the game. Could Eric be right in his conviction that she would not need to spend hours and hours of mind-numbing busy work?

"Because that is what my father would have to do." The tall German leaned forward, his expression creased with earnestness.

"You two," Eric looked around at Dimitri, "have figured out that I've been involved in this appalling obsession of my father's, and you are right, I have been... or rather, I am. But there is no need to worry, I have given them the wrong formula. It will take weeks for my father's scientists to figure that out."

He looked directly at Lindsey. "Please do not submit that paperwork for the Longevive patent transfer. They will get nowhere with the formula or the data I sent to my father's people." Eric was nervous. His speech was rapid and his accent more pronounced than usual, but the relief at getting this off his chest was like an aphrodisiac, he could not wait for things to be back to normal in the labs—especially Ari and Liisa back here working, without him to be sure, but he accepted that. His head pounded.

The three were silent. The silence grew and became oppressive, but neither Lindsey nor Dimitri spoke. Lindsey, because she was afraid to say something that would cause more stress for this man. She was almost certain that she had not imagined that dilated left pupil. But only almost. This was Eric's show, it had to be. So she sat still and tried to look at the distressed researcher calmly and kindly, encouraging him and belying the frantic pace of her thoughts.

"I am not sure where to start."

You figured out that I am involved in this appalling obsession of my father, and you're right, I am and sent the wrong formula to my father, my FATHER, Lindsey's mind was galloping, making inferences as fast as a computer. *Don't file the patent transfer paperwork, there is no need to worry. They will get nowhere with the formula and the data I have sent to my father's people. This was corporate espionage, exactly what I was afraid of...*

Good God, these people—his father is willing to do anything at all to get at the formula...but this kid—she looked at Eric again, realizing that he was most likely close to her own age—he just acted really young, immature. And yet he has figured out a way to fool these creeps...one of whom is someone he called Dad, at one time.

When Eric burst into tears, Lindsey jumped nearly out of her skin.

"My father is Diedrich Braun. He owns Diedrich Gruppe and is one of the richest men in Germany, in the world, really." Eric was sitting with his butt barely perched at the end of the loveseat, it looked as if he planned to run at any minute. No longer crying, the scientist appeared almost collected. One hand rested on his right thigh, the other extended outward as if in a plea. "My mother married my father when she was very young, while still in graduate school."

Looking over at Dimitri, Lindsey saw that the detective had pulled out a miniature recorder, he was taping this. Maybe it was the recorder rather than a gun he had grabbed. Smart, very smart and she wondered what else he carried in that suit jacket. She was grateful he was here, that she was not alone.

Eric's voice had adopted the intonation of a well-rehearsed speech as if this was a story he had told many times. "She was twenty years younger than Father and wanted a whole bevy of kids, she used to say she wanted an entire soccer team." Eric smiled, a facsimile of a smile looking more grim than happy, and the expression stayed on his lips, never reaching his eyes.

His hazel eyes looked empty and lost. Clearly, the notion of a 'bevy of kids' had been an absurd idea in the Braun household. "Father was disappointed in me by the time I was three and detested the very sight of me by eight. Diedrich Braun wanted a replication of himself for a son; a hunter..." Those dead empty eyes looked up at Lindsey and smiled that rictus of a smile again, "a Joe Cairns." At that, Lindsey's gaze snapped to Dimitri, who nodded.

Suddenly Eric snapped out of the intense melancholy he had been mired in and began to explain just what had happened at ASL over the last several months. As if the mere mention of the assassin's name cleared all of the emotion away.

"My father wants Longevive partly because I am homosexual and will never provide him with heirs, grandsons to mold into reproductions of himself. Also because of the money, the one thing that Daddy loves is money.

"I believe, but cannot prove, that Cairns, on the orders of my father, was behind the murder of Matt Adams, and am positive he gave the Longevive formula to my father so that the research company my father took from Adams could develop the drug for humans. Father wants to live forever, or as close to forever as is possible today. Diedrich Braun believes that he is essential to the world and that Longevive will provide him immortality or close to it." Suddenly Eric stood and began to pace the small room, holding Lindsey and Dimitri mesmerized as they listened raptly to a depraved story.

Eric told of a childhood where he was subjected to countless attempts at brainwashing by his father. Brainwashing in the most insidious of ways. A reading list of books like *Mein Kampf, Hitler's Second Book—The Unpublished Sequel to Mein Kampf,* along with *The Speeches of Adolph Hitler, April, 1922-August, 1939* were required reading by his eighth birthday.

Puppies were given to the little boy and then he was forced to kill them to learn his superiority over all creatures. When he refused, the animals were beaten to death by Braun.

Diedrich Braun was an admirer of Dietrich Eckart, the individual who most influenced Adolph Hitler. Eckart was associated with the Thule Society, a German think tank of occult beliefs from which the notion of Aryan supremacy was originally derived, along with the conviction that the Jewish bloodline warranted extermination. Nine months before meeting Hitler, Eckhart wrote an epic poem about the 'German Messiah' predicted by the Society. The poet was convinced upon meeting Hitler that he personified the Messiah. The influence of Eckart on Adolph Hitler is hard to underestimate, despite the fact that Eckart had failed at law, medicine and business by squandering a very sizable family inheritance.

Summer reading included some of Dietrich Eckart's modification of Ibsen's play *Peer Gynt,* where Gynt was reformulated to portray the Uberman—the superior God-man of German folklore, and his ultimate victorious fight against what were parodies of the Jewish people in his trolls. With over six hundred performances in Berlin alone, Eckart's play inaugurated the anti-Semitic epidemic in post-World War 1 Germany. And, augmented Eckart's finances sufficiently to begin his periodical, Auf Gut Deutsch, a blatantly racist attack on German Jews. Both the play and the publication provided the perfect catalyst for influential and moneyed people to support the founding of an antidote to the Weimar Republic, the new German Workers Party in 1919. Within a year, the name was changed to the National Socialist German Workers Party, to become the Nazi Party.

The final break between Diedrich Braun and his eight-year-old son occurred when Eric and his best friend Klaus were found in Eric's bedroom nude, and his mother defended her son's behavior as normal childhood curiosity. Diedrich Braun was so enraged at Eric that he nearly killed him. His then thirty-year-old mother had grabbed her son and infant daughter in the middle of the night, and the three ran away to Switzerland.

When Eric stopped his over thirty-minute monologue, and dropped back onto the couch, Lindsey merely nodded, too overwhelmed and exhausted to think.

"Do you know what happened to Ariana, or where Liisa is?" Dimitri's voice was surprisingly gentle. He had silently moved into the room and had taken a seat next to the researcher, Lindsey noticed with surprise. Dimitri's expression was an intriguing combination of compassion and intensity.

"Ariana found me in the labs as I was taking some of the mice to give to Joe Cairns for my father's people. She rightly thought I was stealing the mice and would not listen to anything I said." Eric shook his head sadly, "Ari fought me with that wicked knife she always carried for self- defense, but cut herself pretty badly. What a nightmare all this is..." Mumbling something in German, Lindsey was shocked out of her torpor when the cop replied to him in German.

Eric's pale skin was flushed with his reply. From the expressions on their faces, Lindsey guessed that Eric had mumbled a series of epithets, and Dimitri had thrown in a few choice selections of his own favorites, all in German.

"Tell us about your sister's heart disease and how she has done on the Reardon protocol."

"So do you know where either of them is?"

Dimitri and Lindsey asked their contradictory questions at precisely the same time.

Lindsey's tone was sharper than she intended.

Eric looked anxiously across the room where Lindsey sat behind Liisa's desk, and then his glance flicked to Dimitri sitting at the opposite end of the couch from him. Plainly overwhelmed, Eric seemed paralyzed.

"Does your sister have heart disease, Eric? And did you have her on Liisa's new TirNan protocol?" Lindsey had forcibly tamped herself down. Her voice was almost as muted as Dimitri's.

His eyes haunted, the German nodded. "Yes. Liisa knew of Gretchen's cardiomyopathy and was delighted to add her to our growing subset of young females on Digipro, who were on her protocol."

Cardiomyopathies are a puzzling and almost-universally-fatal type of heart failure. Thought to be caused by a virus, the actual mechanism of disease is poorly understood. But the course of the disease is all too well known: increasing heart failure and incapacitation over time, and death if not treated with heart transplantation.

Lindsey's drug Digipro had optimized the centuries old drug Digitalis by creating a new molecule which maintained the almost unparalleled Digitalis effects of strengthening the contractile force of the heart while obliterating the toxic impact on the conduction and gastrointestinal systems. Digipro had revolutionized the treatment of acute heart failure.

"Gretchen is in Stage IV failure without Digipro isn't she, Eric?" Lindsey's voice was still intense, but she had forced herself to emulate the same kindness and gentleness she saw in the Swiss cop.

A leading cause of death in children, cardiomyopathy is thought to occur due to a mutation in the DNA of the child, a displacement of one or more of the amino acids of the proteins making up the DNA spiral. Lindsey's mind was racing.

If this young girl's response to the protocol was legitimate...and if Gretchen were alive rather than a fiction of Eric's imagination which Lindsey was beginning to believe. If she was right, this could be all delusion.

"Eric, where are they?" Dimitri repeated his question, this time forcefully enough that Eric started. Eric stared at Dimitri and began to blink more and more rapidly. With heroic effort, the man reached into the pocket of his shirt and grabbed a thumb drive in a badly shaking hand and tried to get it to Dimitri.

Lindsey didn't like what she was seeing, *this guy is in trouble, he's going to seize.* She started to rise out of her chair then all hell broke loose. Eric's eyes rolled up into the back of his head, and he succumbed to a grand mal seizure. Not realizing what has happening, Dimitri had shot to his feet and pulled his gun, aiming it at Eric whose lean, lanky body lost all coordination and motor control. The powerful convulsions slammed his head into the corner of Liisa's desk. The sickening crack echoed through the room precisely when Rich and Toni threw open the door.

A good two feet behind Rich, but close enough to see the chaos inside, Toni decided she could add nothing here. She'd follow a hunch.

Toni had seen Joe Cairns' SUV pulling out of the parking lot as she and Jansen pulled in. Figuring that only a few minutes had passed, she raced to the building where the corporate cars were kept, grabbed a set of keys and sprinted to the lot. She hoped Reardon would forgive the fact that she'd not signed out to take the Taurus sedan. It was a wonderfully unobtrusive car which Cairns wouldn't notice if he saw it in the rear view window of his black SUV unless she was stupid and let him catch her tailing him. But Toni wasn't stupid.

There was only one way out of the corporate offices, and although Cairns was not visible, she felt fairly sure she would catch up to him. But she had to be careful, very careful so she pressed the accelerator and hoped. And then she saw the big SUV about to turn onto Route 1/5 north to Zurich.

Taking a deep breath, Toni worked to slow her racing heart and dried her perspiring hands on her pant legs. *Harvey would not approve of this one, Martinez. This just may be one of the stupidest things you have ever done.*

But Toni could not shake her sense that Cairns was embroiled in this, that there was a reason he had applied for this particular job, so unlike what he had spent most of his life doing. So tame, in comparison.

Last night, she had been online to see if her extensive hacking abilities could reveal anything unusual about Joe Cairns. But after several hours of searching and reading, she'd found only what Reardon had told them, just a little more detailed. Close to twenty years in the Marine Force Recon; the majority of those locations and assignments classified, then a sudden jump to the Cyber Warfare Center in Omaha, Nebraska where he had worked until he had apparently left the government for a job in private industry as head of security. Strange. But possible... sort of.

Now that she was committed, Toni deliberated about why she had taken off alone like this, following a guy she was certain was one of the more dangerous men she'd ever encountered. From the time that Toni had been three years old, she had seen auras. A naturally verbal and happy child, she had begun talking to her grandmother about the almost black aura she saw cloaking her father on the weekends she spent with her Abu in the mountains of Puerto Rico. Toni had seen only one person with a black aura, and that was her father, the night he started molesting her when she was four. The night Abu came to take her to live with her. Joe Cairns' aura was mostly black, with shimmers of gray, a dark muddy gray.

Toni's grandmother was psychic and also a person who sees auras, but her 'sight' had been dimmed by age and sorrow. After asking her granddaughter a few questions about how her father held and touched her, she decided to take her away from her dope addicted son and daughter-in-law, adopting Toni when she was four. Tutored by her Abu, Toni learned to keep her gifts to herself. Abu had impressed upon her young charge that what people do not understand, they fear. And fear is at the heart of every evil act of man.

Although Harvey and her husband Zach Cunningham

knew about her psychic abilities, she had told neither of them about the auras. She had told no one, ever.

Toni couldn't see auras on everyone. But she had learned to use her gifts to bolster the psychic charge she felt upon meeting some people. For example, when Toni first saw Hank Reardon, it was not his obvious Americanisms she was drawn to, it was his aura. She had seen it from far across the village as he walked out of the forest into the center of their small rural town of Aibonito in the San Cristobal Mountains where she lived with her Abu. Reardon wore a deep blue cloak around his entire body. It shimmered and extended from him as it seemed to reach out to her, to call her. Toni had never seen an aura like that before. She knew what it signified; a deep sense of mission and immersion in a cause, one who sought passionately to help others, one who possessed wisdom and was capable of applying it to great ends. Toni was compelled to meet him, talk with him, and maybe learn from him.

Toni blushed when she thought of the silly ruse she designed to gain his attention. She had captured an ordinary toad and claimed that it was one of the rare native crested toads of Puerto Rico, offering to sell it to him for only five hundred dollars, rather than its stated worth of several thousand, in a clumsy combination of Spanish and English. She recalled her absolute certainty that he would not be able to understand a word she was saying. There was no way he could. Nor was there any he should pay any attention to a silly teenager who had lived in a rural mountain village of Puerto Rico for her entire life.

In Spanish, Reardon had calmly asked if he could hold the toad, exclaiming as he did so that it sure wasn't every day that one could hold an almost extinct frog.

His blue eyes were so intense they had almost blinded her as he smiled while asking where she lived.

"About a ten-minute walk away," she had replied nervously. His Spanish wasn't perfect, but better than most of the tourists she had tried to fleece before meeting Hank Reardon.

"Can I go there with you? I would like to meet your parents." They had talked about inconsequential things along the way, at least, they had seemed insignificant to Toni; but within thirty minutes of being in Abu's home, Abu had brought out her Chicken Aspao along with Tostones for the three of them to lunch on. Reardon had charmed the older woman with his praise of Toni, her initiative, drive, and potential.

His arrival to the village had seemed providential. Abu had been talking with Toni about her future, a future, Abu knew, that must not take place in the community, but rather far away. Not yet twenty, Toni faced a dismal future were she to stay in their small town. Neither of them was really surprised when Reardon made the offer to pay for Toni's education while he employed her in his Switzerland business. Toni's grandmother had been praying hard for her young granddaughter. She accepted this gift, sure that Reardon was the answer to those prayers.

For Toni, Hank Reardon was the father she had never had. When her boss, Zach Cunningham told her that Jansen was flying out to Lausanne to help Hank and his family out of a terribly dangerous situation and wanted her investigative skills to help find a kidnapper, Zach had apologized profusely.

"Toni, this sounds like way more than we should handle. Rich was attacked within the first few minutes of being there. He says he needs you, but will totally understand if you say no."

For Toni, there was no decision to be made. On at least two levels, it was a no-brainer. If Hank Reardon's family was in trouble, Toni would do anything she could to help, regardless of how risky it was. Secondly, Rich Jansen had told her boss that he needed her. Toni had to admit that she was flattered. She chuckled as she recalled their inauspicious meeting. Reardon had greeted her and Harvey at the door of his Houston law office with a huge Doberman sitting there. Toni had freaked, insisting that their meeting take place somewhere without that dog and that she never lay eyes on that creature again. Despite the anger she had seen in Jansen's eyes and face, he had acceded to her demands, graciously.

During one of her many talks with the young Toni about her unique gifts, Abu had explained that there were some who looked and acted just like other people, but who were actually deprived of the life force emanating from the soul. This happened, Toni's grandmother explained, when people experienced profound grief, or they were addicted to drugs and alcohol like Toni's parents had been. Consequently, the energy produced by their spirit appeared as gray or black. Abu had emphasized caution over and over to Toni through the years of her mentorship with her young charge. The aura was a sign, nothing more. And always, the information provided by the auras was to be treated as privileged information, not to be shared with others, unless absolutely necessary.

Toni reflected on those long ago lessons as she followed the vehicle which closely mirrored the man. The SUV Cairns drove was black with opaque windows. A black box permitting no window into the contents, just like Cairns' eyes. A muddy gray aura she knew resulted from someone intent on being secretive. Reasonable for sure because of the many years spent in special operations for the federal government. Activities, Toni thought, best left off the radar of public knowledge. The color was also indicative of sadness, long suppressed. All of which made sense if Cairns had spent a couple of decades as a sniper or assassin. But it was his eyes that made Toni's decision for her; opaque, and revealing nothing at all, they were the eyes of someone capable of anything.

Cairns was heading north on the main road out of Lausanne on A-5; it was mid morning so the traffic wasn't heavy, but there were enough cars for Toni to keep two to three cars between her and Cairns. So far so good. The SUV was moving toward the exit to Neuchatel, about forty-five miles northeast of Lausanne. Moments later, Toni took the exit slowly, she didn't want to be spotted. She headed up the ramp and prepared to take the turn onto A-1 when she caught a glimpse of the black SUV, parked off to the side.

OH NO, NO, he's made me. Where the hell is he? Get out of here now girl. Stomping on the accelerator, the car lurched forward at about double the speed she'd been going when suddenly she was in a spin, the car was spinning out of control.

He's rammed me with his SUV... her last thought.

"If you are reading this then I am dead…I guess Father was right about all of us. I am writing this two days after Liisa and Ari's kidnapping, in case my guess is right. I am dying. Weak genes, unfitting for a *Braun.* My mother's suicide after my little sister Gretchen's death at four, and now this brain tumor getting me. Most disappointing for an Aryan wanna-be like Diedrich Braun.

"If I told you that my mother was living, or that Gretchen was still alive and flourishing on the Reardon protocol we named TirNan, please forgive the lie. It was one of the few fantasies I permitted myself, along with the Photoshopped picture in my office of Gretchen as an adult, sitting with our mother. She was so sick near the end, and there was nothing any of us could do. But she never complained, not once.

"Like so many discoveries, TirNan was an accident. Liisa needed help in making sense of the massive amount of data accumulating from patients on Digipro. I volunteered because I was interested in analyzing the nutritional information that we'd begun to collect. Ariana had read the Wahls Protocol and bugged Liisa and me until we read it too. After a long day in the labs, the three of us had kicked back and were brainstorming. I asked Ari and Liisa if we could send a questionnaire out to include with the drug. Basic social science research about what the patient ate. Self-reported data are consequently of questionable reliability, but we got an epidemiologist at the medical school interested and after cleaning up the tool, she joined the study. She suggested targeting kids because they tended to eat what their parents cooked for them. Therefore the data was likely to be more reliable. She suggested we incentivize the parents by giving six months of free medication in exchange for meticulous control of what their kids ate.

"That was nine months ago. We have continued the practice of free meds because some the younger patients had to come off most of their meds if the parents maintained a strict Wahl protocol diet. Basically a strict paleo, but with far more greens. The science emerging about the critical importance of vitamin K, magnesium, zinc and potassium is so very exciting!"

Dimitri was standing next to Lindsey as the three were reading Eric's letter on the computer screen and was bewildered when he saw tears coursing down her face, yet she was smiling. Her husband caught his glance and merely smiled, the love and respect for his wife evident in his expression. Lindsey never noticed because she was so obviously engrossed in a conversation with the dead scientist.

"Dr. McCall, you'll be amazed at the results from the latest analysis I did. Over half of the experimental group has been able to stop all medication. Not a huge number, just one hundred and two girls under twelve, but enough to begin publicizing. Two pediatric cardiologists at Stanford have published a paper in the American Journal of Pediatric Cardiology.

"When I first noticed the tremors and weakness in my left hand and leg, I switched to the Wahls protocol too, I figured I had Multiple Sclerosis just like Dr. Wahls. For a while,

I think the diet helped. But when the headaches and seizures started a couple months ago, I sort of knew where this was heading. And you know now where it ended.

"I don't care whether you contact my father to inform him of my death. But if you do, don't be disappointed if you never hear from him. Most likely you will not get past Claus, who functions as his manservant if that term is still used in this century. I would be honored to donate my body to an academic medical center for any research they might care to do, that way no one needs to wonder about how to dispose of it.

"Enough about me.

"Here's the important stuff. The Longevive test mice are all safely in the first five cages in the room where we keep the new animals. Each cage is labeled with Eric 1 through Eric 5 so you know there will be no mistake. The new guys are the ones I let loose in the lab. Also, the data I gave Joe for my Dad are corrupted for both Longevive and TirNan. It will take his people a while to figure it out, but they do not have the Longevive formula. It is safe and secure in this thumb drive. The only computer with the uncorrupted data set is mine in my apartment, all the computers in Liisa's office and the lab have corrupted data. A pain, but I had to make it look real in case Cairns checked any of them.

"Ari was not supposed to work last Thursday. In the years she worked here, Thursday has always been the day she spends with her parents. When she showed up with Jansen, I had no choice but to knock him out. Ari had been outside of the lab, and when she saw me standing over Jansen's body, I think she thought I was going to kill him. Anyway, she attacked me. I know how ridiculous that sounds, but all ninety pounds of Ariana Dumas can be ferocious, and she carries a wicked knife. In the fight over the knife, she injured herself pretty badly. I did not know what else to do so I called Cairns. I think he brought her to the same place where they have Liisa, it's a farmhouse in a little town about forty miles north of here."

Within just seconds, Lindsey, Jansen, and Dimitri had simultaneously concluded that Eric Braun was dead. Dimitri was the first to grab the thumb drive and stick it into Liisa's desktop computer. Although Lindsey knew what she would find, she went through the motions and found him breathless and pulseless. Both pupils were fully dilated which made any attempt at resuscitation pointless since the best case for him would be brain death. Therefore, she closed the open staring eyes and prayed.

By the time Rich called the emergency number to report Eric's death, they had read enough of the document to begin putting enough pieces together for Dimitri to call in backup for a team to head to Bonvillars. Rich left Lindsey to wait for the emergency personnel to come collect Eric's body and went to collect Hank Reardon at his home and fill him in.

Cairns waited and watched while Toni's little car had been flipped over and over. Then he looked at his watch and decided to get to the farmhouse and the couple. Get it over with. Joe had met them only one time at a private shindig held for Diedrich Braun's "employees." And he guessed that's what he was, an employee, at least for now. He'd been at ASL for about a month when he got the call from Claus, Braun's assistant. Joe was to show up at Braun's villa that following Sunday afternoon.

"Mr. Braun requests your presence this Sunday afternoon for a garden party at his summer villa in Hesse."

Cairns had been engrossed in a technical discussion with Liisa Reardon and a couple of her scientists that he was actually enjoying. One of whom was Eric, but Cairns had not received his 'instructions' about Eric as yet. He had noted the similarity of the last names but attributed that to the frequency of the last name Braun in Germans.

When he took the call, Joe had to work to keep from laughing at the antiquated language used by Claus. A graphic image appeared in his head. A sunny tea party where everyone comes armed with Glocks rather than canapés. There was no humor in the voice at the other end of the phone so Cairns kept his mordant visions to himself. After being given his choice of transportation, courtesy of Mr. Braun, Cairns declined, figuring he would have more control if he drove, it was just a little more than a five-hour drive from Lausanne.

The 'villa' was close to the pictures Cairns' imagined. The house—palace was more accurate —even featured four turrets and sat on five acres of stunning landscaping and ponds. And there really had been a tea party held on the immaculate grounds. There had been over twenty people at the soiree, one of whom was the replacement for Matt Adams, whom Cairns had shot the week before, Dr. Viktor Dragovik. After spending just two minutes with the man, Cairns had smiled, nodded and wandered off. Joe Cairns had worked with some seriously damaged and immoral men in his life, but this guy seemed to personify evil. Although it was a warm sunny day, the air around Dragovik was chilly. Cairns did not understand it but had no desire to try.

The German couple he was about to dispatch had been standing off by themselves. The woman was talking incessantly and with animation to a man who Cairns assumed to be her husband. She was fiftyish and considerably overweight with very course features. She looked like one of the Russian peasant women from one of those epic movies they used to make, like Dr. Zhivago. Braun had been making the rounds of all his guests, but suddenly detoured over to where the couple stood. Placing his hands on the woman's shoulders, Braun leaned down to plant a kiss on both of the woman's cheeks. He had then called Cairns over and introduced them. Braun had been gentle and kind to the unattractive woman. Attributes that Joe assumed were absent from the German billionaire.

Joe wondered why he was thinking about this as he walked up the stairs to the faded farmhouse. About Braun's kindness.

And his bothering to introduce the couple to Joe. Thinking that he was happy he did not remember their names. Unfortunately, they came to him just as he climbed up onto the weathered and rotting steps: Hilda and Bernard.

Not bothering to disguise his presence, Cairns buried the memory and his associated emotions upon opening the screen door and then the unlocked main door, making his way down the short hallway to the kitchen.

Bernard sat motionless at the kitchen table when Cairns walked in; Hilda stood by his right side, leaning down to get close to the right ear of the head her husband held in both hands, elbows on the scarred wood kitchen table. She was screaming. It looked as if she'd been doing so for years. Her voice was like long, sharp nails on a blackboard, worsening the headache incurred from a sleepless night, ramming Toni's car and the surprisingly clear vision of Dragovik at that stupid garden party. Incredibly, Hilda turned to the doorway when Cairns walked in, widened her eyes, turned back to her husband and amped up her rant at him by about four million decibels. Clearly, it was entirely his fault that they would soon both be dead.

Joe reached into the back of his pants, took out the Glock and hit her precisely in the middle of the forehead. She looked surprised that he didn't let her complete her rant and dropped loudly to the linoleum floor; a blackened hole less than the size of his fingertip between her wide-open eyes.

Cairns used jacketed hollow points which assured maximum damage with little blood extruded from the wound. Illegal in most of the world, when hollow point bullets hit a soft target, like the brain, the lead inside the bullet expands, creating a mushrooming effect as it passes through tissue. Therefore creating more extensive damage as it passes through the path of the wound. Jacketing the bullet usually means cuts through the jacket spaced out equidistantly around the perimeters, encircling the hollowed out tip. The cuts and hollow point work jointly to expand in a jagged star-shaped pattern on impact. The diffusion of energy keeps the bullet from traveling through the target, therefore leaving no casing or bullet behind for identification.

The killer turned to the man who sat waiting patiently, arms folded on the kitchen table. His head was down, and his eyes were cast down. He sat motionlessly. Seemingly eager to die. The bullet hit him directly in the heart.

Joe's expression never changed; he looked the same whether drinking a cup of coffee or executing a middle-aged German couple who were no longer useful. He had been killing people for close to twenty-five years, and Cairns had stopped feeling anything for those he killed decades ago. He was supposed to call Braun when it was done but decided to clear the place first.

There was not supposed to be anyone else here, but he decided to make sure that was true. Fifteen minutes later, Cairns had checked the two small dark bedrooms, baths, tiny attic and the basement where the women had been held. The place was empty.

He made the call stating only, "It's done," when Braun answered. Listening for a minute, Cairns nodded. "Yes, I'll dispose of their bodies, no one will find them." After another couple of moments, he replied, "It's a small town, and they were on foot. They could not have gotten very far, I'll find them." Despite the fact that Braun was still speaking, Cairns hung up. Immediately, his phone rang, but he ignored it.

Cairns did not like Braun. He considered him a pompous, condescending relic of Germany's past. But the money was good; actually better than good, and Joe Cairns had his fill of executing Arabs, Iranians and South Americans at the behest of the American government.

Joe Cairns had not made a decision to leave Force Recon to become a paid assassin. It just happened. Once he decided that he was little more than a paid killer for his country, it had not been that large a leap to become a mercenary, a paid assassin. Meeting Braun had been pure chance.

Cairns had been on an undercover job in Berlin. His agency and the Federal Intelligence Service, the German version of the American CIA, were cooperating in a joint op to find and execute a Muslim terrorist who had masterminded multiple successful bombings in London, Mumbai, and Madrid. After three days of tracking the terrorist and dealing with a few too close for comfort screw-ups, the target had finally been found and terminated, along with two of his associates from the German team. Cairns and the German ended up in a small bar favored by the Captain and his colleagues. Bei Schlawinchen located off Kotbusser Dame.

"If it's such a great job, why don't you take it?"

They were seated at the seedy bar that was favored by the German feds. Cigarette smoke hung so heavily in the air that Joe felt as if he'd smoked four cigarettes within fifteen minutes. The place reminded him of a bar in Madrid where he and nine others had been deployed in a failed attempt to prevent an imminent attack on a hotel they had Intel on. He and his group had consumed half the inventory of hard liquor and beer in the bar, trying to erase the images of strewn extremities and burned bodies, when the three explosions took down the Madrid Carlton killing close to five hundred people and more than twenty-five kids.

There was a Playboy calendar hanging between the cluttered bottles of the usual varieties of scotch, gin, vodka, and assorted other hard liquors. Staring at the calendar, Joe wondered if that guy Hugh Hefner was still alive. If so, he must have done okay, since these calendars had been selling since what, the sixties? The place had a weird concoction of old bicycles, a wide variety of instruments, and toy dolls… all hanging from the walls. Could this place be in Manhattan or Philadelphia, he wondered? Joe thought so, there was something universal about seedy bars and their appeal to cops and soldiers.

Cairns was only half listening, while his captain friend had been explaining why he wanted Joe to meet a particular attendee at a black-tie cocktail party the next night. The captain was head of a German task force assigned backup for the protection detail of the European Economic Summit Meeting in Berlin. Several European heads of state would be attending, and as always, there had been several threats to the attendees, including the German Premier. When the Captain invited Cairns, he had casually mentioned some introductions to individuals who may be of interest to Cairns. The two men had shared more than one beer and learned they had similarly low opinions of the people in charge of their respective countries. They were remarkably alike in the practicality with which they viewed their jobs.

Lighting his fourth cigarette within ten minutes, the German cop studied Joe and replied to the question about the job.

"I would take it if I didn't have a wife and a new baby on the way. I'd take it in a heartbeat."

Enviously, Joe watched him exhale the smoke slowly, luxuriously, even almost elegantly. It had been ten years, but Cairns still thought about lighting up a cigarette, especially when he was drinking. Cairns took a deep breath, gladly inhaling the second-hand smoke.

"You said you don't have a family, you're not married, right?"

Cairns nodded; impressed as always with the command of English so many non-Americans possessed. The captain's diction had the precision that most non-native English speaking people had. Marveling at his own insularity and arrogance along with so many of his fellow Americans, Joe surprised himself when he expressed interest in meeting this black-tie attendee. In English, since he knew maybe one-hundred words in German, he said, "Tell me more."

Intrigued enough to rent a tux and play the role of a high-class waiter for the cocktail party at the Berlin Ritz-Carlton the following night, Cairns had been smiling and refilling champagne glasses for over an hour when his buddy came up to him with a terse, "He's here." He nodded over to the doorway where a tall, trim, sixtyish silvered-haired man stood, surveying the room imperiously. On either side of him stood an obvious bodyguard, the bulges of their Hecklers and Koch's apparent under each of their shoulders. Most likely ex-Federal Intelligence Service; good shape, dead eyes, looking capable of anything.

Cairns watched the Captain stare at Braun then nod toward him. Without moving his head, Braun's lips moved; followed instantly by the appearance of one of the two bodyguards directly in front of Cairns.

"Please follow me, Mr. Cairns, Mr. Braun would like to meet with you now." By the time Joe looked back at the doorway, Braun and his one remaining bodyguard had left. Cairns had to move quickly to keep up with the guy leading him out of the reception area. They went into the huge marble floored foyer adorned with gold filigreed pedestals that towered through several levels of the posh hotel. Once outside they walked to a black stretch limousine parked on Potsdamer Platz with the motor running and the rear door open. The bodyguard nodded at Cairns, extended his hand in the direction of the open door and stood mutely at attention.

None of these guys will talk me to death, that's for sure, thought Cairns, as he obediently climbed into the spacious rear of the limousine. Braun was seated at the far end of the plush leather seat talking on his phone and staring straight ahead. After a good five minutes, the German multibillionaire clicked off his phone and placed it back into the left pocket of the dress shirt under his tuxedo. He turned glacial blue eyes at Cairns and said, "Thank you for meeting with me, Mr. Cairns. I am impressed by your background; your skills will fit nicely into the next phase of my organization." Braun spoke precisely with no accent whatsoever. Nor did he reflect the slightest emotion, he was as close to robotic as Joe had ever witnessed, reminding Cairns of a combination of aristocracy and the upper echelon of the former Third Reich.

Their conversation had lasted only five minutes, with Cairns' portion of their talk consisting of only three words: 'yes' to the three questions, phrased more like statements.

"I understand you are looking for a more profitable line of work, Mr, Cairns," was the first, followed by, "And you are willing to do wet work in any area of the world," and the last, "You can begin working for me immediately." Braun had then handed him two envelopes. "This first envelope contains your new credentials for your position at the Cyber Warfare Center in Omaha. You will assume that role the day after tomorrow." The first had been his photo ID as a Director of Operations at the Cyberwarfare Center, and a first class plane ticket leaving from Berlin-Tegal Airport in three hours. The second had been a penciled note stating the amount of money which had just been transferred to his Bank of America account.

Cairns searched the farmhouse and found soap, a bucket, and towels. Donning some rubber gloves he found under the sink in the cabinet, Cairns surveyed the two bodies dispassionately, regarding them as one would refuse. His phone rang again. Again he ignored it.

Recalling the dry newspapers he had seen in the attic, Cairns decided on a more efficient plan to clean up the place. Jogging up the steps with some kitchen matches he'd found by the gas stove, Cairns piled up the newspapers except one thick pile and lit them. Slowly they began to burn. Returning back down to the kitchen, Cairns turned on all the gas burners on the stove, carefully arranged the remaining pile of news-papers at the front door, lit them and ran.

He was about a mile from the house when he heard the explosion. Nodding with satisfaction, Cairns began to survey the road and the land on either side as he drove slowly along the main road leading out of the small town. Mostly farmland ran on either side of the highway, but he saw no farmhouses close by. Picturing the two women running, he estimated that a grove of trees he saw on the left side of the highway might be a good place to hide and rest. Cairns headed toward the small copse of trees.

Bonvillars was tiny, only a little more than three square miles with a population of less than five hundred. The hideous German couple was nowhere to be seen, the town was quiet. Liisa had glanced back at Ariana who had not moved and decided to go for it. As she ran, Liisa tried to ignore the pain in her feet by remembering an undergrad philosophy professor who had listed laughter as one of the characteristics separating humans from other mammals. He had quoted Aristotle, "Humans are the risible species." With his trademark unkempt mass of silver hair, the professor had resembled Albert Einstein in more than a few ways. Fully aware of their physical similarities, he had memorized a seemingly endless store of quotations of the famed scientist. One of his favorites had been, 'You have to learn the rules of the game. And then you have to play better than anyone else.' Liisa remembered being floored by the stark, practical toughness of the statement made by a man who had lived out his life in the rarefied world of ideas. *How fitting that Einstein do a flyby now at this exact moment...yes this is a game for sure. And the only rule is live or die.*

Suddenly Liisa heard the unmistakable sounds of

squealing brakes, grinding metal and a single high-pitched scream. A car crash. And not very far away from the sounds of it. Something kept her from running on the smooth pavement of the highway; despite her bruised and battered feet, Liisa remained several yards away from the highway as she hobbled as quickly as she could.

Abruptly, she heard the sound of a car approaching fast, very fast. Ducking behind a huge tree, she watched an outsized black SUV roar past. *That looks like Joe Cairns' car. What would Joe be doing out here and why would he be leaving the scene of an accident instead of helping…unless… he is a part of this. In that case, he knows exactly where we are! Of course, you idiot, he has to know. Dear God, Ari was right.*

Liisa was approaching the wreck; she could smell it before she could see it. There were no other cars on the road, so she dared to run now on the tarmac toward a smashed silver car that looked as if it may have been rammed, then spun out of control and flipped. The car was upside down, tendrils of smoke drifting out of the exhaust. As she got closer to the wreck, Liisa saw the body of a woman, inside the upside down wrecked car. Running now despite the pain in her feet, Liisa knelt down beside the car.

Hoping and praying to find a pulse, she gently lifted the wrist of the unconscious woman. "Who are you? You look very much like Liisa Reardon...or did that bastard manage to kill both of us and we're dead? What are you doing in my car wreck anyway?" Toni was looking up at a younger, feminine version of Hank Reardon. The same electrifying blue gaze, blonde hair, angular features and one of the reddest auras Toni had ever seen. She blinked a few times to make sure she was actually seeing Liisa's aura and not blood. Then Toni closed her eyes for a few minutes while her mind assimilated

the information just given to her about Liisa: intensely practical, competitive, action-oriented, willful, and physically
active—just some of the attributes about Liisa Reardon that
flooded into her mind. *Thank God, a fighter…this woman is
one tough cookie. Now, how am I gong to get out of this car?*
Ignoring the pain from cuts and bruises, Toni began to slowly
trace the seat belt which held her upside down. *So if I can find
the clasp and loosen it, what happens then? Is that smoke I smell?*
Forcing herself to focus, Toni stared at the upside down face
in the shattered passenger window of the car.

After jumping when the women she feared dead suddenly
started speaking coherently, Liisa merely nodded. The woman
looked banged up, her face was bloody from a few cuts; her
arms and legs were heavily scratched, mostly from road rash,
it looked like. She had odd-colored eyes, were they silvery?

"You're nodding because you *are* Liisa Reardon or that
we are both dead? Which?"

At that, Liisa finally began to laugh, a little hysterically
perhaps, while managing to reply, "Yes, I am Liisa Reardon
and no, we're not dead, not yet anyway. I was afraid you were,
though, so I stopped to see if I could help, or at least not let
you die alone. Glad you aren't dead, but we both will be if we
don't get out of sight pronto. Can you get your door open?"

Ignoring the question, Toni shook her head and tried to
take inventory. Not bad, she thought, then looked at how close
they were to the road and wondered how long it had been
since Joe Cairns had roared off from her wrecked car. And
how much time they had until he returned. She didn't see too
many alternative roads in and out of this place,

"Liisa, we gotta move, we gotta get ourselves off this road;
do you see my phone anywhere?" Putting both bloody hands
on the door and trying unsuccessfully to push it open, Toni

suddenly saw spots and fell into a dead faint.

Too shocked to do anything but stand back up at the sound, Liisa merely stood staring dumbly at the truck that pulled in behind them and the very tall man with the huge dog that climbed out and walked rapidly over to her.

Bending down to look into the wreckage, and Toni suspended within it, he said calmly, "You must be Liisa Reardon, let me give you a hand." Effortlessly, he reached in. With one hand, he pulled open the door, with the other, he cut the seat belt holding the unconscious Toni. Then Gabe lifted a barely conscious Toni out of the car and carried her over and deposited her in the back seat of the truck. The black dog was racing in circles wagging a stupid-looking stubby tail as if he had just found his best friend. "Baron is very happy we finally found you, we've been looking for days." Nodding over at the dog, he said unnecessarily, "That's Baron. I'm Gabe McAllister, a friend of Rich Jansen and Lindsey McCall. Nice to meet you Liisa." This was all said very somberly but at 'the nice to meet you Liisa,' there was the suggestion of a smile.

Ridiculously, Liisa's thoughts came in rapid succession, *He's really cute, I must look awful and smell worse*, and then. *Liisa Reardon, good God, you're thinking about how you look...now?* Calling Gabe McAllister cute was more than a stretch. At six feet five inches tall and two-hundred-sixty pounds, the events of his life were strangely visible in his long rawboned face, which rarely saw fit to smile.

Just as Gabe had assured that both women were as comfortable as possible in the back seat and Baron riding copilot, as usual, Liisa shouted, "Ari, oh my God, Ari! I forgot, she's out there alone, what if he—" She was trying to open the back door.

Instantly Gabe slammed on the brakes, opened the back door of the truck, and placed both of his huge hands on her shoulders and held her down, hard. She was bordering on hysteria,

"Stop Liisa, you're not going anywhere, tell me where you left her, Baron and I will go get her." Gabe's expression was stony. Hell would freeze over before he let this woman leave his truck.

"NO!! NO!! You don't understand, you'll never find her, he may come back!" All traces of girlish fantasy regarding an attractive man had dissolved into a cauldron of guilt, shame, and humiliation.

By now, a bruised and battered Toni was awake, and said, "Listen to Gabe, let him and Baron find her, they'll do a far better job than either of us can. Trust me on this one, Liisa." Looking fixedly at Liisa's bleeding feet, Toni reached over to take her hand. Toni spoke calmly and forcefully.

"Liisa Reardon, please say hello to Baron, who belongs to Gabe McAllister who is now attempting to reason with you. We were all summoned here to find you by Rich Jansen and have been searching for you for days..."

Toni stopped to grin back at the dog, at the evident smile on his long snout as he craned his body to look at the women in the back seat. She had never been a dog lover and had been utterly terrified of Dobermans when she first encountered Jansen's red male named Max. Baron was the picture of unadulterated joy.

Researchers have been debating about the emotions of dogs for decades. And yet Charles Darwin took the existence of joy, sorrow, and grief in dogs as a given. Recent neurological research has confirmed Darwin's conviction and taken it several steps further. Magnetic imaging of canine brains has demonstrated empirically what dog lovers have experienced and insisted: Their dogs feel all the emotions that humans do. Furthermore, they understand and act on the emotions felt by their human owners. The ability of dogs to read, interpret and act on human hand signals and facial expressions has been empirically demonstrated in the scans. In essence, a dog theory of mind.

Toni hugged Baron, her bruised and bloodied arm wrapped tightly around his neck."You are just the most amazing dog, really you are. "Liisa, this boy will find her, I am sure of it." All the while, Baron looked at Gabe with that pure Doberman expression of, 'See how much she loves me?' spread all over his face.

CHAPTER THIRTY-THREE
Copse of Pine Trees, Bonvillars

"Where is she?"

Blinking, confused, thirsty and weak from blood loss, Ariana squinted, trying to see who was speaking. A man stood over her. Tall, his face a blur in the bright sun as it made its way through the densely packed grove of trees. Unable to stay awake, she closed her eyes and once again lost consciousness.

Awakened again from the pain, Ari's eyes snapped open. The man was crouching right next to her; his fingers digging into the knife wound in her side, tearing and widening it, causing blood to flow freely once again, his face only inches from her own as he hissed, "Where is Liisa?".

Blinking away the tears caused by the searing, ripping pain, Ariana recognized the face of Joe Cairns, the Security Director Liisa had hired to protect them from the attack attempts they knew would come. This was the face of the man who was supposed to protect her and their valuable research, Ari thought as she looked into the eyes that were locked on hers. Ariana felt as if she were looking into a bottomless abyss. His face was chiseled, like one of those masks of Greek gods she had seen in the Louvre as a kid. Cairns was a handsome man, but his dark brown eyes looked as if they had seen too much darkness and depravity, there was no light, no sign of a soul.

Staring at the cruel, twisted mouth and empty eyes, Ariana recalled her reply to Liisa when she asked Ari's opinion about hiring Joe Cairns. They had been standing in the foyer of the research lab, the exact place where she and Eric had fought.

"We need someone with the background this man has, Ari. Not only is he experienced within the military but he also has top cyber warfare experience. I think he's a no-brainer." Liisa had noticed Ari's cold reception to Cairns when she toured him through the labs. Ariana's Gallic countenance had been in high gear; she was perilously close to rudeness but had reigned in her apparent dislike of the man, courteously answering his questions. But offering little more than terse replies.

Once again the two women stood arguing in the foyer of the animal research labs after they had accompanied Cairns to his car following his interview for a newly created position as Head of Security at ASL.

"I think he has exactly the experience and knowledge we need," Liisa had said to Ari as they walked back from the parking lot. "I've not seen any resumes to match his background." After a few more moments of Liisa's one-sided conversation, she had become annoyed at Ari's silence, finally demanding an answer. "Damn it, Ari, I absolutely hate it when you act like this cliché of the snarky Frenchwoman, if you were taller, your nose would be hitting the ceiling. Tell me what you think, I want your opinion here, please."

Ari had stared calmly into Liisa's icy blue eyes, so like those of her father, and had sighed. "It doesn't matter what my opinion is Liisa, you have made your mind up." Thoughtfully, she looked up at the much taller woman and said very softly, "I pray I am wrong Liisa. And, as you know, I don't pray. I fervently want to be wrong and you right, but I believe this man is evil. That he will bring evil here with him."

Ari had been born a Catholic; she was French after all. She had been baptized, received her first Communion and had been confirmed at the same tiny church in Rouen where Joan of Arc had been burned during the thirty-year English occupation of France. Upon her confirmation, Ari had taken the name of the female warrior saint as her patron.

In college, Ari had decided that the faith of her parents was mostly superstition and myth, along with the majority of her country and 'modern' Europe. Now, she found herself murmuring the Hail Mary and Our Father as she regarded this man who she knew would kill her, and probably soon. Thinking back to the woman who had claimed defiantly to Liisa that she did not pray, Ari felt sorrow at the ignorance of that statement and sadness for wasted time. She would die here, she knew, yet the prayers arose almost unbidden from somewhere deep within her. Bringing with them a faith and trust she had not experienced since she was a small child.

Wondering at her sorrow for Joe Cairns, more *grief* that felt external to her, all of a sudden she *knew* what had led this man to this life, understood the slow transition from a hope-filled steadfast young Marine to the soulless cynic kneeling next to her. Tears ran down her face. Tears that were not for herself but for this lost man ensnared in blackness and despair. Marveling at the absolute absence of fear, Ari continued the litany of the prayers she had not said since her teenaged years, said now for this lost tortured soul, no longer for herself, she whispered *his* words, "Father, forgive him." She was astonished at the depth of the peace she felt, the complete and total surrender.

"You can kill me, Joe. Most likely you will do just that, but either way, I cannot tell you where Liisa went. You can see for yourself that I'm hurt...in fact, you're doing all you can to make it worse." She smiled slightly. "Liisa was here, she wrapped the wound and stopped the bleeding which you have seen fit to start again. She was here when I went to sleep, she is not here now so I cannot tell you anything...anything at all, no matter what you do to me."

Ari's curly hair was plastered to her head with sweat and pain; her desire for water a living thing, growing and all-consuming. But something enabled her to remain conscious, to stare openly at Joe Cairns as he placed the gun against her forehead. But after a few minutes when there had been no shot, Ari reopened her eyes, flabbergasted to see Cairns walking away. Staggered at being alive to feel the delicious pain in her side.

The hand that stopped his had felt like an iron vise. Instantly, Cairns knew who was there and was unsurprised when he heard the voice he'd not heard for a couple of decades say, " Stop! No more, no more killing. Enough, more than enough killing." He did not want to look because he knew who he would see. But the compulsion was absolute, David. In unadulterated awe, he could merely gape. *You're back, after all these years.*

Hank Reardon was sitting in the library with Rich. The two men were sitting staring at their tepid coffee. They were seated on two of the six overstuffed chairs in the book-filled room, so it was fairly easy to survey the display subjects that comprised the extensive Reardon library collection. The two primary areas of interest were, quite naturally, physiology and business, as Reardon had graduated from Columbia with doctorates in medicine and physiology. But there were also extensive collections of biology, chemistry, and physics related texts; there were even fiction, decorating and gardening collections as well. Rich calculated that there must be over five thousand books surrounding them.

Reardon was up again, restless, and walked slowly over to Rich's favorite corner of this lovely room. The hexagonal corner of the library had been put to practical use by the architect; where the two angles were composed of welded glass with a built-in upholstered bench overlooking the south side of the mountains and the lake below. Hank stood staring at the beauty, and eventually, Rich followed his gaze.

Someone had spent enormous time, energy and money on landscaping. Jansen figured Hank's wife Peg, who had died of cancer, for the artist. The landscaping had been configured in islands of vegetation, yet the overall effect was natural and served to soften and lighten the harsh lines of the unusual house.

Without realizing he was doing so, Jansen breathed out, "These gardens are lovely, magnificent; what a feast for the eyes." It was May, early spring in the mountains of Lausanne. Rich could see roses of every color, interspersed with daisies, veronica, pansies, Russian and perennial sage, and even asters in a bright mix that looked accidental, wild. The colors were so vivid and glorious, they seemed to mock the two men.

Glancing back to Hank, who had not moved in more than five minutes, Jansen doubted that he saw anything but the image of his missing daughter, or maybe now the image of Eric, the dead German scientist. As if in affirmation, Reardon cleared his throat. "You've had quite a morning." Hank had listened without comment but seemed to age before his eyes while Rich explained all that had taken place with Eric Braun, Dimitri, and Lindsey.

"Did Toni stay with Lindsey?"

Suddenly alarmed, Rich stood suddenly. "I haven't seen her since we got to Liisa's office. She must have left during all the chaos with Eric. And gone..." thinking back for a moment, Rich said, "Right when we got to your offices, Cairns' truck pulled out, and he was moving fast." Grimacing, Rich said, "I'll bet Toni followed him. And he must have been going to that farmhouse."

Jansen began to suggest that Hank get some rest while he went back to look for Toni, but stopped himself when he looked at the older man's face. He looked tired, even exhausted but resolute. His wispy blonde hair lay upon the crown of his head carelessly, but his trademark electric blue gaze belied the calm, quiet way he had spoken. Rich understood. He could not walk in the shoes of a man whose only daughter had been kidnaped and maybe killed, but he recognized that look. Reardon had allowed himself to be frightened, cowed and made impotent by these people for close to three days. But no more; the battle was on.

Deciding to take the A-1 because it was faster, Reardon slowed to a crawl because of the construction on Avenue de Montoie. His fingers continued their tapping on the steering wheel. He was suddenly engulfed in memories of taking Liisa to Bonvillars. To the annual truffle festival. For some reason Reardon had never understood, she had loved that single claim to fame of the tiny village of Bonvillars. Each October they made the trek to the festival along with thousands of northern Swiss, Germans, and Italians. They had moved to Lausanne following the completion of Liisa's second doctorate. Reardon had fully intended to retire, until the irresistible challenge of turning around a nearly bankrupt pharmaceutical company captured his interest.

That first October, about ten years ago, they were all on vacation. It was Peg who had glimpsed the Logotto puppy. The dog was sitting in a box by a vendor with some of the largest truffles they had ever seen. After some failed attempts to establish a language, Peg, and the vendor settled on English. Back then, Peg was quite a cook and was intrigued by the immense size of the mushrooms. The man explained that the puppy's mother was a truffle hunting dog and that as soon as the pup was weaned, he would begin training him to be a hunter.

CHAPTER THIRTY-FIVE
Pine Grove, Bonvillars

Baron stood over the motionless form of the small woman and whined as he pawed the ground around Ariana Dumas. Gabe had brought the tech's lab coat with him, and when he gave it to Baron to sniff, the Doberman raced in the direction that Liisa had pointed when she reluctantly acceded to Toni and Gabe's direction to stay in the truck. It was starting to rain and normally Baron hated getting wet, but when tracking he was single-minded.

Panting hard and about twenty yards behind his dog, Gabe spied the still body through the increasing drizzle. His thoughts were a continual plea; *please let her be alive, please let her be alive* as he jogged up to her.

Gabe crouched beside Ariana, gently touching the fresh blood seeping through her shirt. He jumped when Ari's eyes opened, they looked huge and terrified in her small, too pale, face.

"Ariana, it's okay, I'm here to help you. Liisa Reardon is back in my truck, she told Baron and me where to find you."

Baron's tail was wagging so furiously that it looked motorized. Gabe could not keep from smiling as he said quietly, "Ariana, I'm just going to put a makeshift bandage around your wound here, it may hurt, but you look as if you need to keep all the blood you've got."

"What's your name?" Her voice was faint, barely a whisper.

Thinking this a good sign, Gabe's smile widened as he tore off the lower band of his shirt and removed the soaked makeshift bandage that Liisa had applied. *Looks like a knife wound —deep and infected.* The skin around the wound was red, puffy and hot. He frowned as he wrapped her small torso in the cloth.

"Gabe, my name is Gabe."

"For Gabriel, of course, Gabriel." Ariana smiled serenely and closed her eyes.

Liisa was nodding to herself, her eyes fierce, her generous mouth compressed into a thin line stretched taut, like wire. Looking down at an unconscious Ariana stretched out over her lap and Toni's, the tears and despair were gone for the moment. Replaced with anger. "He must have been sent out here to kill them, then he found Ari and almost killed her too."

"Who was sent out here to kill who?" The statement was chorused by Toni, and Gabe.

"The German couple who kidnaped me and were keeping Ari." At the last few words, Liisa glanced at Ari's small body stretched out between her and Toni in the back seat of the truck. She seemed not to notice the silent tears rolling down her face. "She told me not to hire Cairns, she warned me he would bring evil here. I made fun of her, said she was talking silly superstitious gibberish. I insisted that we needed him." Taking a deep, shaky breath, her mouth contorted, "Right, we *needed* him." Palpably energized by her own self-disgust, she looked at Gabe, then at Toni, then back at Gabe. "I'll show you where the farmhouse we were kept at is. I'll wager there are two dead bodies there."

"We need to get you three to the hospital first, so you can all be treated. We'll contact the authorities after we get you some medical care."

Glaring at the back of Gabe's head, Liisa opened her mouth to argue, but was able only to shake her head. She could feel another torrent of tears right at the edge of her consciousness, waiting to take her over. The anger had worked well for a few minutes, but it had faded, leaving in its stead sadness that was unbearable. Liisa welcomed the return of pain in her feet, the macerated flesh was the very least she should have, she wished for knives rather than merely nails with each step she took. Ariana was badly hurt. Because of her.

Toni stared out the window and seemed aware of nothing but the Doberman, who would turn around about every ten minutes and carefully lean his snout as close as he could to her. In reply, Toni would gently caress the dog but said nothing. Her touch calmed him down until the next time, a few minutes later. Now and then, she stared at her arms which were covered in lacerations, and some of the cuts probably had glass in them. But she didn't care, she felt numb. This whole day had been one from hell. Honestly, Toni had been sure she was dead when Cairns had rammed her, and the little car had taken flight. And it hurt her to just look at Liisa's feet. They were bloody pulps. And Ariana was cool, way too cool as she lay unconscious in their laps.

Toni risked glancing to her right to see what Liisa was doing. And was immediately sorry. She was staring straight ahead at nothing, Toni was sure. That usually bright red aura of hers was a vacillating shimmer of four different shades of gray that seemed to reach out to her, pulling her into the dark depression Liisa was experiencing. Usually, Toni could cast off the strong negative 'aural pull' of others, but right now she could not. She closed her eyes and concentrated on visualizing a healing for all of them, especially this diminutive Ariana.

No one spoke a word for the entire drive. Baron seemed to sense the melancholy, even his panting seemed subdued. Liisa's exhausted mind raced feverishly.

These people saved my life. I should say something, I would be dead, so would Ari if it were not for this Gabe McAllister and his silly Doberman that Toni seems to adore. Liisa Reardon was no stranger to intense work and sacrifice, and was not unaccustomed to failure, she was a researcher, after all. However, the combination of her kidnapping, near death for herself and for Ariana, along with the conviction that she was responsible for all of it by hiring Joe Cairns was causing torrential waves of self-reproach.

CHAPTER THIRTY-SIX
Crash site ten minutes later

"This was one of our cars. One that Toni must have taken." Reardon's words sounded hollow, even to him. After Rich had returned to Hank's to update him on Eric Braun and the contents of the letter he had left, both men realized that Toni Martinez was missing. Unable to reach Gabe McAllister or Joe Cairns, Jansen had suggested they drive toward Bonvillars since that was where Dimitri and his team had gone. But as they got closer to the village, they saw the smoke from the farmhouse fire and then the obvious crash site. Had their focus been on the highway heading back to Lausanne, they might have noticed McAllister's truck speeding south toward the city.

Reardon and Jansen lacked the resources to do anything but stand there, trying to find a logical explanation of what their senses were assaulted with. Everything looked lost. After the initial exciting progress and invaluable information provided by Eric, they both felt as if this terrible trial was close to ending.

Jansen was still sub-optimal due to the head injury he'd sustained, and Reardon's earlier vitality had been sapped by the result of one too many stress responses. Although he tried to come up with some way to spin something positive out of the chaotic evidence in front of them, he could not. The women were dead, they had to be. All this, for what?

Frequent stimulation of the adrenals through considerable emotional and physical stress results in overwhelming amounts of cortisol, norepinephrine and the other neurohormonal ingredients of the 'fight or flight' response drenching the body to prepare for battle. In less than four days, Reardon had endured the kidnapping of his daughter, the death of a top employee, two warnings about the fatal consequences of not following the kidnappers' demands to the letter and now evidence that Toni, a woman Reardon considered a daughter, may be dead as well.

But the threats to twenty-first-century man can rarely be solved by fighting or fleeing. Rather than dissipating through extreme physical exertion, these hormonal and neurochemical products are built up over time and can be toxic. The consequences of severe stress and adrenal exhaustion over prolonged periods of time can be fatal, leading to the belief that stress is considered one of the top contributors to the leading causes of death in the twenty-first century, heart disease and stroke, cancer.

Reardon glanced over at Rich and grimaced, his face suddenly waxy with an unhealthy sheen when he silently began to fold, crumpling in a heap. Rich reached over to grab and catch him just as Reardon hit the ground, then knelt and down beside the older man. Quickly, Rich confirmed that he had a pulse, his heart had not stopped, and he was breathing very slow and deep breaths. *Thank you, God.* He straightened him out as well as he could. Fortunately, they had been standing several feet away from the rubble, so Hank was lying on the pavement, not broken glass and bits and pieces of exploded Taurus. Hopefully, Reardon had merely fainted. Rich crouched beside him as he considered that Hank was an unusually fit man, naturally had more energy than most people twenty years younger and carried no extra weight. But Rich didn't like Reardon's gray, pallid complexion nor the feel of his skin, too cool and sweaty for comfort. He was in shock and needed treatment.

As if in sympathy to the relentlessness of the grim series of events which had culminated in Hank Reardon's collapse, the earlier bright sunny morning was giving way to more fitting menacing storm clouds, the wind had picked up, and a few warning raindrops fell in huge cold splats.

When a big black SUV stopped at the side of the road, the window rolled down, and Joe Cairns leaned his head out to ask, "Rich, is Hank alright? Do you need a hand with him?"

Rich's thoughts were chasing after one another, mirroring the huge storm clouds scuttling across the sky. *This day just keeps getting better and better, can't wait to see what will happen next. Okay, hot-shot what now? This guy is most likely a killer, but Hank needs medical attention and fast. The man is close to shutting down from sheer exhaustion. Can I trust this Cairns? No, I absolutely know I cannot. Worst case? Cairns kills both of us. But he's already had plenty of opportunity to do that and he hasn't. I don't think Cairns will kill Reardon or me, at least, I hope not.*"

Rich found himself smiling at Cairns and replying, "Yes, Joe, you sure can help. Thanks for stopping. Hank has collapsed as you can see. I'm pretty worried about him; this latest news of Toni's death has been the tipping point." *I am becoming quite the actor, keep me in cases like this one and I can join the ranks of the best liars around.* Pretending to check on Reardon, Rich glanced away but watched Cairns' to gauge his reaction and was rewarded by a slight but definite twitch in his jaw muscle. Reardon gave Cairns time to play the guileless observer, but to his credit, Cairns said nothing, merely waiting for Reardon to finish speaking. "I think he needs to pay a visit to our friendly local University Hospital ER Doc. Can you help me get him in and drive us to the hospital?"

Joe instantly opened the door, jumped out, crouched down at Reardon's feet and then looked up at Jansen, "Let me know when you're ready Rich."

"On the count of three." Just as they began to lift Hank up off the ground, he regained consciousness and looked anxiously up at Rich.

"What happened?"

"You fainted Hank. Joe and I are going to take you over to see that cute ER doctor so she can check you out. You still don't look as if you feel too swift." Reardon was still pale but the grayish pallor was gone, the dark shadows under his eyes looked like bruises. Rich wondered if he was getting any sleep at all.

CHAPTER THIRTY-SEVEN
Lausanne University Hospital

"I will do just that Dr. Morgan, I assure you." A much revitalized Hank Reardon replied to the American Emergency Medicine physician who stood by Reardon's bed with a knowing smile.

Rich had been impressed by the efficiency of the personnel at the hospital from the moment that he and Joe Cairns had walked an awake, but stumbling, Reardon into the place. There had been little lag time for Reardon. As soon as the nurses had hooked him up to the usual array of monitoring gadgets, this Dr. Morgan had appeared in the universal medical uniform of scrubs. Most likely close to Reardon's age, the man reminded Jansen of a Texas rancher. Big, burly and with a long graying handlebar mustache, Morgan even drawled when speaking to his American patient and two friends. Apparently, one of Reardon's problems had been dehydration. Therefore, one of the early treatments had consisted of a couple of bags of saline.

Cairns had waited with Hank until his cell had rung. Cairns had ignored the first two calls, then had looked annoyed at the third, and mumbled, "Sorry, Rich but I need to get this," and had walked out of the emergency center. Reardon had not seen him since, which was over an hour ago he thought as he looked on at the game being played out by the doctor and Hank. Rich smiled as he watched Reardon charm the doctor, waves of relief crashing over him as he too became captivated by the trademark Reardon wit and intelligence.

"I understand your preference for me to be admitted overnight for observation, Dr. Morgan, I do." Reardon hesitated, took in a deep breath. "I am sure you hear this story every day of your life, Doctor, but some matters need attention back at my company. And if I'm more than a two hour's drive away, I'll not be able to rest as well as I can at home where I can keep my hand on what's happening."

Morgan rocked back and forth on his boots as he listened to Reardon's polite but persistent narrative that roughly translated to something like, "Hell will freeze over Doc before I stay here overnight."

Boots, they are real boots...look like ostrich boots from San Antonio. Morgan caught Jansen's gaze as he stared at the boots and grinned. "I know, I know, not the expected mode of dress for a faculty physician." The drawl was even thicker.

Grinning back at this transplanted Texas boy, Jansen guessed, "San Angelo and then medical school at Southwestern." Rich was talking about University of Texas Southwestern Medical School in Dallas. And figured there had to be quite a story here.

By now, both Morgan and Jansen were standing outside the cubicle so Reardon could dress in private. Morgan asked curiously, "And you know about Southwest Medical School because you're a transplanted Texas doc, too?"

"No, but I'm married to one."

"Here in Lausanne with you?" Morgan asked with a bushy eyebrow raised.

"Yes, as a matter of fact, Lindsey is up working in Hank's research lab now."

"Lindsey...Texas...research...you wouldn't be talkin' about Lindsey McCall and her drug Digipro that half my patients are on by the time they leave this ER, would you?" Morgan's other eyebrow raised in an expression of pure astonishment. "And that guy getting dressed in there is Hank Reardon, CEO of ASL, isn't he?"

Smiling, his natural ebullience pouring out of those incredible blue eyes, Reardon quietly said, "That would be me, Dr. Morgan. Indeed, it would." Hank had slipped out of the curtained cubicle and now stood dressed in a blue chambray work shirt and worn pair of jeans. A far cry from the attire expected of a powerful CEO, Reardon could easily be taken for one of the landscapers working at the ASL grounds.

For a minute, Rich felt sorry for Morgan, who had had no clue who he'd been treating in his ER, but to the man's credit, the doctor merely extended his hand. "Mr. Reardon, it's an honor to meet you. Between this hospital and your company, close to eighty percent of the citizens of Lausanne are employed at one or the other of us. I have heard an enormous amount about you, in fact, my son works as a tech in your labs. He works for Ariana Dumas and thinks the absolute world of her."

Jansen watched Reardon swallow his grief at the mention of Ariana's name and maintain the friendly, open expression on his face as he shook the physician's hand. "Ariana Dumas is the best in her field, he'll learn a lot in her lab." And then he turned to Rich, "Sounds as if Dr. Morgan knows of our Lindsey."

Taking his cue from Reardon, Jansen smiled and replied, "Yes, Lindsey is my wife, as it happens, Dr. Morgan. I'm sure she'd be glad to hear from a colleague, especially one from Texas, who uses Digipro." Rich said the words more out of politeness than anything else. He was shocked to hear

Reardon's next comment.

"How about you come up to the house when you get off, Dr. Morgan? That way you can keep an eye on your recalcitrant patient and also get to say howdy to Lindsey." Hank's eyes were twinkling. Apparently, this man had learned the art of squeezing fun out of even the most slightly positive event, like an ER doc from Texas, who he'd had to negotiate like the devil with. *Wisdom in action, this is what I am seeing. For all the guy knows, both Ariana and Liisa may be dead, but somehow he manages to recognize this doc, his awe at Lindsey and extend an invitation that won't be refused. Hank Reardon should write books or give seminars on how to find happiness at the bottom of the sewer...and the amazing thing is he is not faking...he is enjoying this whole scene...*

"Why, Mr. Reardon, thank you." Morgan was stuttering, fumbling, clearly greatly discomfited and embarrassed. "How generous of you, sir...."

Reardon placed his hand on the physician's shoulder and said earnestly, "Look Doc, you'd be doing us all a big favor. Life has been tough for us all during the last several days, we'd love to have some company with different stories from ours." Then with a wide grin, "I'll bet you have quite a collection of them. And please, call me Hank. When do you get off?"

"Actually, I was off thirty minutes ago, I just stayed around to help out Pete...looks like for once, my good deed does go unpunished! Give me five minutes to change and I'll follow you."

Morgan noticed Hank's peculiar expression, looked at Rich and asked, "Didn't you drive him here?"

"No, I didn't. And the man who did drive us here took off about an hour ago, so this works out great for all of us, Dr...'

"Gentlemen, enough of the doctor business...it's Drew,

Andrew on the birth certificate, but I answer quicker to Drew. And I'd be happy to ferry you both home, it would be a privilege." More relaxed now, Drew Morgan pointed out to the waiting area, "Take a seat out there, I'll be back in a few shakes."

Obediently sitting down in two surprisingly comfortable chairs in the Lausanne University emergency waiting area, Rich turned to look at Hank. Reardon looked thin and tired. But remarkably well considering what he's been through in the last...*had it really only been seventy-two hours?* "You knew Cairns had gone."

Hank squinted. The afternoon sun was pouring through the glass-walled foyer and Reardon was smack in the middle of dense rays of May mountain sunshine. Idly, Rich wondered if he were hot, that long-sleeved shirt looked like heavyweight fabric. "I woke up right after you and Joe so unceremoniously dumped me into the back of his truck. " Reardon's broad grin cut off the apology that began in Rich's head. "And the ride was, what, about forty-five minutes? Or an hour?" Hardly noticing Rich's answering nod, Reardon resumed talking, "Lying there gave me time to think, or maybe crashing helped me see what has been right in front of my eyes since the beginning. It's obvious that Cairns has been in on this. All of it." Reardon still could not meet Jansen's eyes, the sunlight remained intense, but his expression was pensive, not angry at all but reflective. Once again, Rich regarded the older man with appreciation as he watched and listened. Many men Rich had known would be blustering, filling themselves up with fuel from the emotional energy of blame, regret, and disappointment. The force fueled by righteous anger was tempting to grasp at, far more so than the desire to understand, even forgive.

"I knew when you arrived that you didn't like or trust Joe Cairns. Ariana had come to me a few months ago to ask that I override Liisa's decision to hire Cairns. Ari has worked with us for over five years and has never gone over Liisa's head. She was extremely persuasive." Now, Rich could see what could have been the shine from the bright sunlight in Reardon's eyes, but he knew it wasn't.

"And I will live with my refusal to override my daughter for the rest of my life." The thoughtful expression reappeared as Hank thought back. "Liisa had been more than annoyed when I told her about my conversation with Ari. At the time, I thought it strange, because Liisa normally had no problems when anyone disagreed. I remember thinking she was overreacting like this because she wasn't sure about this guy either. Ari had uncovered Liisa's doubts and she was angry at herself but could not admit it."

A cloud cast the waiting room into sudden dusk and Rich could see Reardon's gaze clearly. There was nothing but sadness.

"Joe got a call, didn't he?" Reardon was back. His expression grim and eyes clear and hard.

Surprised that Hank had been aware enough to observe this, "Yeah Hank, we'd not been here very long, maybe ten, at most, fifteen minutes. His phone rang twice. With the third ring, he said he had to take it and needed to step outside. Said he'd be back in a few minutes.

"We won't see him again, he's gone." Reardon's tone was flat, the statement a declaration.

Rich began to ask why he was so sure, but just then, Drew Morgan walked out in jeans, button-down shirt, and boots. He was smiling. "Hope you two don't mind dog hair, I have a pack, a golden retriever, German pointer, and two German shepherds."

When his cell rang, Rich almost didn't take the call.

"Yeah Gabe, what's up?"

"I have them all."

"Have them all…" He could not make sense of the phrase. "What are you saying?"

"Liisa Reardon, Ariana, and Toni. They are here in the emergency room at Lausanne. Where are you?"

Incredulity was written all over his face. Although Rich was too shocked to utter a word, Morgan and Reardon both stopped in their tracks to watch Rich holding the phone, mouth agape.

Fearing the worst, as would be a most logical reaction, Hank Reardon stood still and could almost feel himself draining away. And then he saw Rich's face transform as he said slowly and clearly, eyes fixed on Hank Reardon. "Gabe, they are all safe and are here in the ER; Liisa, Ariana, and Toni?"

CHAPTER THIRTY-EIGHT
Forty miles east of Paris, Same time

Joe Cairns smiled. Feeling the unfamiliar movement of his mouth and the accompanying lightness in his heart, the smile turned to laughter. Cairns could not remember the last time he had laughed.

Braun will have people out looking for me forever, but I enjoyed my last conversation more than any I've had in donkey's years.

Cairns had known Braun would order the killing of his son Eric. He'd been expecting it and wasn't sure what he was going to do about it. The note explaining why he had been employed by ASL had been delivered about a month after he had started.

The penciled note contained the name and phone number and a couple of 'important personal proclivities of my son Eric whom you will contact this week to retrieve the Longevive formula and the data from the Digipro cohort.' There was also a thumb drive 'for Eric's eyes only.' The simplicity of Braun's instructions along with the thumb drive amplified the depravity of this entire escapade in Cairns' head. It was sick. The whole thing was vile. On the thumb drive was a long video of Eric and another man enjoying graphic homosexual relations. After a pause, the video scanned a pastoral scene, then zoomed in on a child. Very young, maybe three and looking ill. Her blue lips were visible as she sat on the lap of a woman; this was Braun's daughter and wife.

Not that he cared about Eric Braun or his little sister, not at all. But he was getting sick of this crap, had been before he even got to Lausanne. But he had not been able to admit it. This private assassin gig was worse than Force Recon. At least with the United States government, there was a reasonably sound purpose behind the killing he had done as a Force Recon Marine. Whether for oil, or choice of dictators, his former job had something more than money to back it up, at least that's how it appeared in the rearview mirror.

Joe recalled the call from Eric about his bungled skirmish with Ariana Dumas. And had been really unhappy when he got to the lab to retrieve the French woman and found Jansen knocked out on the floor. He'd barely gotten back from the farmhouse in time to 'meet' the recovering Rich Jansen and Reardon. At least Eric had given him the mice and the formula to send off to his father, but Eric Bran had been different from what he'd expected. When Joe had called to ask to meet Braun and delivered the message from his father, he'd expected the histrionics, the drama you'd expect from a girl. He was gay and the way Diedrich Braun spoke about this son, Cairns had expected at the very least a transsexual look and all that went with it. Instead, he'd met a very tall, confident man. One who merely closed his eyes and nodded, as if he'd been expecting the visit.

"I work for your father, Eric. He wants you to obtain the formula for Longevive along with the experimental mice on the drug. He also wants all the data on that group of Digipro patients you and Liisa Reardon have collected."

They were seated in Eric's tiny office which was decorated

with one photograph. Pointing to the picture, Joe said, "If you don't provide the information, your father will cut off all support for your sister and mother."

There had been no audible reply from Eric. Merely that nod upon closing his eyes. At that moment, Cairns had felt like trash. A strange feeling, because he had proudly self-diagnosed himself as a sociopath about fifteen years ago. Squirming at this foreign, unwelcome consideration, and maybe even compassion he felt for this guy, Cairns switched to the infinitely more comfortable patina of anger he normally cloaked himself with. His animosity for Diedrich Braun had increased exponentially.

Eric remained mute and motionless, giving Cairns more time to examine the lone photograph. Close up, the little girl looked like a facsimile of her mother. Blonde, blue eyes and beautiful. But when he looked at the girl more closely, he realized she was not a little girl after all. She was probably in her twenties but looked sick, frail. There were bluish tinges around her lips and dark smudges under her eyes indicating some type of heart trouble, Joe guessed. Strange because the girl in the video had been only three, maybe four and looked sick, too sick to make it into her twenties.

Looking at the image of Eric's attractive mother, Cairns had wondered, *What on God's green earth ever possessed you to marry that pathetic excuse for a man.*

He and Eric had spoken only one other time. "I need your help...Ari had a knife...and another guy was here when I came out with the mice..." Eric was breathless but kept himself together enough to provide access to the lab, transfer the mice, and help get Ari to the truck.

Diedrich's son seemed to be someone who should take up space and air on this sick, dark planet as opposed to his father who badly needed to be taken out.

Then when he stopped to help out Jansen and Reardon, Cairns began to guess that his 'boss' would demand that these two be 'neutralized' too. He knew Jansen didn't trust him; that had been apparent from the moment Jansen laid eyes on him. But Rich Jansen reminded Joe of some of the men he'd served with, he liked the guy. And Hank Reardon? What a ballbuster that guy was.

By the time Joe had taken Diedrich's call, he was confident that he knew what Braun would want and how he would handle his order. For some crazy reason, he had hung around long enough to make sure that Reardon would recover, ignoring two calls from Braun. Then when his phone rang for the third time, he'd stepped outside the ER to take it.

"Where have you been? I have been calling you for over twenty minutes, Mr. Cairns. I don't like to be ignored." He hissed the words; they were sibilant as if a snake were speaking on the phone. This was one of Braun's many affectations which Cairns despised.

"I have been extremely busy, Mr. Braun," Cairns replied matter-of-factly. Not that it mattered a whole lot, but Cairns wanted to make sure Diedrich Braun had received what he'd paid for. He reflected on his brief tenure as Braun's assassin.

Back after the black tie dinner, during their less than five-minute conversation, Braun had handed him an envelope. Inside was the typed tracking numbers of an offshore bank, the number of the bank in the Caymans, an account number and login information. Written underneath, Cairns supposed that it had been written by the billionaire himself, was a penciled figure of one and a half million dollars. Next to the note, the phrase, 'This is your first paycheck for the first assignment.' Half a million each for killing Matt Adams and the German couple. Cairns decided he'd delivered.

The silence on the other end seemed charged. Evidently,

Braun was expecting an explanation or perhaps an apology from his paid killer. Cairns merely held the phone to his ear and waited while he wondered if he did owe Braun an explanation or even an admission that Ariana Dumas was not dead, nor was his son.

He'd made up his mind, Cairns realized with more than a little surprise. And knew it had been coming for a while. This jump from the government to the employ of Braun had not fixed a thing. He was sick to death of the killing and not faced the fact until the French girl, Ariana. Cairns could see her face, the repose on the features of a woman who was wounded badly, most likely dying and had expected that he would hasten the process. He had fully expected to shoot her, he had every intention of doing so until David stopped him. Cairns wondered if her prayers had summoned him.

Although she prayed in a mixture of French and English, Joe Cairns knew the "Our Father" and the "Hail Mary" well. His mother, a devout Irish Catholic, had made sure that Joe and his three older brothers had made it to Mass consistently enough to be accepted as an altar boy back in the day when only boys could do it.

The Warrior King of the Jews. He had not appeared to Cairns for at least fifteen years, maybe twenty. He had been a kid, no more than six or seven when he had first seen the man chosen to be God's anointed.

"Who are you?" The little boy Joe Cairns had asked.

"I am the womb of Adonai," was the reply.

Joe knew better than to ask the nuns who taught at the Catholic school his hardworking parents sent him to. But once, when he was a freshman in religion class, the priest was teaching the class about David. And had begun his lecture with the question, "Who was King David?"

Without thinking, Joe had raised his hand and replied,

"The womb of Adonai."

The expression on the face of the priest was enough to make the teenaged Cairns wish he had never opened his mouth.

But after class, the priest had asked that he stay after school.

"Where did you hear that expression, son?" Father MacLeese had asked quietly. "The 'womb of Adonai' as a name for King David is known only to religious scholars." His kind gray eyes were penetrating and curious.

Joe had been supremely uncomfortable. "Father, have I done something wrong?"

"No, son, of course not, I was just surprised that you knew that phrase. Do you remember where you read it or heard it son?"

"No Father, I don't. I'm really sorry." Embarrassment and humiliation were written all over young Joe's face.

That was the first and last time that Joe Cairns had ever hinted at a special knowledge of King David. Over the next fifteen years, David appeared to him countless times. Initially wearing only a loincloth, appearing as a child about Joe's age, he would show up when Joe most needed him. Typically during times of temptation, like the time he started to cheat on a test in grade school. His friend sitting in the chair had even moved to his right so that Joe could read and copy his answers.

"Warriors don't cheat," David had said clearly. Suddenly David stood next to Joe, looking so real that he was sure that everyone heard and saw the short, powerful, long-haired young man clothed in a flowing gauzy dress with a rope tied around his waist. Joe had jumped in his seat and looked around. But all his classmates had their heads down, working on their test.

Then later, he appeared dressed in the garb of a Middle Eastern man. Still later, a warrior. That had been all that Joe had ever wanted to be. He had known it from the time he heard David's admonition. And he had not cheated again, ever. But he had sure killed, had lost count of how many men had died at his hand.

The David who stood in the mists of that small forest was a David such as Cairns had never seen. He was covered in blood, looked as if he'd been in a continual battle for centuries, wearing the blood of all the men he had slain, holding a long spear from which blood, fresh blood, dripped. The coppery smell of blood was in the air, suffusing the mists with its sweetish, metallic fragrance.

Although Cairns had never seen the visionary David's mouth move, he could always hear him, clearly. "Joseph James." The voice was pitched low, a resonant baritone befitting a king. And he spoke in English. Despite not having heard the Israeli king's voice for so long, Joe almost had to forcibly restrain himself from dropping to one knee. And wondering at the reappearance of David at this time and in this place, and at the fact that he spoke English. An Israeli king from a couple of thousand years ago would not speak English. A sardonic laugh at himself...*as if any of the rest of this makes any sense at all!*

Cairns' mother had named him after two saints, she had told Joe before her early death from a heart attack when he had been fourteen.

"Saints Joseph and James will always guard you, Joe." She'd said it again the day she died. The moment the vision spoke his first and middle names, the mists surrounding David had evaporated. Joe could see David's face clearly. And his eyes. Good and gracious God, what eyes— brimming with the dark, awful knowledge of killing and death, enveloped Cairns with grief and regret. Cairns could even smell the reek of all the bloodshed, that distinct cloying, coppery smell of blood, oceans of it. And the dreadful truth of David's words: "No more, no more killing, enough, more than enough killing." They seemed to sear down into the plumbless depths of the soul Cairns had forgotten he had.

Cairns had met the gaze of David and had nodded, not sure what he agreed to, but wanting with all his heart to do whatever it took to ease the pain in those terrible eyes.

"Mr. Cairns, are you still there? I am waiting…"

"Yes, Mr. Braun, I am here." Joe paused for a moment and then asked, "You are waiting for what, sir?"

"To give you your next assignment."

Cairns said nothing, which Braun must have interpreted to be assent because the next statement or more accurately, the command was, "Eric has served his purpose. Please eliminate him. Also, Hank Reardon and his American helper, Jansen. Eliminate them as well. I will wire another one point five million into your account. If you do this within the next forty-eight hours, I will make it two million. Do you understand, Mr. Cairns?"

"I do, completely. But I quit, Braun. Now. Goodbye." And hung up. Then had removed the SIM card, smashed it and threw the phone away.

The drive from Lausanne could be made in a little over six hours, but Cairns went south, along the French coast to Monaco and Nice before heading north to Paris. He had nothing but time.

Lindsey had been partially correct about Eric Braun. Just as the dead scientist had confessed in his letter, the sister had never lived long enough to benefit from the TirNan Protocol. But the story of Diedrich Braun's obsession with Hitler, the principles, and writings of Hitler and of Diedrict Eckart, were frighteningly accurate.

The obsession and paranoia had been intensified by the

death of three-year-old Gretchen. Braun's wife had been telling her husband about the child's blue lips, worsening fatigue and breathlessness. And had begged him to call in a Berlin doctor or, at least, let her take the sick child to a local pediatrician. Braun had not listened. Accusing his wife of hysteria, he barely looked at the little girl and pronounced her healthy. Refusing or incapable of seeing the marked signs of severe illness, Braun was busy building his empire. And convinced he could not father another imperfect child.

The night the child died haunted him.

She had screamed only once. "Diedrich!" A piteous harrowing shout. It was late on a bitterly cold January night, and they were staying at the Villa in Hesse where he lived most of the time now. A restored castle, the villa was magnificent during the summer months of June and July, but gloomy, drafty and nearly impossible to heat in the winter.

He had been working in his office. A roaring fire warming him and the room. Braun had been most displeased at the interruption, but something told him to stop his work and climb the massive staircase to the second floor where the cry had originated. The guilt began then as he slowly climbed the stairs. Braun knew his child was dead before he reached the tragic tableau of his eight- year-old son Eric and his wife sitting on either side of Gretchen's tiny, motionless body. No longer blue but alabaster white and cold, like porcelain.

As he entered the room, his wife turned to look at him. Uttering not one sound, her thirty- year-old face was an ancient mask of grief and betrayal, her blue eyes regarding him without recognition. She had no idea who he was.

That was another fiction of Eric's. His mother had lost all contact with her world and the people in it that night. Despite the best, albeit belated, psychiatric care that Berlin medicine could provide, she remained institutionalized.

Diedrich Braun had never been terribly well-adjusted. Balance and moderation were not attributes of his, even as a young man. His father was a Lutheran minister, strict and uncompromising with his wife and four boys, of whom Diedrich was the oldest. The elder Braun disowned his oldest son when he refused to follow in his father's ministerial footsteps and declared the Lutheran Church, for that matter, religion itself, an absurdity.

In college, he had been known as competitive, ambitious and arrogant, with few friends. But the psychic stress of justifying and rationalizing his actions with his family had contributed to a steady erosion of trust and increasing paranoia. Therefore, when Joe Cairns quit without completing his entire assignment, Braun was unsurprised. He expected betrayal, after all, the man was an American.

The double cross with the mice had not been discovered until last night at his research lab in Berlin. Braun had actually smiled as he'd listened to the panicky researcher who had drawn the short straw and had been the unfortunate soul required to call Braun with the bad news

"No worries, Dr. Palmer, thank you for notifying me."

The man had been pitifully eager to get off the phone.

Despite the devastating impact of his grand scheme, Braun had actually been proud of the ingenuity shown by his son. And the guts. He'd had no idea that his weak and cowardly son Eric would have mustered the courage to make a switch like that. He almost wished things had been different between them, and they could have worked together.

No matter, he had a much better plan. One that would take care of Reardon, his lovely daughter Liisa as well as the interfering Jansen, along with a good number of unnecessary consumers of the planet's resources, like say four to five billion.

Braun had been mesmerized by the swine flu epidemic of 1918. Half of the population of the world had been infected. Strangely, the highest mortality had been in those under twenty-five. Over one hundred years later, no one completely understood how and why the virus had spread so quickly throughout the world and with such devastating rates of death.

Diedrich Braun believed he was the answer to global warming, famine, poverty, and most of the distressingly lengthy list of maladies threatening the world and its inhabitants. And the very best thing about his plan is that there would be absolutely no need for weapons, soldiers, or heads of governments shouting at each other. This would be simple, and painful for many, but would be over within twenty-hours for those who would succumb.

"Pete, this time, I really am going home!" Dr. Drew Morgan scanned the bright sunny foyer of the emergency center. "Just making sure there are no more Reardon people out here before I leave again!" His Texas twang bounced off the walls of the empty waiting room.

"How do I thank you, Drew? You've stayed like seven hours after your shift was supposed to be over, you must be exhausted." Hank thought it best not to mention that he guessed that Morgan was not far from his own age, late sixties. Almost twenty hours on your feet is a game for far younger men and women.

The big, brawny man had not bothered to change out of his flannel shirt and jeans when he had re-joined his coworker hours ago.

"Just doing my job, no need for a thank you. None at all. Look, we're a team here, like you people..." Unsuccessfully stifling a yawn, Drew said, "Pete's done the same for me on many an occasion. And as it turned out, it's a good thing I went back to help. Ariana Dumas and your daughter needed big time help. They were both headed toward septic shock."

Just then, Lindsey walked out of the elevator and walked

rapidly over to Morgan, echoing Hank. "Dr. Morgan, how do we thank you? You've gone above and beyond with caring for all us crazed Reardons and associates."

"Dr. Lindsey McCall, why you're even more beautiful in person!" The ER doc winked at Hank and said, "This is thanks enough, Mr. Reardon. I am sure you know just how famous this Texas lady is."

"Flattery will get you everywhere, but honestly, we so appreciate what you and your staff have done!" Lindsey's hand was extended, and Morgan grabbed it with both of his, holding it while he studied her.

Drew Morgan said, "You are more than welcome, Doctor." His expression was somber and all traces of his earlier fatigue erased.

Lindsey let her hand stay in Morgan's while she continued. "My gratitude isn't just for the excellent care you and your staff has provided our battered teammates, but also for letting Gabe and his dog in to visit them. Those two have been searching for Liisa and Ariana for three days." Clutching the other doctor's hand, there was a sheen in her eyes. "Gabe and Baron..."

"Are professionals." Morgan completed her statement. "I have worked with many a search and rescue team in my years here in Switzerland, but those two are among the best I have ever seen. Course we don't see any Doberman tracker dogs here in Switzerland. Most are St. Bernard's and other high-altitude search type breeds. Much more suited to the mountains, but it must get cold over there too, Afghanistan's mountains are just as high as are ours." Morgan pretended not to see the tears standing in Lindsey's eyes as he chatted. "Baron is extraordinarily well-trained. I seldom run into dogs that well-mannered.

"Gabe McAllister...he was military, wasn't he?"

Not really needing an answer, for Gabe's background was evident in everything he said and did. Morgan asked, "Was Baron in country with Gabe?"

"His namesake was. He was killed in Afghanistan during Gabe's fourth—and last—tour, he saved the lives of Gabe and his entire platoon. This Baron was adopted by Gabe about a year ago, a previous owner had given him up to an animal shelter."

Morgan merely closed his eyes for a moment as he accurately imagined just how the soldier's dog had died. *An IED, bet the dog tracked down a bomb, he would have been leading the soldier and his men. Unimaginable, no wonder the man looks the way he does...that thousand-yard stare is a dead giveaway. Barely thirty years old and living with the memory of watching your best friend do exactly what you have trained him to do: freely, joyfully give his life for you.*

Gabe McAllister had been a handler of military war dogs while in the Marines. They were in Kamdesh, Afghanistan in the appropriately named Landai Sin Valley, in 2009, where the Combat Outpost Keating was overrun by a surprise force of over three hundred Taliban. McCallister was on his fourth and the last tour in the country and had been deployed with nine men to collect and dispose of weapons left behind by the American soldiers who managed to get out alive. The ten men had been following McAllister, who was creeping behind Baron as the dog searched for IEDs in one of the best places to hide the destructive weapons, an Afghan cemetery.

Baron had slowed down that day from his normal fast-paced trot. He was watching one of the tall gravestones on his left, nose up, moving ever so slightly more and more to the left. Watching his dog, McAllister raised his right hand to slow down the men following while he strained to look ahead, to the left where Baron was so intently focused. Suddenly, as if he had run into a cement wall, the big dog skidded to a halt and looked back at McAllister; eyes lit, stubby tail wagging furiously, alive with the knowledge that he'd found the target and was eagerly awaiting the play time which always followed the find. Those sensitive ears were quivering with anticipation: the tell-tale click of the pressure plate was barely audible to any but those sensitive canine ears; Baron knew he'd done it, he had sought and found: mission complete.

The explosion was deafening; McAllister only knew that he was screaming when Samuels, his second in command had wrapped his arms around him so tightly that he could not breathe.

CHAPTER FORTY

Liisa's hospital room early evening

Toni and Liisa had been admitted and would spend the night at the hospital. The ER doc that Drew Morgan called Pete had spent two hours removing the glass from Toni's arms. Thankfully, the worst of the ground in glass had been in her non-tattooed arm, Toni mused, as she surveyed the damage while pushing Liisa's wheelchair down the hall to Ari's room. Lindsey had just called to suggest they come on down to see Ari, who was awake and wanting to see everyone.

Liisa had put up a quite a fuss when the nurse came in with the wheelchair but obeyed when Gabe threatened to pick her up and put her in it himself. Toni had thought the scene one of the funniest she had ever seen. Liisa—not so much.

"No way, I'm not using that wheelchair!"

The young nurse stood there uncomfortably, "Ms. Reardon, your doctor's orders are absolutely clear. You are not permitted to stand until tomorrow morning." She looked up at the clear plastic bag with the mega dose of antibiotic hanging on the pole and adjusted the rate. "Your feet are badly infected, standing on them is...."

Rich, Gabe, and Baron walked back in. At Lindsey's suggestion, they had been headed back to the Reardon house for some sleep, but at the sound of Liisa's raised voice, they came back into her room.

Ducking his head to walk into the room, Gabe walked over to stand next to the nurse. Towering over her, he looked down at Liisa. "Shall I pick you up and put you in that wheelchair? After all, we've gone through to find you, Ms. Dr. Liisa Reardon, you're not about to make any foolish decisions like not listening to your doctor, are you?"

Liisa's face turned as red as her hair. Glaring at Gabe, she swung her bandaged feet over the bed with as much dignity as she could muster, then looked up at the former soldier and muttered, "Okay, okay."

Toni and Rich were staring fixedly at the floor while biting their lips to keep from laughing. The nurse, oblivious to everything but making sure her patient did what she was supposed to, looked up at Gabe and said, "Thank you so much for your help, it's really important that she stay off those feet."

Gabe bowed and smiled at the pretty nurse. With a mischievous look at Liisa, he read her nametag and said, "Happy to be of service, Ms. Ainsworth, Ms. Abigail Ainsworth! That's a very English name, isn't it?"

Blushing at the attention of the good-looking, tall American, the nurse's French accent thickened when she replied, "Yes, my Dad is from the UK."

Liisa interrupted the annoying quasi-flirtation between Gabe and her nurse by hoisting herself to the edge of the bed, and in the process moving the wheelchair farther away. Ms. Ainsworth was instantly attentive to her patient, "Wait, Ms. Reardon, I will help you." In a flash the small nurse had repositioned the wheelchair, had one arm around Liisa's shoulders, the other pulling the taller woman into a semi-crouch while using her own small body as a fulcrum to manage the shift from bed to chair. It was an impressive display of good body mechanics.

Toni had stepped forward then and told nurse Ainsworth that she would be delighted to take Liisa down the hall. Smiling, she had added, "We'll all make certain that she remains in the chair."

When Liisa saw Ariana sitting up in bed, she shocked Ariana, Lindsey, Toni and most of all, herself, by dissolving into sobs.

"What's wrong Liisa? Are you in pain?" Lindsey hurried to her, crouched so she could see her face.

"Noooo, it's just..." She raised a hand and shook her head signaling that she just could not talk.

Toni left in search of Kleenex, she was never any good at crying women.

By the time she arrived back armed with tissues, everyone was laughing. Crisis over.

Despite the fact that none of them knew one another well, that there were economic and cultural differences significant enough to preclude friendship under ordinary circumstance, a bond had been forged among the four women. Between rescuer and rescued, and among those who had been certain they were dying. Staring death in the face and then finding oneself alive would change anyone. But the knowledge that one's existence was due solely to the actions of another severs the facades of independence and control we citizens of the twenty-first-century shroud ourselves in. Toni, Liisa, and Ariana had been altered. Their wounds would heal, but the transformation of their psyches would force each woman to view her world and the people within it with clearer vision.

Surveying the three beat-up women in the room with her, Lindsey said, "Well I could cry too, simply because this seemed..." she looked at her watch, "impossible. Just twenty-four hours ago we had just received the second letter demanding that your Dad transfer the patents for Longevive and TirNan and…" Lindsey interrupted herself because Ariana was looking at the door as if she were looking for someone or needed something. "Ari, do you need something? I'd be happy to…"

"Gabriel, isn't he coming too?"

"Oh for heaven's sake, Ari, you have a crush on the guy too?" And then Liisa covered her mouth in horror.

At that, the four dissolved into hilarity, even Liisa.

The gales of laughter resumed when Toni wryly commented, "We all have a crush on Gabe McAllister, Liisa." But Toni was not joking. She would remember that hand for the rest of her life. Through a dense fog, that gigantic hand reaching through the smashed window, and somehow getting her out of the wrecked little car. Toni could close her eyes and see it reaching through the debris, and she heard that calm voice repeating over and over, "Toni, it's Gabe. You're ok. Don't worry, I'll get you out. You're going to be fine." It had looked like the hand of God reaching through an abyss to save her. She had appreciated Liisa's company, but it was Gabe's presence that had made her feel safe. Hoping that no one noticed, she wiped away the tears.

But Ari noticed. When Toni opened her eyes, she saw Ariana's huge expressive brown gaze on hers. Two strangers who had never met one another. Ari nodded, the movement so slight it was almost imperceptible. But the gesture was one of sisterhood, profound understanding, and compassion.

Quietly, Ari replied to Liisa, "No, Liisa, I do not have a *crush* on Gabriel. That is such a silly American phrase. I just wanted to see him, to thank him." Her right hand reached for the crucifix that she was never without, her eyes widened, but before she could utter a word, Liisa said, "Lindsey, Ari's looking for her medal, her crucifix, do you see it over on that table or maybe in the closet?"

Quickly, Lindsey searched through the sparse belongings. Just as she was about to give up, she spied a chain with a small crucifix in the corner of a drawer, lifted it up and placed it around Ariana's neck. Lindsey kissed her on the top of her curly head. "Ari, you were saying?"

"Yes, I was saying...this Gabriel." Now her small hand searched for and found the crucifix, her second and third fingers rubbed it again and again. "One minute Joe Cairns was there, kneeling beside me in the woods, his gun right against my skull." Ari reached up and placed the flat of her hand on the right side of her head, about four inches from her temple. "And the next thing I knew, there was Gabe. I thought he was the angel Gabriel, come to take me home. And then he spoke his name, Gabe." Ariana spoke in a softly French-accented voice as if she were describing something sacred. The whispered speech intensified her words in an almost painful way. The silence in the room was alive, tangible as if there were other beings there.

CHAPTER FORTY-ONE
Library Reardon's Home

They sat in the exact same places, with Lindsey's Gantt Chart still displayed on the electronic whiteboard. Stella was busily filling coffee cups, while muted conversations took place between Toni and Gabe, and Lindsey and Rich. Only Dimitri and Hank Reardon were silent. Each man was immersed in his own thoughts. The chair where Joe Cairns had sat was empty, no one went near it.

Watching—more sensing—the interaction between Lindsey and Rich, Reardon cleared his throat, twice. As he did so, he thought once more of how indebted he was to these two fine people. Hank recalled the very first meeting with Dr. Lindsey McCall. His good friend, former mentor and then Chair of Medicine at the University of Houston Hospital, Simon Bayer had intrigued him with the tale of a young physician researcher's surprising laboratory success in modifying the digitalis molecule. Although Reardon had believed his red-eye flight from Zurich to Houston to be a fool's errand, he knew Simon to be one of the more practical men he'd ever known. Simon had been honest on the phone with him, and Hank Reardon had just taken over the leadership post at ASL. The company was in trouble. Most of its money-making drugs had reached the limit on their patent, and there was nothing on the horizon.

Hank remembered the conversation. *This may never make it to clinical trials, Hank. But I've watched Lindsey McCall since the beginning of her residency. And have never seen such talent- in research, in the cath lab or diagnostically. She's never doubted her ability to create this new molecule. Never. If this new drug of hers can do in humans what it has done in mice, the treatment of cardiac disease will be revolutionized.*

Simon Bayer had died before the clinical trials had been completed. Ironically, the 'Cardiologist's Cardiologist' had died of a massive heart attack while playing tennis at the age of eighty-six. He never witnessed the tremendous effect of his young protégé's discovery.

Had it been only six years since that meeting? As he mused about their providential meeting and the mind-boggling effects of Lindsey's drug on medicine worldwide and, therefore, ASL profits, he was suddenly overcome. Coughing vigorously to cover the tsunami of gratitude, awe, and joy, Reardon reached out to grab a glass of water. Instantly, Stella was there, topping off the glass with ice water.

"Will you have another waffle now?" Stella had been ecstatic when Hank had asked if she could serve breakfast in the library for the entire group. Finally, people to feed.

Patting his non-existent paunch, Reardon exclaimed, "Stella, if I have a third, Gabe and Baron will have to carry this old man— I'll be too full to navigate!"

Gabe smiled but said nothing. The dog lay at his feet on a thick blanket Stella kept there for him. Studying him, Hank wondered at the former soldier. Although barely thirty, the former Marine had lived through four tours in Afghanistan only to come home to a wrongful conviction and imprison- ment for sexual abuse of the little girl Annie. The child that his dear friend, Zach Cunningham had adopted after Zach and Jansen had proved that the child's abuser had been another man, the boyfriend, and boss of Annie's mother.

McAllister was more than reticent, he'd said maybe five words during the last hour, which seemed his norm. And yet, Gabe seemed at ease with himself and his world. Reardon could find no evidence of the anger or resentment he would expect to see in a young man who had suffered so. Hank had noticed Liisa's reactions to McAllister and felt much happier about Gabe than he had about poor Eric. Although Reardon was careful not to interfere with his daughter's love life, he had known she and Eric had been dating, as had most all of the researchers in the office. Hank had not liked Eric Braun. *Braun—why the hell had that last name escaped him?* The son of Diedrich Braun working under his nose for how many years? He was slipping.

Dimitri surprised himself and everyone else when he asked, "Stella if you are still offering Belgian waffles, I'd be happy to take another one or two off your hands!" The Swiss detective was talking to Stella, but those bright blue eyes were focused on Lindsey, and a slight smile softened the solemn dark face.

Returning his gaze, she invited him to start their meeting. "While you wait for those waffles, Dimitri, do you mind telling us the status of your investigation? And whether you need us to stay in Lausanne any longer?" Lindsey knew that Toni wanted to get back to work with Zach and Harvey. Evidently, there was a new case which would require intensive investigation. Zach had told Rich to take all the time he needed to wrap things up, but there were just the two of them and the two investigators. A big case required the time and energy of the entire team, so she was sorely needed.

Casting an appreciative look at Lindsey, Dimitri leaned

forward. "Director Pierre and I thank you all for your invaluable assistance in this case." His coffee-colored cheeks darkened. "As you know, I was opposed to working with a bunch of—" Dimitri looked over to Rich, "honestly, I never thought of any of you as yahoo's!" The word sounded peculiar with his accent, thicker now because he was nervous, and the detective chuckled along with everyone in the room. "But working with you, each one of you," Dimitri's gaze scanned everyone slowly, lingering on Toni's battered arms, Gabe, Baron and ending up at Lindsey, "has been an honor. You are professionals, and it has been a distinct privilege working with each one of you."

Dimitri's gaze returned to Toni and stayed there. She and everyone in the room waited for the rebuke that would surely come because of her ill-advised decision to follow Joe Cairns. But the cop merely shrugged. "Toni, the same thing happened to me before I transferred to FedPol. We were close to getting enough evidence to nail a killer. I was positive he wouldn't be able to see me, stayed way back and was driving a boring, unobtrusive car. Then he made me. Rammed me with the massive SUV he was driving," shook his head in wonder, remembering. "It was even black, just like Cairns' SUV." His face wore the usual flat, expressionless look of a cop or a soldier. So when he smiled, it transformed his entire face and lit up the brilliant blue eyes. The smile was directed at Gabe and Baron.

"I was in the boondocks, and no one knew where I was because I did what Toni did—didn't tell my partner where I was headed, and tailed a known killer. The car was upside down and smoking, and I was beaten up pretty badly. A few broken bones and nearly unconscious, but I somehow got an SOS out on my radio before I passed out. I woke up to the sweet, heavenly tongue of a German Shepherd licking my face.

The dog is named Kane, and he is still on active duty. His handler is a guy named Jaques. Those two saved my life that day, and I have never gone without my partner or backup ever again." Dimitri let his tale sit for a beat, then two. The silence was beginning to get awkward when he said, "Cairns is a pro. My best crime techs sifted through the ash of the farmhouse in Bonvillars for the last two days. And it's ash."

"An accelerant?"

"No, Gabe. Just plain old kerosene and newspapers do the job just as well."

Looking at Lindsey's Gantt chart, Dimitri pointed to Cairns' name. "He spent twenty years in Force Recon. Has over ten high-level medals that no one will ever know about because he was doing black ops before we all began doing so much of that nasty business that it got its own name. His record is spotless. His last assignment before he went to work for Braun got him a medal from Germany."

Looking at Gabe and then Rich, he asked, "So why does a guy like that go over to the other side? Money?"

"Yes and No." Both men had answered simultaneously. But no one laughed or even smiled at the coincidence. They looked at one another, Rich nodded to Gabe. A non-verbal, 'You tell them.'

"He was ten years in Force Recon then joined the Marine Corps Forces Special Operations Command (MARSOC) and became a Marine Raider in 2006. If Force Recon is run of the mill black ops, then the Raiders are the elite of the lethal small expeditionary teams."

"That's the Marine name from World War Two!" Reardon remarked in surprise. He had not heard of this change, clearly, neither had Dimitri who was listening intently.

"Right, 9/11 got the attention of the people who make these kinds of decisions, and they decided to let the Marines into the sacrosanct corridors of the Joint Special Operations World. They brought back the disbanded Marine Raider name to link those World War Two special ops soldiers—the first with the MARSOC Raider of today."

"Why were the Marines excluded until then?"

Shrugging, Gabe replied to Lindsey, "Because the Army and Navy got there first, I guess."

Listening without comment, Dimitri thought about all those special ops groups in the States: Delta Force, Seal Team, AFSOC, DDI, and now this MARSOC group he had never heard of until now. Add to those the FBI, CIA, NSA and the DOD, and all those he could not remember. Mind boggling, no wonder they got in each other's way. But then again, in fairness to the huge country, Switzerland was about the size of one of the smaller states of the fifty making up the US.

"You were MARSOC, weren't you?"

Gabe's only reply to Toni's question was a failed attempt at a smile, along with a raised eyebrow.

"Okay, thanks for the crash course in the files I could not access. Cairns' file must be redacted, that's why we could not see any of this MARSOC info."

"It is. There are still some people I can call who will pick up the phone."

Dimitri repeated his question." Okay so why did he do it, though? With a background like that, why work for the enemy?"

"He realized that he was a paid killer for the government. Like Marines have since Smedley Butler. That he was doing the dirty work for billionaires that didn't give a damn for this country or for any country. They make more per year than most countries and still it's not enough. He watched good men lose their lives and extremities for a President who refers to ISIS as a JV team." The bitterness of Gabe's words was highlighted by the absence of emotion, he spoke matter of factly, as if everyone understood the truth behind the jarring cynicism.

A decorated Marine, rising to the rank of Major General, Smedley Butler was the most decorated Marine at the time of his death in 1940. During his 34-year career, he participated in military actions in the Philippines, China, in Central America and the Caribbean. Butler is well known for having later become an outspoken critic of U.S. wars and their consequences, as well as exposing an alleged plan to overthrow the U.S. government during FDR's presidency. One of his famed quotes is derived from a speech which was published as a book, *War Is A Racket.*

Rich and Gabe were each silent. Most likely thinking about what the still famous Marine had said. "War is a racket. It is the only one international in scope. It is the only one in which the profits are reckoned in dollars and the losses in lives."

Stella came in with a flourish. Holding Dimitri's beautiful Belgian waffles accented by sliced peaches and raspberries in one hand and a carafe of coffee in the other, she did not notice the heaviness in the room until she placed the plate in front of Dimitri. Eyes widening, she placed her hands on her hips and asked, "Should I leave? Is this a bad time?" Her brogue thick as her nervousness increased.

Soothingly, Hank Reardon said, "Stella, actually your timing could not be better! In fact, may I bother you for a second plate that looks just like Dimitri's?"

Face now wreathed in smiles, Stella replied, "Of course, anyone else?"

Thirty minutes later, they were back at it. "So why didn't Cairns kill Ariana? She said he had his gun placed against her head, that she was saying the 'Our Father' and 'Hail Mary' in French for the first time in many years because she was certain she was dying. In fact," Toni lightly trailed the fingers of her left hand along the healing cuts and abrasions of her right arm. "Gabe, she said she knew you were the angel Gabriel sent to bring her to God, and that she was shocked when she woke up in the hospital."

Although Toni had spoken about Gabe, she was looking at Dimitri who looked nonplussed. After several seconds, the detective replied, "Toni, I have no clue." He was focused on her, his expression was earnest, grave.

None of the others offered an explanation, they merely sat quietly, reflecting on the strange twists of this entire thing.

Lindsey spoke into the silence, directing a new question to Dimitri. "You don't have enough evidence to go after Braun then, do you?"

Relieved to be on the safer ground of evidence, the detective replied, "We are going to try. We have Eric's document after all, and the Chicago police have agreed to reopen that case based on this new evidence."

Rich disagreed. Any decent criminal defense lawyer would throw Eric's letter out as hearsay. If Eric were alive, maybe, but the claims of a dead son against his father with whom he'd had no relationship since the age of eight? Without anything else, he doubted that an American District Attorney would agree to indict. But he said nothing, maybe Dimitri had something else up his sleeve.

Hank Reardon had been thinking about all that had been said. Like Dimitri, he had no interest in attempting an answer to why Cairns had not followed through. He looked at the Swiss detective and asked, "Can you prove that Braun hired Cairns?"

"We have used some of our *influence*" The grim smile

clarified his meaning. "To persuade Cairns' German federal cop buddy to admit that he set up a meeting between Braun and Cairns. We have video feeds of Cairns getting into Braun's limo. Our reluctant informer and Cairns were hired for additional security during The Economic Summit meeting in Berlin. There had been threats against the German Chancellor and French Prime Minister, consequently the German Federal Police hired Cairns. Evidently, Braun's people had approached our unhappy German captain for some private work."

"Have you tracked Cairns once he left Bonvillars, Dimitri?"

"Not after he got to France, Mr. Readon. The SUV was spotted heading to Paris, but we believe that he's dumped that vehicle and is headed who knows where by now." The cop looked at the Gantt chart once again.

He started ticking off points starting with his index finger. "We know that Cairns was hired by Braun to steal the formulas and experimental animals from ASL. We have his son's accusation that Braun ordered the execution of Adams." By now he was on his ring finger, "We have a clear association between Braun and Hilda Schmidt and," holding up his pinky, "we have their bodies identified at the farmhouse, the farmhouse sold to them by Diedrich Braun."

Hank Reardon joined in enthusiastically. "Braun has been trying to acquire ASL for a couple of years. Once Digipro became successful, he started making inquiries to ASL board members but didn't get far. Thank God they had the sense to check up on him. According to their sources, Interpol has had him on their radar for years, something to do with weapons. Like anti-aircraft missiles in the middle east countries.

"Is that true, Dimitri? Have you people been watching Braun because you think he is into weapons trafficking?"

"Yes, in fact, we have evidence but not enough to get an indictment. That's why we are eager to get an indictment in this case." His brow furrowed. "Did you know Matt Adams, Mr. Reardon?"

"Yes, I did, and considered him a friend. I need to call his wife again, she wasn't up to talking when I called before. The news accounts said it was a gunshot wound, and hinted at suicide."

"And you don't believe he would kill himself?"

"No, I don't. There was no reason for it, Matt had just gotten a promising new patent, plus, he was Catholic, and Catholics have pretty strong feelings about suicide." Reardon drummed his fingers on the cup of cold coffee he held. "That new cancer drug patent only sweetened the lure of Adams and Adams for Diedrich Braun." Reardon's mouth was a grimace.

"Hank, tell them what you told me about Braun, your impressions." Rich had been listening to Dimitri and was beginning to understand just why he was ignoring the flimsiness of his case. Braun made Joe Cairns seem like an Eagle Scout.

"Sure, I've been around him several times. There is no nice way of talking about this, and I know it sounds terribly prejudicial. When I think of him, I think of the SS as in Hitler's Nazi police force. There is something so strange about him, so detached. For example, I've called his home twice attempting to speak with him about his son's death. The second time this same man answered. Evidently one cannot speak with Braun unless they go through this Claus. This assistant said Braun is aware that Eric is dead and that there is no need to contact him about this matter again. That Mr. Braun appreciates my taking the time to give him this information. All said as if I had called to give Braun a tip about the stock market."

Lindsey looked over at Dimitri. Neither said a word, but

each had been catapulted back to Liisa's office where they watched Eric Braun die. She felt ill at the precision with which Eric had predicted his father's reaction when told of his death.

Gabe asked, "Dimitri, do you know if the Adams murder was actually investigated by the Chicago police? It wouldn't have been that hard to stage that headshot if the guy knew what he was doing. Someone with Braun's resources could hire the best." Unconsciously, Gabe looked over at the end of the coffee table. Everyone else in the room followed Gabe's gaze. The empty chair where Joe Cairns had sat.

Looking back at Gabe, Dimitri nodded. "That may be why they have so readily agreed to reopen the case, Gabe. Sounds like they bought the suicide note found on Adams' office computer."

"I hate to play devil's advocate here Dimitri, but unless the Chicago cops can turn up new evidence or Joe Cairns surfaces, you'll have an entirely circumstantial case. Even the relationship between Cairns and Braun—all you can prove is that they met Braun."

Dimitri's self-control slipped momentarily as an expression of annoyance crossed his face. He frowned at Rich.

Ignoring the other man's irritation, Rich mused out loud, "But there must have been money transferred between Braun and Cairns. Have your guys been able to locate payments?"

The frown became a scowl. "Cairns received half a million from an offshore Belize account that is a Gordian knot of corporations with nothing behind them except a name. No connection to any of Braun's companies."

Rich nodded.

Liisa's bedroom

Liisa had been released from the hospital, and Toni would be heading home the next day. Ariana was recovering rapidly but needed another day of intravenous antibiotics before coming home. Since Liisa was still advised to stay off her feet, Lindsey and Toni were keeping her company lest she go stir crazy.

Her room was nothing like the rest of the Reardon house. More like a suite than a bedroom, the main room was large enough for a bed at one end with a love seat and two upholstered chairs and a glass coffee table on the other. Toni and Lindsey now sprawled in her bedroom, Toni on the loveseat, bare feet resting on the edge of the table. Lindsey sat in one of the overstuffed chairs, surveying the room.

Behind the chairs and coffee table, a door led into a spacious bath with a dressing table, large bathtub, shower and walk in closet. The area could have been lovely, but instead was neutral, almost plain. The walls were devoid of art. There were not even plants to soften the starkness of the unadorned white walls. The sole concession to aesthetics was a set of long gauzy white drapes covering the large window overlooking the rose garden below which had been installed at her step-mother Peg's direction.

Delighted to just sit quietly as she listened to Liisa explain her research to Toni, Lindsey chuckled as she took note of the similarity of Liisa's taste, or more accurately, lack of it, with her own. Even down to the unadorned Adirondack bedroom suite and matching tables. Exactly the same as she had while working at Houston Medical Center. The bedroom of a woman who merely slept here, one who cared about her work and little else.

The double-L-researchers, Liisa and Lindsey, dubbed so by Toni, had formally accepted Annie into their TirNan subset of females the day before. Annie was the child involved when Gabe had been wrongly accused of sex abuse. Annie was found to have been sexually abused, but not by Gabe. After a lengthy and complicated series of court proceedings, Harvey and her lawyer husband Zach Cunningham had adopted the little girl. Very recently, they had learned that the little girl had cardiomyopathy.

Toni and Harvey were the very best of friends. Consequently, Toni had another agenda— understanding as much as she possibly could so that she could be helpful to Harvey when she returned to Oklahoma.

Harvey had called Lindsey just days before all hell broke loose in Switzerland. Their pediatrician had referred Annie to the pediatric cardiology department at the University Hospital in Oklahoma City. Did she know anyone there? Did she have any advice for her and her husband?

It had all happened at once when during recess out in the playground, Annie had fainted and then seized, all too often the first signs of cardiac disease in kids. Lindsey too had her friends on her mind and discussing the case with Liisa and Toni had brought all her thoughts to mind during the phone conversation with Harvey.

The discovery of Annie's cardiomyopathy had to have felt like a two-ton truck descending on Harvey, Zach, and their two older kids. They had fought through a maze of hearings, judges, and bureaucracy to persuade the state of Texas that this Caucasian child had an infinitely better chance at happiness in this life with them. Despite the fact they were older—Zach was around Hank Reardon's age and black. Then they learn that Annie has a potentially fatal disease. Why is it that the very best people—with the most honorable of intentions, get such a tough break? Here are these two, no longer young who, with eyes wide open, take on a severely traumatized kid only to discover that she has a potentially fatal heart disease? Lord, how cruel this life can be.

Then Lindsey recalled what her childhood friend Julie Grayson had told her about Julie's favorite saint, the mystic, St. Teresa of Avila. The nun had been imploring her Lord about the imprisonment and near starvation of her dear friend St. John of the Cross and heard this reply from the person she called Your Majesty. "Teresa, whom the Lord loves, he also chastises, this is how I treat all my friends." The acerbic Spanish saint had allegedly replied to Jesus, "No wonder you have so few of them."

Lindsey had planned to fly out to Oklahoma City to meet with their Pediatric Cardiologist at Harvey's request. She had trained with Dr. Matt Pierce in Houston and liked him. Lindsey had felt certain that Matt would be enthusiastic about entering his new little patient into their TirNan study. But had to cancel that trip for the one to Switzerland.

At Liisa's online suggestion, Harvey had bought the book by the doctor who had basically caused an almost total remission from Duchenne's multiple sclerosis by adopting a Paleo Diet, along with loads of supplements. Harvey had devoured the book in one evening. Over the sixteen years she had been married to Zach Cunningham, she had tried to persuade him that his beloved carbs, desserts, and chips would bring him to an early death, with little result. But once he understood the rationale behind the protocol, Zach would eat kale and broccoli as if they were potato chips and mac and cheese. Or act as if they were anyway. He, like most great lawyers, was also a great actor.

After listening to Liisa explain the potentially almost miraculous effects of a Paleo Diet along with mega doses of K2 on the subset of early onset cardiomyopathy patients, Toni was psyched because this was something she totally got. Although the terms methylation, transcriptional proteins, genomics, and epigenetics were off-putting to her, she understood the fundamentals of Liisa's explanation. New research demonstrated that disease-causing genetic expressions could be modified, altered, and even retarded. Healthy food like green vegetables, and elimination of wheat, sugar and saturated fats from the diet, had already done so in a significant number of people with chronic diseases.

One of the numerous inroads being made by scientists in the understanding of human health was the critical importance of nutrition to well-being. Of the significance of everyday foods like green vegetables to the health of the cell. Of the switch from the conventional medical focus on particular organ and system disease to an entirely different world-view, the attention to the mitochondria, the building blocks of the body.

Lindsey was listening carefully to Liisa's brief explanation of the cell and the potential revolution about to occur in medicine because of overwhelming evidence which could be ignored only for so long by the mainstream. She thought of her new friend and colleague, Jodi Tamarack, the vet who ran the animal science center at Cal Poly and remembered their last conversation at dinner before all hell had broken loose.

"Cystic Fibrosis a mineral deficiency?" Lindsey was so surprised that she had put down the piece of halibut she was about to eat and gaped at Jodi. "In med school, we were taught that CF is caused by a genetic defect in the CFTR gene. This came from one of the medical researchers who discovered the gene."

Jodi smiled, nodded and replied. "I know. Joel Wallach, either a genius or maniac depending on your world view, theorized via autopsy of captive rhesus monkeys that CF occurs from a lack of minerals, specifically selenium. His findings caused so much alarm in traditional scientific communities that he was fired from his job as a wildlife veterinarian and pathologist for the NIH.

"I was lucky enough to have him as a guest lecturer in one of my post-doc courses. He loved to quote Thomas Edison." Jodi stopped to break off a piece of the fragrant warm bread which their waiter had just placed on their table. "Ummm, this is so good," Jodi eyed Lindsey's largely uneaten meal and her own empty plate and groaned. "No wonder I wear a size twelve on a thin day and you a size four..."

Curious, Lindsey had prompted Jodi, "Edison?" Wondering what on earth the man who invented electricity had to do with a veterinary pathologist.

"Edison said, 'The doctor of the future will give no medication, but will interest his patients in the care of the human frame, diet and in the cause and prevention of disease.'" Watching Lindsey's evident surprise, the vet regarded her carefully. Extending her hand across the small table, Jodi grabbed Lindsey's left hand which lay next to her barely eaten dinner. And smiled when McCall returned the squeeze. "I honestly cannot tell you how excited I am to have you on board, Lindsey McCall!" Lifting her left eyebrow inquisitively, Jodi added,

"But I'm quite honestly baffled about why you are leaving fame and fortune behind to join our mostly unknown program here at Cal Poly!"

"Lindsey, why are you so quiet? Are you feeling alright?" She regarded Lindsey with concern.

"I'm fine, Toni, just fine. I have been daydreaming about my new life."

Studying her, Toni nodded and cocked her head. "New life…back to academic medicine."

It was a statement, not a question.

It was a natural assumption. After all Lindsey McCall had won back her international reputation once she had been acquitted of the intentional murder charge. The Chair of Medicine at Houston Medical had offered Lindsey a prestigious package, including a chair in her name to lure her back. But Lindsey had decided to leave academic medicine for the Medical Director position at Huntsville. Now she had left that job too.

"No, Toni, no more academic medicine." Lindsey thought of the hundreds of reasons that she was leaving clinical medicine, debating with herself about whether she should try to explain. Then she looked at Toni: Tough, stalwart, loyal Toni, and realized that Toni needed all the faith in academic medicine she could muster. Her best friends Harvey and Zach had no choice but to believe in the system. Lindsey would make sure that it didn't roll over them. Consequently, she just smiled and said, "I've started in the animal science center at Cal Poly in San Luis Obispo, California." Grinning excitedly at Liisa, one of her new partners, Lindsey explained, "New job, new city, new house, new partners, you're looking at a brand new person with a brand new career."

Liisa remarked. "Ummm, Linds, you're not starting a new career, I'd say you're returning to your first love. Research. " Liisa shifted her legs and recrossed her feet which were propped up on three fluffy pillows. Hitching herself up further along the wood headboard. "Four days in bed and I'm going nuts, I wonder how people stand to be totally bedridden." Then returning her gaze to Lindsey. "I'm right, aren't I? Dad told me once that you had the same dislike of caring for sick people that he did."

There was a time when the observation would have sliced her deeply to the core, and she would have felt enormous guilt. But today, Lindsey only laughed. A genuine belly laugh. "Yeah, he's right. When your job is taking care of people who feel lousy, it helps to have a personality that can empathize!"

Toni had been waiting for an opening. Both Lindsey and Liisa looked healthy—Liisa's aura was back to normal. Liisa was wrapped in layers of shimmering clouds of red. And Toni was beginning to see a golden aura around Lindsey, a first. *Of course, just like Abu always taught me: "Face your fears. And you will see clearly. Hide them, lie to yourself and you will be blind." This was why she could see Lindsey's aura now but not before. Toni winged prayers of love and gratitude toward her beloved grandmother.*

"Since we're now all good buds, warm and fuzzy and all that, I've got some questions for you, but first, there is some-thing I need to say." Toni was sitting at the edge of the love seat in Liisa's bedroom and looking tense. Suddenly the air was charged, and Toni was staring directly at Lindsey.

Lindsey took a deep breath then regarded Toni calmly, thinking as she did so, that the woman could be attractive if she cut and styled her hair, rather than letting the thick mop of curls have their way in reckless abandon on her head. Some makeup wouldn't hurt either. Her eyes were kind of pretty, or would be if she weren't always looking so fierce. Rich liked and respected Toni, but for some reason, Lindsey decided, *Toni does not like me.* She was wrong, Lindsey intimidated Toni as she did many women- and men, for that matter. But she was eternally oblivious to the fact.

The air in the room grew oppressive as Toni scowled at Lindsey and Lindsey merely waited her out. More than surprised when Toni finally spoke. Astonished.

"I was disappointed when you showed up." Liisa's eyes widened, but wisely she said nothing. "Rich didn't tell me that you would be here, I thought it would be just me, Gabe and Rich." Color began to flood her cheeks, and her right hand began fingering the multiple scabs on her left arm. Toni was exceedingly uncomfortable but gamely continued. "And then you took over—that Gantt Chart…I'd never heard of a Gantt Chart. So that silly stunt I pulled was to show you that I was as good as you." Toni gulped and cleared her throat. Lindsey sat in awe at the naked uprightness of this woman, her candor, guts, chutzpah. "That wholly stupid move nearly cost me my life. All because I decided I needed to compete with you." Her expression was bleak, a study in self-disgust.

This time, the silence was restorative, almost cleansing. Toni met Lindsey's gaze. "Harvey thinks the world of you. She has been telling me how gifted you are for months. Now that you are helping her with Annie, too, I guess I was afraid that you would take my best friend away from me. When I couldn't get to sleep last night, I called Harvey to tell her this entire ugly story. Harvey made me promise to tell you, and to thank you for all that you are doing for Annie and for all of us here."

While listening to Toni's heartfelt confession—there was really no other word for it, Lindsey had been reflecting on her own demons. While the need to prove herself to others had never been something that Lindsey had battled, loneliness and self-condemnation certainly had been. She recognized both in Toni's soliloquy and knew there was no facile phrase she could use to make the feelings disappear. The vital thing Toni was doing here was listening to herself. The very act of saying the words out loud to another person could result in immense relief, the very basis of the sacrament of confession.

Consequently, Lindsey continued to meet the dark brown eyes of the woman who had decided to pour out her heart to relative strangers and made a decision. It was time she decided. Eighteen years was long enough, she would finally meet her daughter, also named Lindsey, and would confess to her that she was indeed her mother and had walked away from her at her birth.

Just then, Lindsey realized she'd missed something. The energy in the room was different, light. Both Liisa and Toni were staring at her, expectantly.

"Umm sorry, guys, evidently I've been elsewhere, what did I miss?"

Laughing now, Liisa asked, "Why have you never asked me, Lindsey?"

"Asked you what?"

Now Toni and Liisa were dissolved in gales of laughter. Finally, Liisa was able to get the words out between bouts of hilarity. "Why I spell Liisa with two i's!"

Lindsey stared at the gleeful women, shaking her head. "Why would I? And why is that funny? I don't get the joke."

Damn good thing I have no friends. They would tell me I have finally lost it; hell, I am telling myself that I'm crazy, a complete loon. Nuts. Goneza. Ready to be in a padded room with a straight jacket. But he was as clear as he was back in the days when I was an altar boy, and I'd see him, hear from him, at least, weekly. King David is back in my life. And I'm walking away from a million dollars. And did I mention that I now have made an enemy out of one of the most powerful people on the planet? Braun will not forgive that level of affront. I doubt that many people have done that to him and lived. And I'm happy… is that right? Happy?

Cairns was driving to Greece because he had been told to go to Delphi. For a rest. A rest he would need in the upcoming battles. Plural.

The voice had so startled him that the SUV had swerved close to the side of the freeway and shuddered as Cairns fought to regain control. Once the car was stablized, he glanced over to the passenger seat. There sat David, washed of any blood, and clothed with a one-piece single linen shift, regarding him calmly. Joe slowed the speed of the SUV and pulled over to the side of the road.

Despite the clarity with which Cairns could see the Israeli King sitting right next to him, he felt like two people. One sat serenely conversing with King David, the other was screaming denials, epithets, and dire predictions.

You complete and utter fool! This is not real but only that undigested pizza you ate for breakfast, this guy isn't real…you're living on borrowed time, Cairns, if Braun doesn't kill you, the cops will. By now, that Swiss cop, Reardon, and Jansen know you murdered the German couple and probably Matt Adams! A cacophony of bombast.

"Perhaps." The Israeli King watched him serenely, hearing and answering his thoughts.

Perhaps? No way could he disappear from the radar of Interpol.

"Get rid of this car now. Find a small car that will not draw attention. Then drive to Delphi. Then rest."

Dump the car, of course, and do it now. You are losing it, Cairns.

Ignoring the chaotic internal chorus, Joe found himself asking, crazily, "Why do you call yourself the womb of Adonai?" And found himself relieved at the reappearance of this vision, spirit or apparition or whatever he was. This was the David who had been at his side during the early years, the years when he had felt a commitment to something bigger. Someone. As he waited for the reply, Joe Cairns felt the sting of tears, the first since his mother had died. Relief. Gratitude. Peace. But more.

The clarity of the personage of David was startling. Brown, curly hair, about shoulder length, a long, strong nose, full lips and those eyes. They were brown but not exactly brown, more amber with flecks of gold. As Joe gazed at David, he felt himself being drawn in, almost as if those eyes were whirlpools, mesmerizing whirlpools.

That generous mouth in the handsome and ever young face turned upward as if to smile. "Three sets of fourteen generations." And David's face began to shimmer, he was leaving.

"Wait!!!"

"Yes?"

"Why me?"

"You are a warrior." There was a long pause where David studied Cairns. He felt as if his very soul was exposed. Long-suppressed memories and wounds began to rise to the surface causing pain the likes of which Joe Cairns had never experienced. Just when Cairns thought the pain would kill him, he heard David repeat the command. "Go to Delphi. Heal. There is much work to be done. Many battles ahead."

Liisa Reardon stood behind the pulpit of the Notre Dame Church in Rouen, France, preparing to deliver the eulogy at the funeral mass for Eric Braun. The church was packed, her father had offered free transportation for the four-hundred-mile trip from the corporate headquarters in Lausanne, and it looked like most of the over three-thousand employees had taken him up on his generosity. People were standing at the rear of the church.

Rouen had a checkered history. The capital of Normandy, the city, had been one of the largest and most prosperous cities in medieval Europe. It was one of the capitals of the Anglo-Norman dynasties, ruling England and much of France during the eleventh to the fifteenth centuries. During the Hundred Years War in 1419, the entire city of seventy thousand surrendered to Henry V of England, becoming the capital city of occupied France. And in 1430, Rouen was the site of the trial of Joan of Arc. After a lengthy church trial, the saint was sentenced and burned at the stake in 1431. The subsequent centuries were consumed by religious and political wars, culminating in the destruction of almost half the city in World War Two.

Miraculously, the Notre Dame Cathedral was spared destruction. Made famous by Impressionist French painter, Claude Monet, paintings of the Cathedral hang in the Musee D'Orsay, National Gallery of Art in Washington DC, and in the National Museum of Serbia in Belgrade.

This was an unusual Mass. Maybe even unique. Whether Eric Braun had ever been baptized was something only God knew. And He had not told Father Renee Dubois, the Pastor of Notre Dame Church. But Father Dubois had listened carefully to the tale told him about Eric Braun, his brief life, the circumstances of his death and the heartbreaking non-reaction of his father when informed of the sudden death of his only son. The priest had made no promises to the four women seated in his small office at the back of the church. But he had accepted the written information about Eric, translated by Ariana into French, with a graceful smile, nod, and handshake to each. Then he promised a decision by the end of the next day after he consulted with the Archbishop and reviewed the Canon law for Funeral Rites for non-Catholics. The priest had repeated twice, that even if permission was granted, Canon law prohibited his mention of Eric's name during the Eucharistic prayer since that would imply that Eric was in full Communion with the Church. He had said this in English as if to emphasize the grave import of what he was saying to the women. He hoped they would understand, but that was a non-negotiable ritual condition of the Catholic Church.

The whole thing had been Lindsey's idea. Or rather, she had inadvertently supplied the setting. The day Ariana had been released from the hospital, Lindsey had insisted on driving to get her because Liisa's feet were still painful. The infection was gone, and the IV antibiotics were done, but Liisa was still nowhere back to normal, consequently she didn't argue. After Lindsey had received Dimitri's permission, she had printed the contents of the letter Eric had written two days before he died and given both Ari and Liisa a copy to read privately. Neither woman had said a word about the contents or had mentioned his name.

Once Ariana was seated comfortably in Hank Reardon's roomy Bentley, Lindsey said, "Liisa, we are going somewhere for a drink. Just us girls. Where can we go for some nasty, unhealthy appetizers and good drinks?"

Liisa turned to Lindsey, a look of wonder on her face.

Intentionally misinterpreting her expression and its unstated implication, Lindsey looked in the rear view mirror at Ariana who was watching her boss and Lindsey with an amused smile. "So, let me guess. No one drinks here in Lausanne, or you and Ariana don't believe in fraternizing outside of the workplace? Which is it?"

Fifteen minutes later, they were seated in Pierre's, a lively pub in Old Town.

After ordering their drinks and some appetizers, Ariana and Lindsey looked quizzically at Lindsey, but when she did nothing but smile and raise her glass of Cava in a non-verbal toast, they both looked around the bar as if seeing it for the first time.

During one of her recent conversations with Kate Townsend, Kate had confirmed the rumor that Toni had heard from some of the techs. Liisa and Eric had been an item. In fact, Kate had said, they had all gone to this bar together. Kate had described it in detail as a Canadian sports bar with free popcorn, a ceiling adorned with sports jerseys and loud music. So this was the place. Kate had also told Lindsey that Ariana and Eric had been extremely close friends. Eric had come on board right after Ari. The German researcher had grasped the reasons behind Ariana's total redesign of the animal research labs. A redesign which transformed the formerly black box of phase one and two clinical research into open areas where investors could see the scientists and the animals. Although the redesign cost ASL close to a billion dollars, the payback occurred within a year. Once investors could actually see where their money was going, they were far more willing to believe the promise of the research. Evidently, the two had been instrumental in selling the considerable changes which needed to be adopted by the other researchers.

Both of these women had loved the dead German. Combine his loss and the dreadful way it had happened with the dark circumstances of his family, then add it to their own recent kidnapping, and the trauma would exceed the coping skills of most people. Before finally signing off of his almost twenty-hour shift at the hospital, Drew Morgan had given her the name of a psychiatrist he knew because he thought one or both of these women may need counseling and maybe medication to get through the next several weeks.

Lindsey had thanked him and kept the card in case he was right, but she hoped it would be unnecessary.

Both Ariana and Liisa sat looking around as if it were the first time they had ever seen the place. Watching both women gape at the people and the noise with an almost vacant stare, Linsey began to worry. Maybe she should have called the psychiatrist, maybe these two were headed for trouble. But suddenly, they looked at one another, this time, their eyes bright with animation and high-fived one another across the small table. Their shout of "WE DID IT!!!" was heard over the loud music and most of the other patrons turned to stare.

Inwardly breathing a smile of relief, Lindsey asked, "Did you read the material that Eric had written in the case of his death?"

Instantly the smiles disappeared, and Ariana stared down

at the table while Liisa focused up at the sports jersey covered ceiling.

"I met him when I was here at Christmas for just a minute or two. Do you remember that Liisa?"

It seemed like five minutes but was probably more like ten seconds before Liisa looked back at Lindsey, nodded and said, "Yes, Lindsey, of course, I remember that meeting. Eric, actually his entire team, were all excited to meet you."

"Have you thought of what you will tell them? Eric's team?"

Maybe she was cruel, but Lindsey would not wish the years of anesthetizing medications and often ineffective counseling she had seen people go through—especially her sister—on these two. If they could speak it, she was pretty sure they could move on.

Liisa's expression was a riot of conflicting emotions. Sadness, guilt, and grief were the primary feelings demonstrated by the silent tears rolling down her cheeks.

But then she did something completely unexpected. Leaping up on her still very sore feet, Liisa swung around the wooden table and took the empty chair next to Ariana.

"Can you ever forgive me, Ari? My stupid decision to hire Joe Cairns over your wise advice nearly cost us our lives. None of this would have happened if I had not brought him in."

Lindsey thought otherwise but said nothing. She didn't totally understand what was happening here, but she didn't need to. Finally, these two were talking. Her goal had been realized, Liisa and Ariana would be fine. They hugged and cried while Lindsey sat gratefully sipping her drink.

Liisa asked, "So Lindsey, do you think that Eric died from a brain tumor like he suspected he would? Understand it's just a guess but is that what would fit?"

Lindsey nodded. "Yes, most likely a glioma, one of the

fastest growing brain tumors there is. And from his letter to us, Eric would have researched his symptoms. Obviously, a very bright man, once he noted the rapid increasing severity of the tremors, the changes in his pupils along with the headaches, he reasoned that he had been wrong in his initial belief that he had MS.

"From his letter, it sounds like everything accelerated very quickly. Did either of you notice anything?"

Liisa shook her head no, but Ari said, "The tremors. Yes, I noticed them a couple of months ago and asked if he was alright, but he claimed he'd just had too much coffee. The next few times I saw them along with his unnatural gait, I said nothing. Eric made it clear that he did not want to talk about anything related to his health."

Lindsey studied both Ariana and Lindsey wondering if she should tell them exactly how he died.

Ariana's pixieish features looked sad but composed. Liisa's cheeks were flushed, and her eyes were red but also composed. They had loved this man, each in her own way. They deserved to know. There would be no family members mourning Eric Braun.

"The tumor did not kill him. It would have and probably very soon, but he had a grand mal seizure. The intensity of the seizure literally flung his body off the loveseat and onto the floor. In the process, his skull crashed into the corner of your desk, Liisa. Dimitri and I could hear his skull crack. He died instantly."

Still looking at Ariana's brown gaze and Liisa's blue one, Lindsey kept talking, despite the flood of tears coursing down each woman's face. "I did not know Eric, I just talked with him once and then met him the day he died, but I think of him as heroic." Ari and Liisa both startled. Wet eyes staring at her.

"He sacrificed everything for you both and for those drugs, you know. There had to be immense psychological pressure to obey his father in that irrational sense children always have when desperately hoping for the love of a parent, regardless of how hopeless it is. But he resisted. He defied his father in a most clever way. He loved you, the company and the research. He achieved your protection from his father whom he obviously knew was evil, but as his son, he loved him anyway."

Both women sat quietly, thinking about what Lindsey had said. No longer crying. After several moments, Ari spoke up. Lindsey smiled as Ari said her name, her French accent made Lindsey's name sound almost evocative. Her expressive brown eyes danced as she declared, "We have decided exactly what we are going to tell Eric's team, Dr. Lindsey. We're going to tell them we have changed the name of TirNan. We are changing it to The Eric Braun Protocol.

"What do you think? Is that okay with you?"

Now Lindsey almost shouted. "Yes, what a completely splendid idea!"

"There's more." Now Liisa looked edgy.

"You are still in agreement, yes?"

At Liisa's answering nod, the diminutive Ari declared, "We're going to have a funeral mass at my Rouen church for Eric!"

Liisa looked down to the front row and spotted them. Lindsey and Rich were on their knees, eyes closed. Ariana and her mother were beside them with Hank and Liisa Reardon seated next to Gabe McAllister. Gabe looked up at Liisa and winked, she could feel her cheeks heat up but could not suppress her answering wide smile at him.

The mass had been in French, and the elderly priest had insisted on introducing her and her father, thanking them for their support of the Dumas family. He added a commendation to Hank Reardon for providing transportation for ASL employees to this funeral mass for Eric Braun.

Liisa stood waiting for the subdued hum of conversation and movement to cease following the remarks of the priest, getting more and more anxious.

Grasping the sides of the wooden pulpit and scanning the cavernous church, Liisa wished she had never given into Ari and her mother and agreed to do this. She knew nothing about this faith. And had never cared to learn. Catholicism seemed to be an odd mixture of superstition, myth, rules and weird symbols.

But suddenly, for a moment, Liisa swayed, thinking of the kidnapping, the sheer miracle that she was here, capable of delivering this talk. There was no other word for it—that she was alive was miraculous. The least she could do was deliver this eulogy for Eric, as Ari had asked. As she surveyed the Gothic turrets and stained glass windows with the morning sun making subtle rainbows and casting beams of muted multicolored hues throughout the church, Liisa could sense the presence of others. Not those alive in the pews, rather those who had lived and worshiped here. Breathing more slowly and deeply to relax and open her mind, she inhaled the incense which had been dispersed throughout the entire mass. And sensed the generations of prayers which had been said here, the holiness of this space.

The church had quieted. Hundreds of pairs of eyes were on her as she began to speak in French, "Quel honneur, d'être ici en ce lieu saint…

San Francisco California Airport

"Home, we are home!"

The Swiss plane was landing. They had left Lausanne almost exactly fifteen hours before and had fortunately grabbed a nonstop flight. Still, the flight was over twelve hours long. Even in first class, two flights of that many hours in five days took a toll on the body. At least on most people. Except for his wife. Jansen could feel the jiggling in his seat and bet McAllister in the seat behind him could also.

Lindsey could hardly sit still, she was so excited. Rich smiled dully and tried to clear the fog out of his mind. Like her, he was happy to be home, but the residue of the last five days hung heavily on him. How many days had it been since he had slept, really slept? He had listened to the snoring of his wife for most of the flight. And envied her the sleep. Each time he entered a deep sleep, the nightmare returned. He and Cairns were digging graves in a huge gravel pit for two bodies while a bloody apparition watched. If that weren't awful enough, a man dressed exactly like a Nazi Storm Trooper stood on the edge of the pit. Next to an oversized black SUV with the back doors open. Diedrich Braun. Jansen had never met the man but knew who stood by the car. Waiting. It felt like a premonition.

"You don't feel well, do you?" Lindsey's eyes searched his face as the flight attendant announced their arrival in San Francisco and people around them stood to search overhead compartments for belongings.

"I'm fine, Linds, just tired." He reached up to get their overnight bags, grabbed them and kissed her on the tip of her nose. "Let's get out of this plane, grab Max and get home!" Turning to Gabe, who stood right behind them, "So we'll see you and Baron this weekend in Pismo for the party then, right?"

"You bet! That party sounds great, you guys. Thanks for inviting us!" Gabe would fly on to San Diego, where he and Baron would get their fifth wheel they lived in and drive to Pismo in time for the party.

Walking out the gateway to the airport, Lindsey glanced at Rich. *He looks exhausted. Worse than those first few months in criminal defense. And thin, his face looks gaunt. But no wonder, we've both been through hell, but him more than me. He is the ultimate Marine, this husband of mine.* Chuckling mordantly, she thought, *He hasn't seen all the deaths I have seen, especially one right under his hands. Maybe we should have put off this soiree for a while...in just four days, we're having like thirty people in a practically empty house! What on earth was I thinking?*

"All will be fine Linds, stop worrying...so we don't have any furniture, who cares?" Rich could read her mind with uncanny accuracy.

They were on the down escalator heading out to the private car having passed through customs in record time.

"Yo, Rich and Lindsey!!"

Kate Townsend stood at the bottom of the escalator holding JH on her right hip.

"What a sight for sore eyes you are!" At the sight of their friend, Jansen felt some of the weight of the last few days peel off his shoulders.

"Did you know Kate would be here to get us?" he asked Lindsey, just as they stepped off the escalator to share excited hugs, kisses with Kate and her little boy.

"So how were you able to manage getting here, Kate? I thought we agreed that we'd grab a cab?"

Lindsey was looking curiously at Kate, who said, "I thought about that and decided we'd all come to get you—Max too." Shaking her head, "From the tiny little bit I know about this whole story, a ride where neither of you needs to think or make decisions, plus another great dinner at the Townsend-Coopers would be just what two exhausted detectives need." Tossing her curly mane of chestnut hair and shifting the weight of JH over to her other hip, Kate checked her watch. Then continued, "Steve left the office a couple of hours ago and should be home preparing dinner, that is if you can eat a steak cooked by Dr. Cooper?" Laughing, she was looking over at Jansen.

"You know what Kate? Right now, I could eat a steak cooked by almost anyone!"

The four sat outside on the patio outside Steve and Kate's Palo Alto home. True to their word, the Coopers had prepared everything. Rich had done little other than to comment on what a super job Steve had done on the New York steaks as he ate hungrily. Max was parked right under his feet, clearly intending to remain there. The dog had been joyous when Kate returned with Lindsey and Rich in tow. And was still smiling. At least Rich saw the smile, Kate and Steve weren't so sure.

The air was chilly with low humidity. Strangely not all

that different from the mountain air he and Lindsey had breathed the last night they were in Lausanne.

"Soooo let me get this straight." Kate swung back and forth to the rhythmn of JH's breathing on the baby monitor. "Eric, the tall German guy I met when I spent a week at ASL doing research for *Murder in the Medical Center* is, in fact, the son of the German billionaire. A father from hell who black-mailed his own son to steal the formula, data and experimental mice for Liisa's new life-extending drug. But despite the fact that Eric is close to death, he has the wherewithal to falsify all the information so that his father ends up with nothing. The industrious Diedrich Braun manages to insert an assassin, an ex-special forces Marine, who tries to kill all of you. And the assassin is gone, who knows where. Eric dies as he hands you all this information on a thumbdrive." She stopped the porch swing for a moment to study Rich and Lindsey, who were seated close together on a long couch sipping wine.

"You realize how implausible this sounds, right? I mean if I didn't know you guys better, I'd swear you were sharing some kind of delusion."

Rich and Lindsey smiled and nodded. There were a few details they had omitted, but Kate's take on the last five days was exactly what they had hoped. Their reporter friend was on a leave of absence from the Houston Tribune, but they knew her. Had her investigative sense been roused, there would be no stopping her. On the never ending plane ride, Lindsey and Rich had prepared a story. One which adhered closely enough to the facts of what had happened that the case against Diedrich Braun that Dimitri was buiding would not be compromised by early publicity. But it did all sound a little crazy. Like one of those Jason Stratham and Mollie what's her name movies. That kind of crazy.

Shrugging, Kate rose, walked over to Lindsey, and hugged

her for the fourth or maybe fifth time that day, sighed heavily and said, "In the last couple of years, you've become my best friend. Since it took most of my life to even have a best friend, I'm euphoric to know that I don't need to replace you!" Crouching down to Max, who lay on a bed Kate and Steve claimed would always be there for him, she crooned, "You are the absolute best dog I have ever known." And stroked the big Doberman's belly as he rolled over on his back and exposed it to her. "He missed you guys I know, but with a dog like him around, I'd never have to worry about the baby. Max watched him like a hawk."

"There's just one thing about your story I'd like to ask if that's ok?"

Jansen stiffened and hoped she did not notice, while Lindsey casually asked, "Sure Kate, what is it you'd like to know?"

"Gabe and Liisa...you think they may be an item?"

Grinning with delight and relief, Lindsey and Rich both said, "Yeah, " Rich added, "We'll see this weekend, right?"

Kate reached into the pocket of her jacket and pulled out a pad of paper. "Glad you reminded me. Lindsey, after you called, I reached the entire list except Monica and Luke. The Philbins will not be here either. Marguerite is in the hospital, quite ill, Eleanor said. But they both send their love to you and Rich and hope they can come to visit later this year." Kate smiled at her husband who had been quietly listening to his wife. "JH and I can come with you all, that is if you'd like an extra pair of hands to help get ready, and Steve will come down as soon as he finishes rounds Friday morning."

Completely overjoyed, Lindsey clapped her hands. "Kate, that is awesome! You can help us furnish a few rooms!" Looking over at her sleeping husband she quieted her voice. "I'll bet he's not had more than ten hours of sleep in total since he left San Luis Obispo.

Jansen had entirely forgotten that this coming Saturday, June 11th, was his birthday. Laughing and smiling at his good friend Kate, he said, "You knew about this the whole time, didn't you?" At her answering nod, he continued, "Were you the mysterious decorator?"

"Goodness no, Rich—I know what I like but not until someone puts it in front of me. Your realtor and I spoke on the phone a few times when Lindsey was too busy to deal with basic stuff like furniture selection." She looked at Lindsey, now seated close to Rich on the short L-leg of the grouping facing the Pacific. "Did I even talk to you about any of this furniture?"

"Nope. But I love it, love it love it! You guys could not have done better. The colors, design, simplicity, lovely."

Lindsey drained her glass of wine and held it out for a refill. She regarded Rich as he filled her glass. "You remember Eileen Simmons, the realtor who sold us the house, right?"

"Yep, I do."

"While Max and I were at Kate and Steve's,—" at the mention of his name, the big Dobie got up off of one of the four new beds which were distributed throughout the house for him, sat in front of Lindsey and gave her his paw. Leaning forward to meet him, the dog tilted his nose gently toward her face until his snout touched her mouth. Dobie kiss.

Grinning broadly, Lindsey hugged the dog, "Max, I sure did miss you! Am sooo glad we're all together again!"

Both hands caressing the dog, she continued speaking. "Anyway, after dropping you off at the airport, I thought about the close time frame I had made for us with planning the party for June. And also, dear husband, that you are the one with the color, texture and design skills, not me." Laughing now, she added, "Liisa Reardon and I could start a club for smart women who lack all sense of decorative style.

"So I called Eileen. Surely, we're not the only new residents of Pismo who lack the time but have the money to hire an interior decorator with a willingness to do more than merely advise. Voila. Alicia introduced me to Shirley Heathcock, another transplanted Houstonian, who decided to start a little business after her third husband died.

"That little business has grown to include more than fifty employees and an annual revenue of more than twenty million." Lindsey stopped petting Max to pick up her wine glass. At that, the Dobie returned to his bed, circled three times and lay down, heaving a loud sigh as he did so.

"Shirley's folks arranged all the dishes, cooking gear and bought the food." Taking a deep swallow of the wine, "this is delicious wine—Kate you and Shirley told them what to stock in the wine cellar, right?"

"Sure did. I love spending money, especially when it belongs to someone else!" Kate asked, "Lindsey, will Shirley be at the party? I would like to meet her in person. If only to tell her what an awesome job we did with your house."

"She will, said she wouldn't miss it for the world. By the way Kate, where is that list? Rich needs to see it and make sure

I haven't forgotten anyone." Wrinkling her nose, she quipped, "Course it would be obvious that they were forgotten if I don't call until four days before the party!"

CHAPTER FORTY-SIX
The Party, three days later

It was nine at night. The party had been going for two hours, and all but nine people on Lindsey and Rich's list were there. Unfortunately, Luke Preston and Monica Bradbury had been unable to switch their schedules when the date of the party had been shifted to the second weekend in June. Monica had called Friday night for both of them expressing their regrets and claiming they would come out together later in the fall.

Hank and Liisa Reardon had flown in Friday morning with Stella and George on Hank's private plane conveniently landing at the airport at San Luis Obispo. Stella and George had steadfastly refused Lindsey's entreaty to merely enjoy the party, a fact which both Lindsey and Rich were exceedingly grateful for because the Pismo home invited intimate groupings in more than ten places. The pool, extensive deck, library, great room, media room, wine cellar and kitchen dining areas were all filled with groups of two to five people. Attention to all of these groups would have been impossible for Rich, Lindsey, and the couple from Shirley Heathcock's agency.

Once Stella and George made it crystal clear to Lindsey that they would not be comfortable if they were not working the party, they spent five minutes with Juan and Rosa, the agency employees, and organized territories for each of the four. The result being that each of the small groups received an offer of drinks or canapes every five to ten minutes. That way Rich and Lindsey could focus on being host and hostess.

Rich roamed his large and still unfamiliar home for a specific face. Out on the deck near the rectangular lap swimming pool, stood Steve and Kate Cooper with a woman he did not know.

Spying Rich, Steve called out. "Yo, Rich! Can I buy you a drink?"

Rich smiled broadly as he approached his two friends. "Sure, what are you drinking?"

As if on cue, Rosa approached with a tray of champagne flutes. The tiny young woman deftly balanced her tray of flutes with one hand. With the other, she carried an assortment of hot canapes which she placed on the small table beside a white upholstered wicker chair. Turning back around, Rosa faced four people staring at her.

"Have I spilled something on myself? Or do I have spinach in my teeth?" Rosa Flores had a presence that was not diminished by the fact that she was waiting on a group of wealthy people. Quite the contrary, her bright smile matched the warmth of her large expressive brown eyes. Jansen was more than impressed with her.

Laughing, Rich said, "Hardly Rosa, we're each wondering how you manage to defy gravity with those trays."

The others were nodding their agreement as they accepted a flute of Cava. When Rosa turned to Rich, she asked, "Would you prefer a Grolsch? We have plenty of them chilled. Or would you like one of your reds opened?"

This lady is a class act, she misses nothing. How has she figured out what I drink in two hours?

As if reading Jansen's mind, Rosa said, "Your wife and Stella told Juan and me what everyone here likes to drink." Further explaining, she added, "Before I married Juan, I worked as a bartender in San Francisco at the Sugar Lounge for about five years. Maybe you've been there?"

As Rich was shaking his head no, Kate was studying Rosa. "I thought I recognized you, Rosa." Kate extended her hand as she said, "There were very few Friday nights when I wasn't at the Sugar with one of the other journalists at The Chronicle."

The petite Hispanic set the tray on the table beside the platter of canapes as she regarded Kate. Then her thin face lit up. "Stoli martini on the rocks with a bunch of olives!"

All four including Rosa cracked up.

Recovering first, Rich asked only half- joking, "Ever thought about becoming a lawyer Rosa? We need more brains like yours in law."

Straight-faced, Rosa said, "You know I've learned to consider all options in my life. But law? My Dad is a lawyer in Mexico and tried to get me to go to law school so we could practice together. But I didn't want to spend all that time in school." Wrinkling her nose, she added, "And I'm too restless to be able to do all the research...can't sit still.

"So what will you have?"

Forgetting the question, Jansen looked puzzled. "Sorry?"

"To drink. Grolsch, a single malt or one of your reds?"

Jansen shook his head chuckling. "Thank you, Rosa, very much. I have no idea of what the inventory of single malts is but, please choose one and I'll have it on the rocks."

While they waited for Rosa to return, Steve said, "Alicia Simmons, please meet Rich Jansen, our host and our friend the criminal defense attorney Kate and I have spoken about."

Jansen started. The mantle of criminal defense lawyer still hung heavily on him. And the nagging feeling that he had gone to the other side, the wrong side, after ten years as a homicide cop simmered still. Shoving those unwanted sentiments to the bottom of his psyche, Rich extended his hand to the tall redhead. "Nice to meet you, Alicia. I hear you're having some pretty grim boyfriend problems that you and I need to visit about shortly."

She was not unattractive but looked uptight, stressed. Dark shadows washed out her blue eyes and emphasized the angular planes of her face. Jansen could feel the fear surging from the woman as he grasped her dry hand.

This woman is terrified. Plainly scared to death.

Changing his intended schedule for the next couple of days in midcourse, Rich held on to her hand and gazed steadily at her. "I can meet with you first thing on Monday, here in my office and we'll put together a plan for you."

Just then, Rosa approached with his drink.

"Aberlour on the rocks. Shall I wait to make sure it's ok?"

"Aberlour? Nope—perfect. Thank you, Rosa."

As he took a sip, he smiled and gave her a thumbs up. Pretending to focus on the scotch, he sensed the relief among the small group. Kate and Steve had evidently promised Alicia nothing, not even a meeting with him. He was grateful to them for that and appreciated the consideration of his good friends. But the woman needed help, that was evident.

"I'm going to continue roaming guys, I'll see you later."

Moving back into the house, Rich saw an intriguing group sequestered in one of the seating ensembles in the great room. Liisa Reardon, Gabe McAllister, Lindsey's new partner Jodi Tamarack, and two priests. Seated on a dark brown leather couch was a massive man in the robes of a Franciscan. Beside him was Gabe, engaged in a vigorous conversation. And standing in front of the men were Jodi and Liisa, so tied up in what was plainly a passionate discussion that only one person even saw Jansen approach.

Father John Tobin, dressed in his usual attire of a black long sleeved shirt and black trousers, stood by the open glass doors to the deck watching the ocean below. Or rather listening. The surf was better heard than seen at nine in the evening. Midsummer, some light remained as the longest day of the year approached, but the sun had set, and the dry southern California air was cooling by the second.

Without turning, the priest emitted a long low whistle. "What a splendid home for you and Lindsey, Rich. I could not be happier for the two of you. I hear that it was quite a week for you both in Switzerland. Kate filled me in on the details. By the way, they both look gloriously happy. It isn't often that I get to see a couple I married a year later." Still studying the unseen ocean, he said so softly that Rich had to lean in close to hear,"These are perilous times for couples and their children. The war on the family has intensified."

Now turned to face Rich, John added with a nod to the big man in the robes. "I had no idea whether Blaise and Lindsey would hit it off, but I knew if they did they could complement one another." Suddenly, Father John's solemn face split into a grin. Jansen's guess at the source of the grin was affirmed when he felt Max nudge his left side.

Crouching down a bit to get on a level with the Doberman, the priest said softly, "Well Max, I have sure missed seeing you, big boy."

Max was sitting in front of the man and grinning. "I am getting dangerously close to getting a dog because of you, you big lover boy."

Standing once again, the priest nodded over at the massive man in the robes. "He's a hagiographer."

Rich looked over at the priest out of the corner of his eyes and chuckled. "You guys..." shaking his head in amusement, "That guy's a Franciscan priest, has a doctorate in chemistry, another in physics, and in his spare time writes about the saints?"

Noting the puzzled look on Father John's face, Rich asked, "What?"

"The last time I spoke with Blaise, he was a Jesuit. But you're right, those are Franciscan robes." Shrugging, John turned his piercing gray eyes to Rich and then toward the other side of the room where Lindsey was talking with Julie and Ted Grayson. There was a young girl standing with the three adults. She suddenly turned and saw him from across the room. Rich drew a sharp breath. He had not seen her in almost two years. Time rolled back as he stood there, remembering.

Rich Jansen was the newly appointed Chief Warden at the Huntsville Prisons. Hired by Texas Governor Greg Bell to solve the rapidly escalating problems partially caused by a newly imprisoned female Cardiologist. Once Rich began to investigate the strange case, he decided to risk his new job by helping his former law partner prepare an appeal. In the process of his investigation, Rich had met with Julie Grayson and her four children. It was Julie who had found Lindsey's sister Paula and the suicide note that exonerated Lindsey.

She looked like a facsimile of Lindsey's dead sister Paula, small, maybe five foot two or three, long dark—almost black hair. She looked nothing like his wife, except for those emerald colored eyes. But in this young girl Lindsey, her eyes were startling, almost unnerving.

Rich turned to Father John who seemed completely unperturbed. Lindsey had not told him that the Graysons were bringing their daughter—also named Lindsey—with them from Texas. Or that she planned to tell the girl who her biological mother was.

"She's going to do it, isn't she? Makes sense really Rich, don't you think?"

Rich smiled because he had no clue what made sense to this priest whom he loved, this holy man. Or that she had told him about the baby she had not seen until this evening. But this was an evening of many surprises. And so he waited in silence for the wisdom he was confident he would hear.

"You and Lindsey have been through so much in your own lives before you met one another. Each of you has fought many wars: injustice, betrayal, the loss of dear family members. Each battle unique to you and waged the way the most important ones are; in the dark and alone.

"Your battlefields are varied, actual combat, the streets of Houston, courtrooms and of late, what sounds like pure evil." The priest exhaled a long slow breath. "Lindsey's are incompetence, stupidity, greed and the burden of her God-given genius. Different battles, but warfare all the same. Lindsey saw death frequently in her work at the hospital and then at the prison. But watching a young man die in front of her eyes and be powerless to stop it, and participating with you in revealing the person behind what sounds like pure evil. And to beat him…this round anyway." Now the intense gray gaze met Rich's. "It puts everything in perspective, doesn't it?" They both watched the three adults hugging and crying far across the room. "It makes what once looked unforgivable, bearable, even perhaps, laudable."

Suddenly Father stood, smiled and extended his arms as if to embrace the house. "You both need this beautiful place because so much is asked of each of you."

Both men watched as his wife Lindsey, her daughter and the Ted and Julie Grayson, hand-in-hand, walked over to them, their faces radiant. Two sets of impossibly green gazes were trained on them.

PROLOGUE
MALTHUS REVISITED

Berlin, Germany

At Braun's command, Dr. Viktor Dragovik entered the cavernous living room where his boss, Diedrich Braun stood as if posing for an SS recruitment poster.

"Does it work?"

"We are on the third set of mice. All were gone within forty-eight hours."

Braun nodded, the motion hardly discernible.

The Serbian doctor waited, knowing better than to assume anything where his boss was concerned.

Still maintaining his ramrod posture, Braun asked, "How much can you make and how will it be dispersed?"

"Enough to eliminate at least six billion people. The dispersion will be through cattle via ingestion. Once in the human intestine, the virus will mutate and be aerosolized. But this has not been tested, so far this is just theory."

"When will you be able to test it? And where do you plan to do it?

"Within the next two months, we will be ready. We have a Chinese prison population of fifteen hundred men for the first test, as soon as you give us the go ahead.”

This time, the nod of the silver head actually moved several inches, and the bloodless lips smiled. “Well done, Viktor, well done. You may go now.”

Same time. Delphi, Greece

Joe Cairns ambled toward the center of town. Time for his nightly beers. His five o’clock date with the bartender, Demetrius. The kind of sullen brother-in-law of Rafael, who owned the small café.

“Yassas, Demetrius.”

It had taken three evenings, but now he got a smile out of the depressed sixty-something-year-old bartender.

“Kalispera, Jusef!”

With all the time in the world and enough money to live comfortably for the rest of his life, Joe should have been the happiest man in the world. But only when he got to Delphi did Joe understand why David had told him to come here.

Along the fifteen-hundred-mile trip, he had stopped at small hotels and bars in Italy, Slovenia, Serbia, and Macedonia. In most of them, a woman usually sat in the bar alone. And within ten minutes or less, made it plain that she found him attractive. After a while, they all started to look the same, despite their age, language and body type differences. Cairns had no interest in any of them.

Delphi. Heather Malone’s favorite place on the earth. Heather Malone. Who knew why he was thinking of the one girl he could have married, had things been different.

Heather had been enthralled by the Greek myths. She could speak for hours about the gods and goddesses, but her favorite of all was the oracle at Delphi and the well-known maxim carved into the Temple of Apollo in Delphi, *Gn thi Seautón*, Know Thyself. Joe Cairns thought of her and the admonition now each day in this ancient place filled with the whispers of prophets and prayers.

There was a place Heather had told Cairns about. One unknown by tourists. She had explained very carefully how to get to the rock that Zeus had split. There would be a yellow strip across the path into the forest prohibiting access. But she had said one day after they married and had at least five kids, they would go there together and pray. Because Zeus was simply another name for the god with ninety-nine names. Heather had read so much about the place that she had described it perfectly.

There was nothing but forest. Just as Heather had predicted all those years ago, the night before she was killed by a drunk driver on the way home from school.

Each day, Joe walked the half mile or so away from the tourist sites and past the yellow strip. And got on his knees in the forest and prayed to an unknown god. And cried.

Joe had not cried since he had been a small boy, but in this place, this sacred place, the tears washed away years of sorrow and regret. He had begun to run again for the first time since he had left the Corps. The Greek food was the healthiest on the planet, consisting of fish, fresh vegetables, olives, and moussaka. Each dish seemed better than the last.

On the tenth day, he sensed before seeing the sandaled feet, that he was no longer alone. And when he opened his eyes to see King David, he was unsurprised.

Same time, Pismo Beach, California

"Hank Reardon, how are you on this beautiful morning?

Sure is here, anyway." Jansen was sitting on their deck watching the ocean, sipping coffee. He never tired of this view of the constantly shifting shadows playing in the waves of the Pacific Ocean.

"One day, I swear, Jansen, I am going to call you and Lindsey just to chat, is she there?"

Rich put his coffee down and stood up, alert. "No, she's at Cal Poly, she's pretty excited about the early effects of Longevive on a test group of dogs. Dobermans with markers of cardiac disease, I might add." Realizing that he was chattering to postpone what was most assuredly bad news, he got to the point, "But obviously, you have not called to talk about that. What's happened?"

"Dimitri was found dead at his home this morning. Without him, the case against Diedrich Braun is toast." Reardon exhaled a long slow breath that sounded more like a sob. "Lindsey will not be testifying Monday."

The Swiss special ops detective had persuaded the Switzerland office of the Attorney General to indict Diedrich Braun for two criminal felonies: the murder of Matthew Adams and industrial espionage, specifically the robbery of the animal research laboratory of Andrews, Sacks, and Levine. Lindsey had been one of the main witnesses for the prosecution's case.

Rich had been surprised when Dimitri had called a few months ago, exuberant. After months of painstaking work on his part, the Swiss AG's office had agreed to indict. With the influence of FedPol, the case was fast-tracked. The evidence against Braun was wholly circumstantial, resting entirely on the written claims of Eric, Braun's dead son. A decent criminal defense attorney could find hundreds of holes in the case and Braun had all the money he needed to hire the very best. Rich had tried to dissuade Dimitri before he and Lindsey had left Switzerland. Despite the days spent sifting through the ruins of the Bonvillars farmhouse, the Swiss CSI team came up with nothing. Although the Chicago police agreed to reopen the Adams case based on the claims of Eric Braun about Adams' murder, there had been no new evidence forthcoming. Nothing to suggest that Adams' death had been anything other than suicide.

"Bet it wasn't a faked suicide, this time, Hank."

Instantly aware of Rich's inference, Reardon's answer reeked with derision. "Heart attack."

Dimitri Vlasov had been a fit, forty-something man. The Ukrainian had worked out almost obsessively and ate like an ascetic.

"Are they buying it?" Rich was asking about the people at FedPol.

"It was Director Pierre who called me this morning. No, he and the DA think it was a hit ordered by Braun. Not terribly difficult to fake a heart attack if you know what you're doing."

Standing at the splendid panorama displayed before him, Rich felt profound sorrow for the loss of this good man. Over the few days he had worked with Dimitri, Rich had developed a friendship with him, one that transcended their significant differences. His death left a vast hole among the ranks of the soldiers fighting this war. It was a war, and Diedrich Braun had won this round hands down.

"Have you heard anything from him?"

Rich smiled. "No, I didn't expect to."

"Do you think you will?"

"Yep, I am sure I or we will."

"You ended up liking the guy, didn't you Rich?"

Taking a sip of his now tepid coffee, Rich squinted into the bright sun. "Like?"

At the other end of the line, there was only silence. Hank waited for the younger man's answer.

"Put it this way Hank. Ari told us that Cairns had been about to kill her. She felt the barrel of the gun against her skull."

"But Rich, she was in shock from blood loss, infection, and fear. She could easily have imagined the entire thing."

"Is that what you think happened, Hank?"

"What else would explain it?"

Rich merely smiled. Ariana had been as lucid as he and Hank Reardon. But for a man without the experience of God to believe her conviction that her prayers had changed the heart of a killer was too much.

AUTHOR'S NOTE

A small collection of large homes which overlook the Pacific Ocean can be seen while traveling south on Route One to Pismo Beach. Although there is no address there named 37 Bluff Drive, the house that Lindsey McCall and Rich Jansen buy in Pismo Beach looks very much like one of the homes there.

This book is a work of fiction, written for purely entertainment value, all characters and institutions are imaginary. Consequently, there are no such drugs as Digipro or Longevive, nor is there a protocol named TirNan. The characters and the story are plumbed wholly from my imagination. Lindsey McCall does not exist nor do any of the other characters in this book. Although there are Medical Directors at Huntsville Prisons, there have never been any with the names of Lance Pettigrew or Lindsey McCall. Similarly, the Institutional Effectiveness and the Institutional Compliance Departments do exist within the Texas Prison System, but my characterization of these departments is derived entirely from my imagination as justification for Lindsey's departure from prison medicine. Nor is there such a person as Senior Medical Director, Dr. Stanley Nixon, DO.

I thank Shirley Heathcock and Eleanor and Marguerite Philbin for the permission to use their names and hope they enjoy their fictional characters.

Many of the elements of this story are indeed based on fact. Epigenetics is real, exciting and progressing at an astounding rate. The much quoted Joel Wallach is a veterinarian and was able to cure cystic fibrosis in the lab and in his animal research. One of the first epigeneticists, Dr. Wallach, has been writing for decades about the critical role of minerals and nutrition in the prevention and treatment of many chronic diseases afflicting much of the world. Developmental Biologists like Rhonda Patrick at Stanford are revealing the astounding effects of nutrition, minerals, on longevity on an almost daily basis.

There is a book titled *The Wahls Protocol.* Based on the diet that Dr. Terry Wahls wrote about her defeat of Progressive Multiple Sclerosis., the nutritional plan is similar to what was described in this book—a paleo diet (more or less what humans ate before we manufactured synthetic foods: meat and vegetables.)

The One Health Initiative is an organization of veterinarians, epidemiologists, ecologists and public health physicians. Its mission statement is stunningly consistent with Pope Francis' encyclical on the environment and human ecology.

Several major corporations are funding massive studies on longevity, Google is a major investor of researchers in an anti-aging project. Some of those scientists claim that a 140- year average lifespan is very definitely within the foreseeable future.

When I wrote the first novel, *The Fragrance Shed by A Violet: Murder in the Medical Center*, it was not with the idea that there would be subsequent books with the same characters. But once I completed the book, Dr. Lindsey McCall and the people in her world did not disappear. Quite the contrary in fact. Since she and the others had taken on flesh and bones during the process of creating them, these fictional people continued to take up residence in my mind, psyche and… heart. Therefore, she is back, in this third book and will appear in a fourth, with a working title of Malthus Revisited.

Had I listened to the advice of a few mentors when I was very young and become a medical doctor, it would have been the field of Cardiology in which I would have specialized. And if I'd had the fortitude and the money, I would have entered the MD/Ph.D. program. My field of study would most likely have been Cardiovascular Research. But I doubt that I'd have had the foresight and guts to leave at the peak of my career like Lindsey.

The appeal of hard science is just that, the belief that it's hard, meaning lasting and true. But those wise enough to plumb the realities of science know that it is all theory, and, theories change. Nothing lasts, not even hard science.

Thomas Kuhn published *The Structure of Scientific Revolutions* in 1962. In the book, Kuhn described how culture and human thought interact with science by returning to Galileo, Copernicus and the radical consequences of those revealed truths on certain institutions and society as a whole. We tend to think that science equates with truth, unalterable truth and disregard the human factors.

To combat the increasing prevalence and mortality from heart disease, President Lyndon Johnson declared his "War on Heart Disease" in 1964. Five years later, Renee Favaloro revolutionized cardiovascular surgery with his use of the saphenous vein to bypass obstructed coronary arteries at Cleveland Clinic, making bypass surgery the most commonly performed cardiac surgical procedure in the world. Then in 1964, for one out of every two people with heart disease, the first symptom of cardiac disease was death. Fifty-two years later, death is the first sign of heart disease for one out of every two people. The data are unforgiving and the gloomy numbers apply to almost the entire medical system.

Like many of the closely held paradigms of the twentieth and twenty-first centuries, the one- hundred-year-old model of treating human beings as if human organs are separate and distinct from one another is beginning to crumble. Too much evidence, hard evidence, is mitigating against the "medical model." The ways that medicine is organized, taught, practiced and incentivized is proving to be fallacious.

We see the problems only around the edges, spoken by the rare few who see through the rigidly institutionalized systems to the realities: That the medical outcomes of Americans rank at the bottom when compared with most other Western countries. Despite American medical expenditures that are triple those of other countries, their populations are healthier than Americans. Moreover, wholly preventable diseases like Diabetes and Obesity are at epidemic proportions here.

In my first novel, Kate Townsend writes an investigative series called "Murder in the Medical Center." In the second edition of the novel, extensive sections of her series are found in the book. Much of her data are based on my dissertation research. Data which have existed for decades now, revealing the illusion of scientific objectivity, the power by pharmaceutical companies over medicine and the financial incentives to maintain that power.

Change happens incrementally, at a glacial pace. Until the tipping point occurs and then everything changes, seemingly all at once. In the intervening years, where we live currently in the early part of the twenty-first century, it is resisted. The reasons are as diverse as is the population of medical doctors and personnel administering what is called American health care in September of the year 2016. But fundamentally, it's about power and money.

I understand. To this day, I recall the feeling of watching a fibrillating heart return to normal sinus rhythm, restoring life to a person who was clinically dead. There are few greater highs than that. Over time, one can believe that she does actually hold the power of life and death in her hands.

Multiple studies have demonstrated that psychoactive drugs are no more effective in creating a sense of well-being than is sunshine and exercise. Yet the percentage of Americans on these drugs is increasing at an astonishing rate. IMS Health reveals that close to eighty million Americans are on some type of psychiatric drug—over one million of these people are between birth and five years of age. A Mayo Clinic study revealed that seventy percent of Americans take at least one prescription drug, the most common being psychoactive drugs, opioids, and antibiotics.

Lindsey's decision to leave medicine and return to research mirrors the dreams of some former physician friends and colleagues. Many, although certainly not all, were disillusioned after five or twenty years of clinical practice. A return to the lab would be a relief, particularly in these days where basic sciences have the potential to do exactly what Lindsey says they will do: revolutionize medicine.

Scientists worldwide are studying the effects of non-medical variables of health. The effects of adequate sleep, exercise, and a diet different from the SADS (Standard American Diet) are revealing astonishing differences in people's health. Wheat-free diets have been found to cure arthritis, irritable bowel syndrome and many more diseases of the western world.

The animal research lab at Cal Poly in San Luis Obispo is fiction, as are the characters Jodi Tamarack and Fr. Blaise Roderick. However, Dr. Jamie Noland, Head of the Animal Science Department at Cal Poly was kind enough to give me a tour of her department, including the expanse of land where the Cal Poly sheep, lambs, and other animals are cared for. The barn where Lindsey takes over the feeding of baby lambs for new mother ewes does exist. There is, however, no shower there.

The writing of any book is a group effort, and this one is no different. I must first thank Nancy Cleary at Wyatt-Mackenzie for her consistent excellence in design and depth of knowledge in this chaotic publishing world. She makes the writing a far less solitary endeavor. Her design of this cover nailed the major elements of the story. Also, I thank my husband for his willingness to listen to plots as they develop in my head and help me out of dilemmas with certain characters who manage to corner me. And once again I am grateful to the readers of the manuscript: my husband John, Susan Toscani, and Rachel McClure.

No book is produced without excellent editing. For *A Price for Genius*, I am most grateful to Cate Baum for her line editing of the first iteration of this book. Her challenges about the plot and my writing style caused me to dig more deeply than I had before, answer questions about exactly whom I am writing about and why. I thank Cate for that. Also for what feels like a new economy in my writing, although it is no easy task to revise a completed book. This shorter, leaner version of A Price for Genius is, I hope, a far better read.

And Lori Hawkins, thank you for your excellent proof read of this book—it has been a real pleasure to work with you.

9 781942 545682